David Leddick is the author of numerous works of fiction and non-fiction. His previous novels include *My Worst Date* and *The Millionaire of Love*. A famous beauty guru, he is former Worldwide Creative Director for Revlon and International Creative Director for L'Oreal, Paris. Other past jobs include ballet dancer, officer in the US Navy and advertising television commercial director. He lives in Miami Beach, Florida.

never eat in

....

David Leddick

Library of Congress Catalog Card Number: 99–63334

A catalogue record for this book is available from
the British Library on request

The right of David Leddick to be identified as
the author of this work has been asserted by him
in accordance with the Copyright, Designs and
Patents Act 1988

First published in 1999 by Serpent's Tail,
4 Blackstock Mews, London N4 2BT

website: www.serpentstail.com

Printed in Great Britain by Mackays of Chatham, plc

10 9 8 7 6 5 4 3 2 1

For Tom Love

I would like to thank:

Casey O'Blondes, my true and beautiful friend, who first suggested that I send my book to the freelance editor . . .

Florence Ingleby, so witty and astute, who guided me to . . .

Peter Ayrton of Serpent's Tail, who thrilled me by accepting my book.

And also Patrick Gale, dashing and undaunted, who streamlined my manuscript, no small task.

On the American side of the ocean many thanks to:

Kathie and Alan Nengel, who struggled with my original manuscript until it was finally neatly committed to paper.

chapter 1

....

mr bigge

The man I loved so much, the man I love so much, I saw for the first time in my son's bedroom.

I was cleaning it. Actually I rather liked cleaning Freddy's bedroom. After spending all week tottering around in Chanel at the agency trying to keep everyone calm it was a relief on Saturday to muck out his room. Knee deep as it always was with inside-out blue jeans, unmatched sweat socks, smelly underpants and dilapidated motorcycle magazines. I did not even mind those cruddy towels that just had to have been masturbated into.

Freddy, of course, was not home on Saturday. Tennis lessons. Then skateboarding at the Bethesda Fountain with his gang of little creeps. Then the movies. He swears there were no recreational drugs. One can only hope. Everyone I've known who did drugs always swore they didn't. That's why I prefer your average alcoholic. At least in the midst of a terrible hangover they don't try to pretend they don't drink.

What did Dick Beaver say to me so memorably last winter in Palm Beach? 'I'm a drunk but I'm not an alcoholic.' Of course you're not, darling.

So as I was assembling the soiled, the worn and the torn I dragged a cassette from under the bed.

'Oh, God,' I thought. 'He rented a movie and forgot to return it. Probably about three months ago, the little rat.'

I looked to see what it was. On the box was a photograph of a husky man with a crewcut in blue jean cutoffs. With something quite large jammed down the front of them. It read:

Bob Bigge

in

Big Things Come in Bigge Packages

Whaaaa? On the back were several pictures of Mr Bigge in the all together doing astonishing things with a variety of people. A young blonde woman. She'd had her breasts done I noticed. A black man. A young dark-haired couple.

It made me a bit gaga. First, I wanted to see it. Secondly, what was it doing under my fifteen-year-old's bed? Thirdly, should I be outraged? Fourthly, should I tell Bertrand when he came home from art directing *Attraction* magazine? A magazine that only seemed to be fully functional on the weekends.

One step at a time, I thought. First things first. I'll go down and look at it. A fatal step. That's when I fell for Bob Bigge. Mr Bigge. Big.

So I watched it. I'm not going to describe it to you. Actually it was pretty gross. Not to say I haven't done some of that stuff, but I'd never watched it. There really isn't that much difference between two men doing it and a man and a woman, you know. At least not the way they did it in this film, face to face, legs up. From a fashion shooting standpoint, it was *awful*.

In principle these people did this kind of movie a lot, right? You'd think they would learn where to put the lights. And develop some taste as to where the camera should be. And if you're going to rent a room, why not rent one that looked like something? What gives with all those fireplaces? Evidently in the porn business a fireplace spells class. Those were my thoughts at the time.

Finally it was just about protuberances being shoved into orifices: What did that Englishwoman say at Oscar Wilde's trial: 'I don't care what anyone does, as long as they don't do it in the street and frighten the horses.' Not much of this would have frightened horses. It just wasn't very sexy. No one looked like they were suddenly overwhelmed with excitement or passion or beauty.

Which brings me to Mr Bigge. He was beautiful. I don't mean his penis, which *was* big. And . . . what's the expression? 'Perfectly formed.' It looked nice. But a penis is a penis. Like a breast is a breast. There are differences but people get hung up on nuances. I often think of extraterrestrials coming down and trying to figure out why we think Cindy Crawford is so much more beautiful than say, Janet Reno. There they are. Large, two arms. Two legs, two breasts, two eyes, two ears, covered with skin. Pretty much the same color hair. And people are raving about one in preference to the other. In terms of galaxies and moon craters, these are very subtle differences we're talking about here.

But style, that is something different. Somehow I think extraterrestrials would spot the difference right away between a Grace Kelly and a Kim Basinger. One so glittering with posture and confidence and being amusing. The other, well, you get what I mean.

Mr Bigge was like that. You felt he was in the wrong movie. He was so beautiful and blond and perfectly wrought and moved among those other pieces of flesh as though he thought it was funny to find himself there. They all seemed so physically small in comparison. Something like acolytes surrounding the priest. It was like a kind of ritual. Now I will put *this* in here. Now I will put your mouth *there*. I had this feeling I wanted him to come to life and make love as people make love when they're alone together. Not worrying about the camera angles. Do I have my leg out of the way so the camera can see my crotch? That kind of thing.

What did I know? The only man I'd done anything sexually excessive with was my husband. And I don't think you could say what we did was excessive. Don't you often sit around a dinner table and wonder what the couples there really do sexually? Do they sit on the edge of tables, kneel over each other upside down and backwards? Maybe, maybe, maybe. But there's something about the way they deal with each other that suggests not. A kind of weary, pleasant condescension. They like each other and what the two of them know about sex you could put in your hat.

I was a bit that way myself. Certainly I'd had sex before I got married, and with guys other than Bertrand. But, you know, I never really got a good look at their penises. Their penises. Both of them. Fred Bartlett and Leslie Tannenbaum. My two boyfriends in college. I slept with nobody in high school. Other girls did but my boyfriends never really made any great effort to. Maybe it's because I'm blonde. Too lovely. Too nice. Anyway Fred Bartlett managed it, and it was fun. But we were kids. He just wanted to get on top and pump up and down until it felt good. And it didn't take much pumping up and down to do it either. Why don't people face facts? Most men just want to get that friction going until they feel good, and that's it. Most women don't mind the friction and they like the fact the men feel good, but for themselves it's just okay. They've got other things on their minds.

And we take that simple little thing and make such a big deal out of it. Leslie Tannenbaum wanted to make more of a big deal about it. I remember after the first time we made love he said, 'Look, I've got some hairs on my chest. I must be becoming a man.' And he was gorgeous. I was so flattered that he wanted to go out with me. A football-playing poet. With long blond curly hair. He wanted to get all our clothes off and make the whole thing more visual. In retrospect I think I idolized him but I don't think I loved him. I was just so thrilled that he wanted me to be his girlfriend, the rest of it went with the territory. That's probably why he broke up with me and started going with that terrible Colleen Kennedy. He deserved her. She really wanted to screw and wasn't impressed that he'd been published in the *Kenyon Review.*

So I thought I was lucky when I met Bertrand while I was first working at *Vogue.* Franco-American. So lively. So charming. Such a good job at *Estrella* magazine. A Senior Art Director at his age. I'm not going to be all sourpuss about my marriage. It really wasn't like those awful things in Gail Sheehy's *Passages* where everyone said 'I got married because all my friends were,' and 'I got married because we'd been going together a long time and he wanted to and I couldn't think of a good reason not to.' And so on. I was really crazy about Bertrand. Bertrand was a good kisser. When we first met, should I say? That's not fair. He still could be when I made the effort to get him in the mood. We both held on to our bodies. He always worked out and so did I when I could. Thank God I have good thighs. I got that from my mother. She got it from her mother. The Morton legs. Good hair and good legs have been my stock in trade. You could do worse.

I always liked to sleep with Bertrand. He was usually very tempestuous. That must be the French part. But there was an inner reserve there. There was never any question of Bertrand crying in my arms and telling me how much he needed me. That's the French part, too, I suppose.

What was there really to complain about, that Saturday when I saw Mr Bigge? Bertrand was now Senior Art Director at *Attraction.* I was senior writer on the Nixtrix Beauty Products account at Campanella Co. and earning a lot more than many of the men on the account. We had a house on East 81st Street. Our son went to Dalton. We were paying our bills and had money left over. Not just running from one payday to the next like a lot of these people. Bertrand was even able to buy that Dubuffet he wanted so much.

I put the cassette back under the bed. Finished cleaning Freddy's room. Went downstairs and did the breakfast dishes. Took a bath. Washed my hair. And kept thinking about Mr Bigge. I thought, 'This is ridiculous. I'm a mother of a fifteen-year-old boy. I should be concerned that he's watching filthy adult videos which are going to put all the wrong ideas in his head. That guy was so beautiful. Especially that scene where he's standing and holding that woman's ankles in his hands and that long, flat muscular torso is moving back and forth, those hard thighs battering her body. How does that joke go? 'Stop it dear, you're making mother hot.' Exactly. I was making myself hot.

So I straightened myself out. Made a cup of tea with lemon and honey. That's what I do instead of eat. And went for a lie down and to read the *New Yorker*. Let's not get into that. I was just hovering on the edge of stopping reading it.

And then I sat up and thought 'Screw it'. And went and fished the cassette back out from under the bed and threw it into my office carryall. I didn't really want to see it again but wanted to see if Mr Bigge had done some other videos. This was not at all like me. But I certainly can't be the only married woman in New York who has rented videos.

Sex videos that is. Freddy came in just before dinner. Bertrand didn't come back and I didn't really expect him to. I could just imagine them down there at *Attraction* trying to decide if the sub-paragraph on the story about the new hair-dos from Brazil should be in two-point or three-point type.

Freddy and I ate our well-balanced meal. He got a piece of apple pie. I didn't. And then he was out to go across the street to watch television with the Hinkle girls. I let him go because it really was just across the street and the Hinkle girls were A-level students who still wore braces. I was probably all wrong. They were probably a pair of little ravers who never wore underpants and had tried every drug known to man. What's a mother to do? They certainly never *looked* like they weren't wearing panties.

I went to bed early. God, I love to sleep. If I've held on to my looks in any major way it's by sleeping a lot and using Mario Badescu products. Slap that night cream on and sack out, sister.

Sunday morning I tried having some impromptu sex with Bertrand and I think he was very appreciative. I can be imaginative when I have to. But it really didn't do the trick for me. Bertrand never liked to fool around too much. He just wanted to get at it. Sort of that French idea of the *baise de santé* I suppose. Wouldn't want those little semen droplets to get all backed up and go stale on you, would you?

Monday I girded my loins and was determined to go into the video store down Third Avenue on my lunch break. It was something like taking your first parachute jump. You just step up to the open door and leap out. Or in, I guess.

My boss, Edwina Gray, was in fine fettle. She usually was on Mondays. It can be exhausting trying to be chic and witty enough for Edwina. She's tall, she's blonde. She has a big nose and excellent legs and wouldn't have it any other way. She had the Nixtrix people all wrapped up. If she were to die they would probably have committed suttee and thrown themselves on her funeral pyre. Very cagey, Edwina. And a very good egg. I've always loved her since the day I had to go in and tell her I had to leave because Freddy was being sent home sick from school. We were in the throes of some major mascara push. The client had resisted Edwina's new name of Forty Lashes so we were in frantic rewrite. Edwina looked up and said, 'Your private life comes first.' And she meant it. Her favorite saying then was 'It's only advertising.' That and 'If it's only on the air for thirty seconds, how long could it take to write?'

This morning she was wearing her gray duck-eye suit with no blouse and a large Bulgari bracelet and earrings. She's quite adamant about necklaces. 'Only in the evening and then no bracelets' is her rule. I worship her. Nothing pleases me more than when people call me 'Little Edwina'.

On Monday mornings we used to meet and plan the work for the week; the only time we really got to see the boss in a group. Three writers, three art directors and two juniors. A big group. Nixtrix brought in much dinero to Campanella and the agency pretty well gave Edwina her head. The account people kept a low profile. And had done since the day the Nixtrix advertising manager, Carlton Carlson, went on a rampage and was striding around the room shouting, 'You people have had it. You are the shittiest agency in New York. You know nothing about advertising. You're stupid. You're jerks. [This was one of his calm days.] The only reason you people have this account is sitting right there!' He pointed in a dramatic way to Edwina, who was putting on Chapstick, staring into space. I know, I know. Head of the biggest beauty account in the country and she wears Chapstick. Lipstick only at night. She says you never know who you might want to kiss in the elevator during the day.

She looked up at his ringing words and said into the silence, 'I think we should leave now.' And we all filed silently out. Like people leaving a sickbed.

It's her example that I held in my mind when I went to the video store. I know if Edwina wanted to rent a sex video she would go rent it. March in and get a really good look about before deciding on her purchase. And would walk right up to the counter and slap it down. No bones about it. Yes, it's me and this is what I want to see and what about it? So I did the same thing, to the best of my abilities.

Have you ever been in the porn section of a video store? It's mind-boggling. Never did so many different people seem to be doing precisely the same things with the same lighting and cameraman on the job. At least that's what the pictures on the outside of the boxes suggested. I was at a loss to find Bob Bigge. He wasn't under the 'B's'. You can imagine that section. Boobs, Balls, Butts.

A clerk was passing by. A really good-looking black guy. Maybe they choose the clerks to look like they could have stepped out of one of the films. I must say I had to admire the clerk's demeanor. You could be shopping for eggplant or garden hose. I held out the cassette I had in my bag and said, 'Do you have any other films . . . videos . . . by this performer?' He took it and looked at it. 'Oh, yeah,' he said. 'He did a couple under that name. I think he changed studios. He's called Chase Manhattan now. I think he's over here under "C".'

'Why do you file them under their first names?' I said. 'They're known that way by their fans. Most of them wouldn't know how to spell Manhattan,' he said. I hoped I looked like I could spell Manhattan.

He gestured down the line and I immediately saw that my new friend had been busy. There must have been ten videos to choose from. *Chase 'Em Down. Chase and the Chaste.* How literary. *I Want to Be Chased.* There was quite a list. I was torn. Finally I took three because I liked the pictures of my honey on the cover. There was the torn-off jeans one, shot in the country I guess, called *Wild Animal Chase.* And one in a tuxedo. At least the tuxedo jacket. Nice legs. And after dithering, my last choice was called *The Size of the Chase.* You can well imagine the cover.

At the desk I said, 'I'll rent these three for a week.' The clerk, a rather pretty young woman, registered nothing. To her it was three pairs of pantyhose. Or more like the complete film oeuvre of Charles Manson. 'Can I return this?' I said, holding out my son's video. She looked at it. 'I don't think this is from us.' Waving it over her head she called out; 'Hey, Charlie. Is this Mr Bigge video ours?' Fortunately the shoppers have their protocol down just as cold as the clerks. No one turned, no one looked. Evidently Charlie mumbled or signaled negatively, as she said, very politely, 'This must have come from some other store. Are you returning it for a friend?' I think she must have gotten the signals that I was a first-time shopper. 'In a way,' I said.

'You'll have to check with them about where it came from,' she said, tossing it into the pink and black plastic bag the others were already in. At least the bag wasn't blazoned with SEX VIDEO on the side. I placed it in my carryall bag and went back to the office.

'I am becoming so duplicitous,' I thought during the afternoon, while I was leafing through foreign magazines, cutting out pictures. Trying to get ideas for a new television commercial for Sunset Shampoo. Edwina's new thing was that products should do more than one thing. This one not only lightened your hair when you used it, but also left a residue to make your hair easy to set. Sun. Set. Get it. I hope you do. I hope you do. Actually I tried the lab sample and it was pretty good.

While I was thumbing through shoals of pictures of European blondes on yachts, riding horseback on the beach, covering their breasts with one arm while reaching for a drink on a chaise longue in St Tropez, I felt a little thrill of excitement about my videos. Right there. Under my desk in my carryall. And nobody knew. Who would think? This nice young woman in a black suit with pearls (I don't always follow Edwina's no necklace dictum) and medium-height heels rents porn films.

I stopped and looked out the window across Third Avenue. Not much to see, we were on the 37th floor. Edwina's office was on the other corner looking over the East River. Whenever people exclaimed at the view she said, 'It's only Queens.' And she wasn't being funny. She was right. A view over Queens isn't exactly a view. One night we were walking home together and you could see the sky was a brilliant red beyond the Hudson. She said, 'New Jersey is burning. At last.' That was funny.

Back to my thoughts. Just when *was* I going to look at my videos? I was never alone. If I had to wait until next Saturday that was going to be a lot of viewing in one afternoon. Should I stay up late? But I never did that. And what if Freddy or Bertrand got up and wandered in. They'd think I'd gone mad. Or worse. They would probably want to call in an exorcist.

I could get up early but that was just as bad. I wouldn't be in the mood and Bertrand was always lurking around doing his exercises. I could go home on my lunch hour. I could rent a hotel room. No, I'm just going to lock them in the bottom of my office armoire. (My office was in French Provincial. Real. Big spenders the Campanella Company.) Good idea. I did not want them around the house. There's always that terrible bit of bad luck when someone is looking for their ski sweater and stumbles upon your sex videos, isn't there?

chapter 2

....

my mother and i

Do you love your mother? Would you say that 'love' is hardly a word that can encompass how one feels about one's mother? It's like standing so close to a mirror you really can't see all of yourself. My mother is so close to me I really can't get a good look at her. Not that I have ever tried, really.

My Uncle Fred (my son Freddy is named for him) once told me that he was talking to my mother, his sister, and she said, 'I didn't know that you were so fond of cats.' He had two at the time, gifts from a male friend. He told her, 'I'm not really, but now that I have them I feel responsible for them.' My mother replied, 'That's how I feel about Nina.' And that's exactly how she was with me. Very responsible, competent, steady, always there for a decision about what to do. She was demonstrative in her own way, always kissed me good night. Insisted upon it. But once I kissed her on the mouth and she said, 'Oh, don't do that. I don't like that.' Hmmm. Makes you think.

Well, my cool, now widowed mother, who lives in the Turtle Bay area right behind the office, called and delivered me from my quandary about the video. 'Nina, I'm going down to Florida to visit my friend Millicent Anderson in Jupiter. She's depressed. Can you run by and water the plants while I'm gone? Say on Monday? The maid comes on Thursday and she can do it when she's here, but they really need watering twice a week. If you could come by on Monday, that would do the trick.'

Out of the blue, Mom delivered. I'll go over to her flat and watch my videos. *Quelle bonne idée!*

'When are you leaving?'

'Tomorrow dear. For two weeks. You don't really have to come until next Monday.'

'How are you getting to the airport?' I asked her.

'In a taxi. I always hate taking people to the airport and picking them up there and I certainly am not going to impose that on people now.' I knew she meant it. And she's perfectly capable of it. She's only sixty and a very fit sixty. She goes to the gym, more often than I do. And I see her looking at my rear end reflectively when we're together. It isn't sexual. I think she sees women as racehorses that have to keep fit for the long run.

'I'll come by on Friday just to make sure Paloma hasn't forgotten,' I said.

'She won't, I'm sure. She's good about that,' she said.

'It's really no bother,' I said. No bother. No bother. I could hardly wait. And a great explanation when I got home. If anyone asked. Which no one was going to. The old shoe would be there to get the meals on the table and that was all that was ever noticed.

So Friday I was really excited as I left work. I thought, what if I get struck by a car and they find me carting pornographic videos around? I put it out of my mind. Anyway, I didn't have to cross a street. My mother lives right next door to Katherine Hepburn. Just around the corner and down 49th Street. She has a floor-through flat. Katherine has a whole house. I had worked around the corner for five years and never seen Katherine. I asked my mother if she had ever seen her and she said, 'Only once. She looked exactly like Katherine Hepburn. Only more crumpled.' My mother isn't a witty person. Just a direct one. And people often take it to be wit. She always assures them that she isn't being funny at all.

It was strange to enter my mother's apartment when she wasn't there. It had that empty quality that all New York apartments have during the week when their owners are at work. Do you know that feeling when you're home sick during the week? You feel that you're intruding on the privacy of the place. It wants to be alone.

My mother's apartment is largely in navy blue and maroon. Not big. Somewhat severe. But secure feeling. Like a large warm blanket you pull up over yourself on a chilly night. Pretty isn't the point.

She has lots of things from our family home in South Orange, where I was brought up. My great-aunt Emma's china cupboard and marble top table. The French dining table and upholstered chairs. The chairs are more Biedermeir. Mother got them from an emigré friend who had brought them from Vienna. She has some unusual friends. For such a conventional woman she has eclectic taste in people. I know why they like her. Stable. Do you hear me? Stable. Stable. Stable.

She has some paintings Bertrand did in art school. Not bad. Sort of big, figure studies in a loose style. I don't know if mother liked Bertrand, but she likes his painting. He usually gave her a little watercolor or something at Christmas or on her birthday. She always framed them and put them up, too.

So, there in the murk of mother's apartment, I saw more of Bob Bigge. Or to use his real name, Chase Manhattan. I wondered what his real name was? Something like Hector Mazursky probably. I popped in *Wild Animal Chase*. Sixty minutes. I stopped the machine and went to check the plants. Paloma had done her job. Back to the machine.

Well, what can I tell you? Quite a display of virility. I fast-forwarded the parts where lesser mortals were grinding their bodily parts together.

That seems to be the routine in these videos. The star does some major stuff, and they cut away for a break here and there where the hired hands or people in a bar or the neighbors get down and dirty. What a beautiful body. It's on the order of Leda and the Swan, or the Eagle and Ganymede, or the Rape of whoever the hell she was. Europa. He was a God descended to have intercourse with we mere mortals.

The story? A writer goes to a farm to work on his great American novel. Arrives in a tweed jacket and an open convertible. Carries in a computer laptop. All very modern. Needless to say he didn't get much writing done.

What with the housekeeper and her husband. Some housekeeper. And some husband. He screwed both of them if you can believe it. The husband surprised them on the kitchen table, and they jumped him and tore his clothes off, and you know.

As in the other film there was a kind of gymkhana quality to it. No one seemed to be actually interested in their partner; it was just sort of like a big bake-off. Or fuck-off. Wasn't it Tallulah Bankhead (again and always) who, when some man asked her 'What would you say to a little fuck?' threw her hair out of her eyes and answered, 'I'd say, "Hello, Little Fuck" '?

That was sort of the style of these videos as far as I'd seen. I watched my hero handle two unwary ladies who stopped by for directions and a really cute young man who had come by to be interviewed for the job of new hired hand. They actually seemed to be having the most fun together.

I put all the videos in a suitcase in mother's closet and left them there. Should I be struck down and mother find them there someday it would give her something to think about. I wouldn't care. I'd be dead.

I had something to think about on the long bus ride up Third Avenue, however. Hard stomach muscles. Real biceps.

Double shields of muscle on a rising and falling back. This is really weird I thought. I'm becoming a pervert.

And so I went home and made cheeseburgers and tomato and lettuce salad. They loved that.

You're never really out of doors in New York. You just go from one space to another. Out of your apartment, into a bus or taxi or subway, into your office. Then into a restaurant or a theater or a movie, back into a taxi, and home. Like little rats scurrying from one box to another looking for satisfaction.

That's what I thought about as I scurried rat-like into my mother's apartment on Monday after work. The plants needed watering this time. Chores done, I settled down to watch *The Midnight Chase*. I guess the producers thought their audience would get bored easily as people had their clothes off about two minutes into the story. Chase owned a nightclub in this one. The idea being that the audience fantasized what they'd really like to see the strippers, male and female, doing. And voila, they did it. Much better lighting in this one. Two adagio dancers took it all off and screwed standing. Front and back. Head to toe. You know. You probably don't. Then five male acrobats got very acrobatic. Then two female belly dancers. Who makes these films? Who works in them? These people weren't at all bad-looking. Although definitely mere humans. Then my Chase entered and did unspeakable things with a blonde stripper and someone who looked like a garage mechanic. They both paid attention to the blonde at the same time. Actually it looked like quite a lot of fun. I mean, don't you think part of the fun of fucking is to reduce some man to a state of blubbering collapse? And two! You can imagine. At least I can.

Later Chase went to a society party after the club closed and there he led the revels in which everyone got naked and the camera panned across heaps of limbs and lips thrashing about in every direction. Something like a butcher shop. I don't think *that* would be fun.

It's strange, these movies got me excited but not particularly excited sexually. I wasn't interested in seeing any of these other people except Chase. And I'd probably have enjoyed it just as much seeing a film of him walking down the street. Well maybe not quite as much. There was one shot in the last scene where he pulled off his dress shirt and then pulled his undershirt over his head. Talk about rippling. Pretty great. Oh, God. What *was* becoming of me? I didn't think women were voyeurs. (Or is it voyeuses?) At least I have never heard of such a thing. Voyeurs are always dirty old men. And here I was. A dirty old woman. Not quite old but getting there.

At dinner Bertrand apologized for having had to work most of the weekend. He said this issue was particularly tough because they were doing a whole new layout style with broken up typefaces scattered about. I didn't mention to him that Italian *Vogue* has been doing this for some time. I'm sure he knew. What is it about the magazine business that is so profoundly interesting to the people who do it and so completely incomprehensible and boring to those who don't? I could tell Freddy was miles away when his father talked. He was probably wondering which of us took his cassette. Maybe he was blaming the maid. Poor Mabel; she's so religious she'd probably have had a heart attack if she'd fished that thing out from under the bed.

So went my week. Dreaming up hundreds of new names for a new fragrance during the day, looking forward to my next screening date *chez maman* during the evenings. Nixtrix was launching a new fragrance and was very nervous about it. We met every evening at their offices at 5.00 to present names and see how they liked them. Their staff was doing the same thing. We must have gone through several thousand. I was trying to focus them on woman as the aggressor, rather than temptress. Being men, they didn't cotton onto the idea too much but Edwina was all for it. But I didn't really have my mind on it.

chapter 3

....

edwina's story

Edwina asked me to lunch. Curious. We'd often had lunches with clients and with the other writers and art directors, but we'd never had lunch all alone. It made me a little edgy, even though we knew each other well after five years of working together.

Except it was the kind of knowing each other well that New York specializes in. We'd always been cocooned within the framework of work. The perimeters were clear, our personalities well-defined. We didn't go outside that. Edwina seemed to be very open, but not really. For instance, I'd been to her home once. To a party. I had no idea about her love life. Or if she even had a lover. She could be a raging lesbian for all I knew. So many New York lesbians are like that. All chic tailleur and big jewels.

Edwina once asked me 'Why are bull dykes, Chinese cooks and wives in the suburbs so much alike? You know, all short hair, sun tan chinos, baggy shirts and no makeup.' One could ask that about New York lesbians, too. All check jackets, black hose on good legs, spike-heeled, closed-toe shoes, a slash of lipstick. Chic, but you can never imagine them locked in someone's arms. Anyone's arms.

So we went to Bice. I wore all black. I knew what I was doing. I'm blonde. The room is blonde. I wore black.

Edwina came to pick me up in my office. She was wearing navy and black. Always one step ahead of me. She smelled of Je Reviens. 'I love your perfume,' I said. 'Daring of me, isn't it, wearing such an old hat fragrance,' she said as we headed towards the elevator. 'But I like a fragrance that makes people draw back when you step into the elevator.' We did and they did. In an elevator Edwina always continues to talk in a normal tone as though people don't know her but know of her. 'Who wants a discreet perfume?' she said. 'I wear it for my own pleasure and if I can't smell it what good is it?' I, who usually wear St Laurent's *Paris*, which couldn't be more ladylike, said nothing. I hung my head a little. One doesn't need to rise to Edwina's level of audacity when with her. She rather likes a slightly stunned response.

We took a cab. She has such a nice way of getting into an awkward New York taxi. She sits down backwards on the edge of the seat and swings her legs in, knees together, legs looking great. The men passing by appreciated it. I copied her but didn't let my skirt fly where it might as she did.

When we got to the table I said to her, 'There's something French about you, Edwina. You get into a taxi with total assertiveness.'

She narrowed her eyes at me over her menu. 'What a strange thing to say,' she said. 'Actually I am French.' And then proceeded to order tagliatelle verde with a green salad and a glass of red wine. She never drinks white wine. She thinks it makes you acid. I wasn't such a suck-up that I ordered red, too. I ordered white. Pouilly Fumé, my favorite. I had mozzarella and sun-dried tomatoes first. Then sole. I like sole primarily because eating it is like performing an operation. First this side, then lift out the spine neatly. Leave no bones behind. I would have loved to have been a surgeon.

'I'm taking you to lunch because I feel I've been neglecting you,' Edwina said. 'I rush in and ask you to do four thousand names for a new shampoo and rush out and don't even tell you what a good job you've done on a project. Often when I'm home lying in the tub I think "Poor Nina, she's home rustling up some grub for that kid and her husband while I'm relaxing. Soaking and reading about Danish country houses or something." ' I smiled. 'And I realized we've been working together for years and I know zip about you. I've met your husband once at the office. And I've only seen pictures of your child. What's his name?' 'Freddy,' I said. 'Frederick. After my uncle.'

Then we discussed where I had been born, went to school, siblings (none), parents (one dead) and the rest of it. Edwina knows her stuff on drawing people out.

'And what do you do for fun?' she said as we stared at the figs we had both ordered for dessert. With cream. God, I would have thrown up if my mother had tried to get me to eat something like that when I was a child. And here I was ordering it.

I realized I was really very unhappy and said, 'Watch porn films.' Without blinking an eye Edwina took a sip of her coffee and said, 'What kind?'

'Just one kind,' I said. And I told her about my sneaking over to my mother's to watch my forbidden inamorato. As I talked I felt great misgivings. I didn't know Edwina that well. This could be all over the agency before I even returned home. Then again, if Edwina wasn't sophisticated enough for this, who in the hell was?

'Obsessions are great, aren't they?' Edwina said. 'They're like a great wind out of the North blowing through your life. Everything else is easy and of no importance in comparison. So what's next?'

'I don't know,' I said. 'I guess I'll go rent some more of his videos. My mother came back last week, so I haven't the foggiest idea where I'm going to look at them.' 'You can go to my place,' Edwina said. 'On your lunch hour. I don't mind.

I won't join you. Although I'd kind of like to. He must be hot.'

'He is,' I said a little sadly. I felt half-mad and ashamed of myself now the truth was out.

'What does your husband think of all this?' Edwina asked. 'Oh, he doesn't know.' Edwina looked at me a bit pityingly. 'Of course he doesn't know. But doesn't he sense a lack of enthusiasm on your part for making bamboola?'

'Actually it makes me feel a bit more like making it,' I said. 'But I don't think he particularly cares one way or another.' 'What do you mean?' Edwina said in that flat tone of voice she used in the office when you had to explain yourself.

And I told her that Bertrand was completely in love with his job and worked right through the weekends often and that we hadn't so much drifted apart as entered completely separate orbits, in which we were each completely absorbed. 'Do you think my obsession means I don't love my husband anymore?' I asked Edwina. 'No,' she said, 'I think perhaps you're becoming another person. I think you've had enough and you want out.'

'I'm not aware that I want out,' I told her. 'We seldom are,' she said. 'We so seldom are. Until we get cancer or they drag us off screaming.'

On the way back to the office Edwina told me something about herself. Surprising things. I think so that I would feel reassured about my confession to her. She was putting some very personal information in my lap as security.

Edwina *is* French. She was born in Vendome the year World War II started. 'There,' she said. 'Now figure that out. The Germans were invading and my parents took my older sister and fled to the Massif Central. Curious isn't it that they left me behind? They left me with my grandmother, who lived in an outbuilding at the Château d'Aigremont. I think she had once been a lady's maid or worked in the kitchen there. She took care of chickens and things like that, I guess. Later I wondered if perhaps my parents thought they could get rid of both of us by leaving us behind. I can't imagine what they thought we would eat.

'But the Germans were wonderful to us. They used the château as their headquarters. They baby-sat me. I can remember riding on their shoulders and the coarseness of their uniforms chafing my legs.'

We were stuck in heavy traffic at 53rd and Park. I was staring at Edwina. 'Edwina, how could you remember this? You were a tiny baby,' I said. She turned towards me and all the smoothness of her face seemed rumpled, like wind across the flatness of water. 'Strangely, I remember everything of my first year on earth,' she said. 'I know no one else does, but I do. More clearly than any other year I've lived. I remember the dusty, oaty smell of the barns at the château. The German soldiers carrying me about. My grandmother cooking over a little iron stove. The old quilt on her bed, red and black. A boat that they used to take me out on on the river. The soldiers. I suppose my grandmother was afraid to tell them they couldn't carry me about with them.' In the shadows of the cab Edwina's eyes had no color. I felt I was looking right through them, as though looking through the eye holes of a mask, out into a night sky where the stars were gathering. Even though it was broad daylight outside the taxi.

I reached over to put my hand over hers on the plasticized taxi seat. 'Edwina, what are you doing here?' I said. 'What are you doing here working on these silly things at this silly agency?'

She looked away, putting her face in order. 'Well, that was quite a start for a life, wasn't it?' she said turning back. 'Shall we get out and walk? We'll be here until sundown if we don't.'

As we walked she said, 'My parents soon came back of course. They used to come out to the château at night to see us. In the darkness. My grandmother was probably giving them food. German food. I was there all through the war. I didn't start school until the Germans left. I went back a few years ago. I found the boat, sunken into the reeds along the shore. So small. I remembered it as some huge barge.

'I hardly remember anything of France anymore. After the war I remember we lived in Blois and my mother's best friend ran a *bandagiste* shop. Can you imagine? They sold all kind of things for the *mutilés*. All those wounded in both wars, I suppose. It was full of artificial limbs. And the shop window had dummies with all kinds of bandages. Bandages for parts of the body you couldn't even imagine needing to be bandaged. The husband of the owner only had one leg himself. When we visited them there were always three artificial legs in the front hall. Each one had a different shoe and sock on it. So he could just strap on a suitable one as he was about to leave the house. The last time I was in France I went past that shop. It's an antique store now. I wonder where all those artificial limbs went?'

I could only stare at her. She was talking looking at the tall glass facades across the street that were so far from her memories. She turned towards me. 'And I knew France had really changed when I was in the Metro in Paris and they don't have those little Walnetto candy machines anymore. For a franc you used to get five little square, tough nut-flavored brown squares, each one with waxed paper folded about it. I used to love those. Sometimes I survived on them. I can remember being so hungry in the Metro, waiting for a train. I went to school there before I left France.'

I went into her office with her when we got back and asked her, 'But how did you get here, Edwina? And you have such an English name.' And sitting calmly at her desk she told me that her real name was Edwige Grisebon, which no American could pronounce. And that she had come to the United States in her mid-teens, running off with an American soldier, had lived on the West Coast. And here she was. Later. Much later.

'You really don't have any accent at all,' I told her. And she

said, 'My French is ridiculous now. I speak with all the awful
kid slang of the 1950s. French people laugh at me. But I
worked hard to get rid of any accent. I hate those "Frenchies"
whose accent gets worse every year. And I've lived in England.
I've lived all over.'

'And what about love?' I said, leaving. 'All my gods are
dead,' she said. And looked down at her papers.

I came back in. She looked up at me. Her face was very
calm now. 'Time tore them out of my arms,' she said.
'Everyone you ever loved is dead?' This was kind of heavy for
three o'clock on a Wednesday afternoon. 'Not all of them,'
she said. 'Sometimes they want to come back into your life.
There's always that possibility if they're still living.

'But I have no desire to sleep with someone with withered
buttocks just for old time's sake,' she said. 'And those old
World War II cocks, men think a woman doesn't care what
their body is like. That's not true. Some women just ignore
it. I can't. I would rather just remember. The sweet *nuage*.
And you know, I don't even think about it all that much. I
have no desire to live in the hollowed-out shell of my past.'

I said, 'But what we do is so unromantic. It doesn't really
mean anything. We do an ad or a commercial and it's gone.
No one remembers it. It's totally unimportant.'

'But I have you and all the rest of the staff,' she said. 'I
find you all very interesting. And the job is fun.'

'Everybody else thinks it's a nightmare,' I said. She said, 'I
pretend I'm a nurse in an insane asylum where all the patients
think they work in advertising. My job is to keep them calm.
If you disagree with them and argue it only makes them
worse. And I never make the mistake of thinking I'm a doctor.
I am always the nurse. Just the nurse.

'Beauty and fashion is interesting work. It defies mortality.
Sick, old, infirm, we still get up and put on a new dress and
do our hair in a new way and paint up our faces and inside
we're still the same. Young, ready to do battle. Men know

nothing of this. Homosexuals do, of course, but most men never understand this. They think we do it for them. So silly. 'Coco Chanel said she never designed a good dress until she didn't care anymore. That's how I feel. I don't have to care to know my business. I know what good is. And we do good work. If the client doesn't want to buy good work, that's his business. You offer caviar and they prefer peanut butter, so you give them peanut butter. That's why I don't allow awards around the office. When they say "This stinks", you can say, "That's your opinion." And do it again. But put an award on the wall or a prize on a shelf and you've accepted that their opinion counts for something.

'They have their opinion and they're paying the bills. But once you accept that they are better judges than yourself you've had it. There. That's my lecture for the day. You're not going to hear that again for at least a year.'

'Even so, Edwina, you've made me feel sad,' I told her.

'It's not sad. Yes, maybe it is sad. But life is a mixture of muddy sadness and glitter. There's nothing wrong with enduring great sadness as long as you've had enough of the glittering bits.'

'Speaking of glittering bits, are you going to the *Escapade* magazine lunch tomorrow?' I said, really leaving her office this time. 'They have a new English editor.'

Edwina said, 'What would an English woman know about fashion? They can't even do their own hair.' And she turned to her typewriter.

I worked all afternoon tightening up a Gleam 'n Flow commercial. Seventy-three words is all you get in thirty seconds and a good writer doesn't kid themselves they can squeeze in a few extra. And I did some voiceover tests with half a dozen announcers. Amazing the suave, sensual voices that come out of these men, who for the most part look like they should be refereeing a rugby match. Maybe it's like opera singers. You have to have a belly to get that tone.

I went in to say good night to Edwina. We had rushed into a kind of intimacy during our lunch hour that had left me feeling a little shaken. She looked up, saw me in her doorway and said, 'I've been thinking about you. We're going to be shooting that "Girl With The Glow" commercial in Los Angeles next week. I think you should be on the shoot. That old bat Merida McCall is probably going to give us all kinds of trouble with the script and we don't want to have to struggle with her over the telephone.'

I said, 'But you were going to go.'

'It's high time you started taking over some of these projects. You wrote the original script. It's your idea, shooting it at the Huntington Museum in Pasadena. Those French rooms and the rest of it. You should go,' she said.

'I'd love to,' I told her. 'Freddy can stay at his friend Jacob's and Bertrand won't even notice I'm gone.'

'Come here and sit down a minute,' she said. 'I had another idea, too. I have another old friend out there who used to be a dancer. She's a casting director now. I just called her and she's going to track down this fellow who has captured your fancy. She said she's heard of him but has never worked with him. I want you to call her when you get to the Sunset Marquis hotel and see what she's found out. Just tell her that you've heard his name and you're doing some casting for that new Jamaica Wind fragrance project while you're there. You can see him that way. See what's cooking.'

I sat there numbly and nodded. And nodded. And nodded. Edwina was being very cool. She was handling this like just another project. I was almost out the door when she called after me, 'We'll talk about love some more another time. I have a lot to say on the subject.' Of course everyone within earshot heard her. But Edwina's door was never closed. Whatever she said was for the world to hear. And ponder upon.

chapter 4

....

in hollywood

I stayed at the Sunset Marquis in Hollywood. West Hollywood, actually. It had gotten all rather swank recently. Over-
decorated rooms with the bed sitting at an angle to the corner.
Lots of chintz. All the furniture of an English country
bedroom crammed into a smaller space. Not bad, but I liked it
better when I first started coming to Los Angeles for television
shootings.

It was so seedy then. Rock groups always stayed there.
Figuring they couldn't trash it much more than it was trashed
already. Everything looked sun-faded. Those big, low motel
beds with the bed covers that feel as though they have asbestos
in them somewhere. And big prints of large flowers on the
walls. I loved it. Total anonymity. You could check into one
of those rooms and no one would ever find you again.

That cheesy swimming pool in the middle of the three
stories of rooms. The pool in which Van Heflin died. Swimming in the night, probably under the influence of various
mood enhancers. The hotel said it was a heart attack. Or
used to say so. Now they denied all knowledge of it.

I love the feeling of sinking without a trace when you check
in at the Sunset Marquis. And I love that uphill street, deep in
foliage, the buildings hiding behind hedges, the greenness and
the freshness, always the same no matter what time of year

you arrive. Flying in from New York, traveling across the wasted streets from the airport, up La Cienaga and off to the left. And then, this hideaway, especially magical at night with small lights flickering deep within the dark green leaves that engulf the entrance. A bored desk attendant who couldn't care less who you are or what you're doing there. And if you drive into the parking space underneath, there's an elevator that takes you directly to your floor. So you can come and go with partners of any race, creed or place of national origin. Great.

And then room service. And no television. I never watch television. I was reading *Cousin Pons* by Balzac. Edwina prefers that for the most part her staff don't watch television. The Glorious Amateurs she called us. Since we didn't know what was going on, what we did looked fresher was her theory. Frequently she told us a wonderful idea that had come to her in the bathtub. Something about blondes in the snow. And we had to break the bad news to her that Clairol had been doing exactly that for the past two years. The television department was always agog at what we didn't know.

The next morning I got to the studio at six o'clock with the talent and hair and makeup two hours before the crew. They never have the talent ready before ten o'clock anyway, but I'd hate to come in at eight and be told 'We didn't know whether you wanted her hair up or down so we waited.' Petitfour St Albans was doing hair and makeup, so I had less to worry about. But Merida McCall was the talent and we'd really have to be two against one to get her ready and looking like something.

Merida was almost one of the Charlie's Angels once. And then she got lucky and had a series. *The Wild Corral?* A western of some kind. She was the blonde. And now she was the hostess of that dreadful show *Stargazing*. Petitfour always referred to it as *Starfucking*. Actually I rather liked Merida. She doesn't have a sense of humor but at least she knows she should have. I think she was originally from Orange County somewhere. Probably hasn't lived more than fifty miles from Sunset Boulevard in her whole life.

So I was up at five, out of the hotel by five-thirty and at Raleigh studios by six. We'd decided finally not to work at the Huntington Museum. I think Merida thought Gainsborough's *Blue Boy* would distract from her. Dawn was breaking. It wasn't so bad coming from New York. The three hour difference makes it kind of a normal schedule. As long as you go to bed early. Which is always impossible.

I got in the door about ten minutes ahead of Merida. Petitfour was already there with all his little utensils set out on the dressing room counter. He's short. He's dark. He's cute. He's good-tempered. I think he liked to work with us because we didn't take the whole thing very seriously. Edwina's slogan 'It's Only Advertising' has run through the industry. He told me the last time we worked together that before he met Edwina he knew he was short but he didn't know he was out of proportion. Edwina doesn't care so much about advertising but she does care about perfection.

Petitfour and I kissed and got our cups of coffee and croissants from the food table in the studio. As usual groaning under the weight of enough food to feed an entire village on the Indian sub-continent. And Merida arrived, with her secretary and chauffeur. Who rushed towards the food table as though it was a mirage. Delighted to distance themselves from Merida probably.

You had to hand it to those Hollywood people. Whatever she might or might not be, Merida was on time, had clean hair, and didn't complain about the hour. The fact that she was probably making about fifty thousand dollars for a day's work might have had something to do with it.

Up close she wasn't bad. There had to have been some discreet pulling and tucking, but she looked good. Trim. Like an Olympic skater ready to hit the ice.

First we tried on clothes. We had commissioned a strapless dress with a large bow on one shoulder from this Hollywood designer that did all her clothes for her show. Larry Marmoset. That's not his real name. It's Marmosan or something. He hated us and with good reason. We went to great lengths to get around him. Edwina saw a wonderful Ungaro dinner suit with pants she thought would make Merida look like a lady and had had it sent from Paris. Merida met Ungaro once at the Paris shows and went on about how handsome he is and how he really likes women. 'Yes, my dear, of course,' was all Edwina would say, but gave me the pitch for when I got into the dressing room.

Merida had on the Marmoset dress, which made her look like something out of *Destry Rides Again*. Her plain little face under her hair curlers looked quite satisfied. Because the dress made her bosom look enormous. Just what we didn't want.

'Merida, I have a surprise for you,' I said. She looked at me in the mirror with a look that didn't welcome surprises. 'We were talking to Paris and Mr Ungaro asked if he could send something for you to look at that he had designed thinking it would look wonderful on you.'

This was not entirely the truth, of course, but there wasn't any harm in lying with this particular strategy. I held up the garment bag. Merida did not demur. The Ungaro name had done its work. We released her from the bondage of her Marmoset gown and got her into the Ungaro number. He knows what he's doing. A wonderful purply-dark blue sequin jacket, no revers, nothing. And trousers in the same shade with a sequin stripe down one leg. 'Cobalt blue,' said Petit-four. 'Pretty fabulous. I'll do shadow that works with it, it'll make your eyes cobalt blue. It's the best for blondes.' It was like working on a good volleyball team. I threw the ball up and he had it over the net before anyone knew what was going on. Merida didn't even discuss it, and there were no forlorn looks at the other dress, drooping on its hanger. She did say,

'You don't see my legs.' I let Petitfour field that one. 'Everyone knows you have fabulous legs,' he said. 'This is throwaway chic. You're so fabulous you don't have to show them every-thing.' She ate this up. I rather admire her, actually. Unless she was a large ten-year-old when she was up for *Charlie's Angels*, she's got to be pushing fifty. And still has the hutzpah to want her legs to show. Once a starlet . . .

When we got to the jewelry part I showed her the Bulgari sapphires I'd brought out for her. I hadn't had to have an armed guard with me because they were only worth 200,000 dollars. I just brought the earrings and a bracelet. If I'd had the necklace, too, I would have had someone with a gun around.

I said, 'These are the jewels we have for you. Of course you might want to wear some of your own.' She laughed without moving her lips, which Petitfour was painting. When he got done she said, 'I don't have any. I remember when I was doing *The Wild Corral* that Yvonne DeCarlo asked me if Dentley gave me jewelry. I was Mrs Dentley Breeding then.' Everyone remembers when she was Mrs Dentley Breeding. He did her over. Suddenly there were cheekbones and breasts and blondeness.

'I told her he didn't and she looked at me and said, "Big mistake." That was hardly my biggest,' she said looking back at us from the mirror with the 'Blame me for anything. I can take it and I can survive' look you only see in Hollywood. They're toughies that bunch. I guess they know that there's nothing you need to be ashamed of finally as long as you can pay your bills.

We sailed through the day. Roger Flint was the director. He can drive you crazy but nobody makes a woman look more beautiful. And Merida knew it. And Roger was a Hollywood person. There is always respect for someone who has climbed out of the morass.

Merida knew her lines. She did glow, thanks to Roger's

lighting and Petitfour's makeup. She was even pretty adorable when she said, 'Let the glow on your face put a gleam in his eye.' That's been the *Girl With A Glow* line since the Civil War. She delivered value for money, our Merida.

And away she went at six o'clock. Which was pretty miraculous, considering that Roger considered the day misspent if we weren't there groggily trying to stay awake at midnight. I noticed that Merida took all the flowers, all the champagne, even all the special catered lunch that was left when she departed. I'd like to imagine that the chauffeur, the secretary and she made a light supper together tonight with the leftovers. What a woman.

On my lunch break I had called Ninthe Eliot, the casting director, to check on the casting we had planned for the next day. She said, 'I have eight great men coming in starting at ten. We'll give them each a half an hour so we can videotape them and you can talk to them a little.' I felt nervous. Had she actually gotten Chase Manhattan for the casting? I couldn't ask her. That would really look dumb. I told her that it sounded great and I would be there.

I had never met Ninthe Eliot. She was all business on the telephone and she was all Milwaukee in person when I met her the next day. Los Angeles is so much like a foreign country you're brought up short when suddenly a Ninthe Eliot appears. Short, dumpy, glasses. Not at all discomfited by her appearance. I guess in Milwaukee being good-looking is highly suspicious and not all that desirable. And yet. And yet. Edwina said Ninthe had been a dancer. And was a good friend. That put me on guard. She was obviously no sap.

'Where did you dance?' I asked her right off as we waited for the men to show up. I had asked to see the list and ran my eye down, finding no Chase Manhattan. I showed no disappointment. In my own way I'm well trained. How much did Ninthe know? She wasn't showing me any cards.

'I was a soloist with Ballet Theater,' she said. 'During the last days of Alicia Alonso and Igor Youskevitch. I used to alternate roles with Yvonne Chouteau. She was Indian, you know. Like the Tallchief sisters. And Mocelyne Larkin. God, could they dance. I saw Yvonne do the Dawn variation from *Coppelia* when she was eight months pregnant. Had to completely readjust her balances and everything. Wore a kind of shorty nightgown costume. She was incredible.'

'Well, you must have been pretty good yourself,' I told her. She said, 'I had attack. I was compared to Preobajenskaya. From the old Imperial Ballet. I was short and had good pointes. Still do.' She stuck out her foot and pointed at the wall in her espadrille. 'But you can only fight weight so long.'

'And you wound up out here how?' I said. 'I knew Dick Beard from Ballet Theater and he was dancing and choreographing in the early television shows. You should have seen him. Quite a fabulous-looking guy. Nobody at all like him around now. And he put me in his shows. And I helped him with casting. And one thing led to another and here I am.' She seemed quite pleased with where she had ended up. Dancers are so sensible I've found.

'Our first guy is Danny Buck. Very handsome. Can do lines. Has been working for Disney in those shows they do. Very built.' And he was. Those Hollywood guys are so much larger than life you can hardly imagine they're real. Here is handsome Danny Buck. Without a flaw. Jeans and a plaid shirt. Nice manner. Nice pictures. How is he different from Tom Cruise or Brad Pitt? I started thinking seriously about our Jamaica Wind commercial. Would he be right? 'Do you want me to take my shirt off?' he asked as Ninthe put the video camera on him. '*I'd* like you to take everything off,' Ninthe said, 'but actually you don't have to take your shirt off. Mrs de Rochemont showed me the board. You can keep your clothes on for the test.'

'Are you French?' he asked me, as he turned this way and that, giving his profiles and three-quarters. 'No, my husband is,' I said. 'He's a lucky guy,' he said. Was this young man coming on to me? 'Luckier than he realizes,' I said. Not knowing exactly what I meant. I never flirted well, even in school.

'What did you think?' Ninthe asked me. 'He's very handsome. And charming. Why isn't he a movie star?' I said. 'He probably will be. Too many good-looking guys and not enough movies. It takes time. Everybody you're seeing in the movies today is older than you think they are. Only Harrison Ford admits it. It takes time to climb up those golden stairs.'

Then we saw Phillip Fried. And Montgomery Anderson. And Jack Hannibal. All so good-looking. All so charming. All with wonderful bodies and wonderful smiles. 'Can you see one more before we break for lunch? Graham Grant. He asked especially if we could see him now because he's booked this afternoon.' And there in the door he was. My Chase Manhattan. Va-va-voom. Ninthe didn't register a thing, although she had to know who he was and what he did. He stepped up and shook our hands. He handed us his composite. One picture by Bruce Weber I noticed. Nice hands. Great hair. But not overly groomed. Somehow he looked a little less plastic than the other men we'd seen this morning. He was wearing chinos and good lace-up shoes and a T-shirt. Perfect.

On camera Ninthe asked him to tell us about himself. He said he was from Baltimore originally. He had graduated from St Johns University in Annapolis. Had started acting there. Had done bits on soaps in New York. Had been in Los Angeles for four years. Had just done some regional theater in Kentucky and was going to Hawaii for a pilot next month. How much of this was true I wondered. He certainly had something the others didn't. You could see it on the video. Was it the eyes? He was hot. You couldn't take your eyes off him on camera.

Ninthe, who had said nothing in front of the other men, said, 'I've never had you in here before, have I Graham? I think you're very interesting. Very interesting. Who's your agent?' She glanced at his card. 'Doris Dinard. I'll call her this afternoon. I have a couple of other clients who would like a look at you, I'm sure.' He smiled at her and said he thought that would be great. I, of course, had said about three words after we were introduced. Finally I roused myself and said, 'Would you like to see the storyboard?' He came over and sat down beside me in a folding chair. I could feel the heat from his body. I was going to start acting nervous in about one minute.

'If you're not having lunch with anyone why don't you come with us?' came from Ninthe's mouth. My thoughts exactly. 'Sure,' he said. 'I'd like that.'

We went to lunch at Butterfields. We walked. Ninthe's office is just up Sunset. We walked down that long, long staircase into the foliage. You never hear anyone speak well of Los Angeles and Hollywood. Only LA has this sort of deluxey small-town kind of place. Plants, fresh air, uncrowded. I love it.

I liked Chase. But now I was calling him Graham. I could see that Ninthe liked him too. Not in the same way. There was something almost professional about him. Reserved. As if he'd been taught to be social but it wasn't natural. Quite different from his pals of this morning. 'So what are you reading?' he asked me as we unfolded our napkins and looked at the menus. '*Cousin Pons*,' I said. 'That's one of my favorites,' he said, telling the waiter he wanted a chicken salad and iced tea.

'It's a particular point of view,' I said.

'It's a Hollywood point of view,' he answered. 'I like the concierge. She had never done anything bad before because she hadn't had the opportunity. She didn't drift into badness, she did a complete about-face when the chance came. That's human, don't you think?'

'I think it's also human not to be bad when given the chance,' I said. 'Ah, but that takes brains, don't you think? The brains to look ahead and see you're not going to like yourself and what a high price that is to pay,' Graham said.

'Don't you think brains are everything?' I asked him. 'One of my friends says that if you have a problem that someone else has solved, the real problem is that you're stupid. I have so many friends in analysis who talk endlessly about their problems and I wonder if they were just a bit more intelligent they'd figure it out,' I said.

'Sometimes our emotions keep us from being intelligent,' he said. This was only too true. I saw Ninthe eyeing me. She was following all this and not saying anything. 'So when do you go to Hawaii?' she asked Graham and he began to explain that it wasn't set definitely yet, but it looked like it would be the end of July.

We talked a bit about the Jamaica Wind commercial we were casting and I told him I'd been inspired by Jean Rhys' book *Wide Sargasso Sea*. That the images of the dark woman in the carriage traveling through the tropical trees and along the cliff edge looking out over the sea were images from that book. And the man walking out of the sea to meet her on the beach was her fantasy.

'You're the writer then?' he asked me. 'I thought you were the account person.'

'That's because she's wearing pantyhose,' Ninthe said.

'And high-heeled shoes,' he added. 'That's a pretty romantic scenario. I thought you said we didn't have to take off our shirts because there weren't any body shots. Is this guy coming out of the water wearing a suit?' 'Actually he's naked,' I said. 'But you don't see anything because it's against the light. He's just a silhouette.' 'They get to see my face a little bit don't they?' he wanted to know.

'Mr Grant, with a face like yours they are certainly going to see some of it,' I told him. 'Does this mean he's got the part?' Ninthe asked, looking up from her sherbet. She was being good today. No cake.

'This is so preliminary. Who knows if the client will even give a final okay on this commercial. But yes, I think Graham is the best suited for it so far,' I said. 'And you haven't even seen my body yet,' he laughed. I thought this was getting a little heavy. This was what I'd come to Hollywood for and now I was getting cold feet. I didn't really mind being a slut, I just didn't like *acting* like one.

He walked us back to Ninthe's office where he'd left his car. I asked him where he lived. He told me. In a little complex just above Sunset uphill from my hotel. I told him he lived very near where I was staying. I think I managed to do this in a nice 'married lady with a child' manner. Just two people perhaps planning to work together. Nice. And he left. I felt a pang. This could have been my only contact with my sex god. Would I have been more up front if Ninthe hadn't been there? Let's face it, if Ninthe hadn't been there I wouldn't have been there. What a good egg. What a saint. I wondered how he thought I looked. A tired blonde?

After lunch we saw Chad and Ched and Ted and Fred. Or was it Ned? No matter. All charming, all handsome, all doomed to be that three-second shot at the end of a beauty commercial. Mr Right. Having just found *my* Mr Right, I wasn't interested.

As I was leaving Ninthe said, 'Do you think he's homosexual?' I didn't have to ask her which one she was talking about.

'He's everything,' I said.

'I guess in his line of work you have to be,' Ninthe said.

'So you know what he really does?' I said.

'I'm the one who found him for you,' she said.

'Am I crazy?' I asked her.

'Is getting what you want crazy? Just remember, once you get what you want you've got to be a good sport about it,' she said, running the video tape back. 'I'll make you a copy of this and send it to your hotel so you can take it back with you. When are you heading for the airport?'

'I'm on the Red Eye.'

'That's actually better than arriving in the dead of night.'

'Thanks, Ninthe. For everything.'

'It's nothing.'

'How'd you get the name Ninthe? It's almost like mine, Nina.'

'Weird, isn't it. I was the ninth child, believe it or not.'

'Was the one before you Eighthe?'

'Please. Don't be smart. The rest of them had quite normal names, if you consider Calvin and Eunice normal. I was the last. That's how they got the money together to get me ballet lessons. They'd moved into Milwaukee from the farm. And here I am.'

'Wild.'

'You're pretty wild yourself, Nina. You don't look it, but you are.'

That was nice of her, I thought in the cab back to the Sunset Marquis. Wild Nina. My new monicker.

I was packing when the phone rang. It was the desk. 'There's someone here to see you,' they said. 'Who?' I wanted to know. (I meant 'whom'.) There was some mumbled conversation. 'Your friend Graham,' they said. 'I'll be right down,' I said.

I didn't give myself time to think about it. I just went right down. He was sitting in a chair by the door. 'I was impulsive,' he said, getting up.

'How nice for me,' I said.

'I thought you might like to have dinner,' he said.

'I'm taking the Red Eye at midnight,' I told him. 'Why

don't we go out by the pool and have something to drink? Maybe I could have dinner on my way to the plane.'

My heart was beating really fast. What was I supposed to do now? Did he find me interesting? Was he trying to make sure he got the part? What was going on? I could imagine why he hadn't been available this afternoon. Screwing fifteen people and a goat.

'I was just driving up the street in front of the hotel and I thought that you were in there and so close and maybe I would never see you again and I didn't want that to happen. I don't get to meet many people like you out here. Or anywhere. And no, I don't care if I get the part in your Jamaica commercial or not. Some guys would do this to get a commercial, but not me,' he said as soon as he was sitting under the umbrella. Looking off at nothing in particular.

I thought I'd make it hard for him. 'That's exactly what some guys would say, too,' I told him.

'Oh, come on,' he said, turning towards me. There was something definitely working class about him, which wasn't bad. He was as nervous as I was. I wanted to think that anyway.

'It's so hard to have a conversation like this without sounding like daytime TV,' I said. 'But actually I'm pleased you came by. And yes, we will definitely have dinner together. And yes, I am a married woman. And no, I haven't done this before. There's another well-used line. I'm not the kind of woman who picks up men at castings.'

'I know that,' he said a little patronizingly. 'It's obvious. You're a nice, smart person from New York and I'd like to know you better and I kind of have the impression you wouldn't mind knowing me. And we'll see where it goes. Okay?'

I said that this was okay.

He went on, 'I decided a couple of years ago that if I wanted to know somebody I'd just step up and say it. And if

they turned me down flat, so be it. Being humiliated won't
kill me.'

'I certainly do want to know you. It's just kind of scary for
me. It seems a little slutty,' I said.

'We don't have a little slutty here in Hollywood. We only
have a lot slutty. And that's just the beginning. I wouldn't
worry about it,' he said.

So I went back to my room and finished packing while he
had a drink by the pool. And we got in his car. A Porsche.
As they say in Hollywood, if you've got twenty thousand
dollars you're either driving it or wearing it. And we went to
the Lampedusa. Suitably unfashionable. And I love the chairs.
That's me and food. The Lampedusa has these wonderful
chairs that look like carved bamboo and are kind of a dusty
pinkish color. And they're comfortable. The tables are far
apart and I can see what I'm eating. *What* I'm eating is less
important. And there were no candles. I haven't had a
romantic dinner in some time but this wasn't going to be one
of them. Dramatic, maybe. Romantic, no.

I did my part. We talked some more about Balzac. I told
him how I thought Balzac's life was. He worked himself to
exhaustion to make enough money to marry his Polish
countess and bring her to Paris and then he died. What he
really wanted wasn't love but prestige. When are people going
to wise up was what I wanted to know. And I meant it.

'Poor things,' he said. 'They just want other people to think
well of them.'

'Don't you want to be well thought of?' I asked him.

'Which one of me?' he said. 'No, I don't particularly want
to be well thought of. I can't imagine anyone thinking of me
at all if they're not actually with me. I just want to live. And
I don't know how.'

That made me want to cry. 'Do you think I do?' I asked
him.

'Certainly a lot more than I do. Look at you. Sitting up

straight. Perfect table manners. Interested in Balzac. Working in advertising and not even touched by it. Yes, you're doing something right. I can tell by looking at you. You know who you are. And what you will do and what you won't do. Don't you?' He was leaning across the table with his hands in his lap looking me very hard in the face.

'I don't want to disappoint you but I'm not sure I know what I'm doing in regard to you,' I told him. 'I think, I think, well, what do *you* think of obsession?'

'You don't mean the perfume, do you?' he said. 'That's like that old joke about someone asking Nancy Reagan what she thought about Red China and her answering "Never on a pink tablecloth." What do I think of obsession? I think you're lucky, that's what I think.'

'You're just like my boss. That's what she said,' I told him. 'She said she thinks obsession *is* love.'

And I told him about finding the video and watching it and becoming obsessed with Mr Bigge and Chase Manhattan. His face didn't move. Graham Grant seemed to be gone. No one was there.

When I got done he said, 'So, do you want to fuck?'

'No, I don't think so. Not now anyway. It's more I want to explore you and find out who you are. Like Siberia. Or the Sahara.'

He laughed. And the real Graham Grant seemed to have returned to the table. 'I think you'll get your chance, if that's what you want. But that's the hard part. The fucking part's easy. Let's get out of here. If we don't leave now I'll never get you to the airport on time.'

He took me to the gate. He carried my bag but he didn't try to hold my hand. I rather wanted him to.

'Maybe I could kiss you good-bye,' he said as the counter girl looked at us. 'Did you have sex with someone this afternoon?' I asked him. 'Yeah,' he said. 'Well, not really. It was a shoot for one of those stupid magazines where my cock is just about to enter her vagina. But it never does. That way you don't have to show condoms.'

'Strange job you have,' I said.

'Strange but the kind of job I seem to be cut out for,' he said. And then he put his arms around me and gave me a really nice kiss. Lips shut, but nice. And I really wanted to kiss him back. We were a good kissing team. With some people kissing doesn't do anything. With him it did plenty.

'I think this is going to be fun,' he said. 'How do I reach you?'

I turned back from the door to the plane. 'You know my name. I work at Campanella on the Nixtrix account. Are you listed?' The stewardess checking me in was really enjoying this, holding out her hand patiently for my ticket.

He shook his head. 'I'll call you,' he said. And was still standing there when I looked back just before running down the passageway. I was the last passenger. They clanged the door shut behind me as I boarded. And begin looking for my seat. Most of the passengers already had their sleeping masks on.

Would I sleep as I was whisked over Iowa? Looking down in mid-flight it was never black. There were always lights on somewhere all over America. Maybe all the love-obsessed were up in the night. Like me.

chapter 5
....
jamaica wind

I went straight home from the airport. It was dawn. Bertrand
and Freddy were just getting up when I arrived. My arrival
was scarcely noticed as they lumbered sleepily from bedroom
to bathroom to the kitchen.

From the looks of the kitchen, strewn with pots and pans
and a garbage can jammed with the remains of pizza boxes and
TV dinners, they had managed to survive. I fixed some bacon
and eggs for them, which improved their moods a little. The
attitude was that I had neglected them by going to California.
I could have made pancakes but enough was enough. They
left and I took a shower, unpacked and wondered if I had
actually done what I'd done. Maybe it was all a hallucination
and I actually had never left New York? No, there were my
dirty knickers tumbling out of the suitcase. I had to admit I'd
been somewhere.

I was late getting into the office but I knew Edwina wouldn't
mind. She'd rather that you were late than not look good
when you got there.

As soon as I got in I typed a final script as it had been
recorded, with the little changes I'd made for Merida. She
was a stickler. Didn't want to say 'that' when it should be
'who'. Rather than argue I just put three dots in the script
instead of the word and tell the talent to take a breath there

and leave out the word. 'As you would in ordinary conversation.' That always seemed to work and avoided arguments
later.

Edwina put her head in my door, checked out my plaid
skirt and black cashmere sweater, said 'Very collegiate,' and
'When do we get to see rushes?' I told her they'd be in
tomorrow morning and we could look at them on the lunch
hour at Dreamboat, who usually did our editing. So discreet.
Not a word about the Jamaica Wind casting.

I went to the gym on my lunch hour. It was time to start
again. Robert Fitzgerald. He's all the way to hell and gone
on the upper West Side, but worth it. Faye Dunaway was
there. And my old pal Nanette Waffle from *Vogue*. Nanette
said she was going to call me. 'Are you listed?' she asked. 'Of
course,' I said. 'I need every call I can get.' 'Me, too,' said
Faye, puffing at the next machine.

At the end of the day Edwina passed my office door and
actually came in. Didn't sit down. She was wearing a new
cobalt-blue suit. She must have gotten our conversation
about cobalt blue with Merida on her ESP receiver. 'Do you
think we could rush the Jamaica Wind job into production?'
she said. 'If we want to do it in the Caribbean we ought to
shoot next month before hurricane season. And if we wait
until September it's too late. Do you have the casting?'

'I do,' I told her, reaching into my carryall. I can be as cool
as she can. She taught me everything I know. She must have
talked to Ninthe Eliot. 'Can we take a look at it before you
leave?' she said. 'Now?' I asked her. 'In about fifteen minutes.
I have to tell Myrna LaFay that I love her but she gets no
raise until Christmas. It wasn't my idea that she buy a co-op.'

We looked at the casting together. I had the composites
with me and put them in front of Edwina one by one. Edwina
doesn't 'Um' and 'Aw' over male models' pictures. She's only
thinking of how they're going to fit into the film she has in
her mind.

She made little notes on her pad. I think she knew which one was Chase Manhattan from her conversation with Ninthe but she didn't let on. She crossed her swell-looking shins and asked, 'Which one do you like for the job?' 'Danny Buck is very good-looking,' I ventured without looking at her. 'I like that man Graham Grant best,' she said. 'Far and away. The girl is going to be Bernice Barucci, unless I can talk them out of it. She's the contract girl. A cow, but there you have it. Very dark. He's very blonde. They'd look great together. Anyway, that's my recommendation.'

'You do know that's the man I wanted to see, don't you Edwina?' I said to her, still looking down at my papers. 'I guessed it was,' she lied. 'You have good taste. Even so, he'd still be my choice. Honestly. He looks like a handsome blonde Prince Charles. But not really a gentleman. With just the suggestion that he'd be good in bed. Like Gary Cooper. He'll be my recommendation to the client. We should be able to shoot before the end of the month.' Going out the door she turned and said with a wild look she puts on to feign excitement, 'And I'll bet he's divine fucking.' 'I didn't, I didn't,' I said to her back. I know she believed me but she continued to say, 'You say, you say', as she disappeared into her office. As usual the staff was agog but can never piece these little outbursts together.

I packed up my things and stopped once more at her door. 'You're not doing this just for me are you?' I asked her.

There was no one else around. 'I want to do this commercial. I think he's the right guy for it. I am not inconveniencing myself in any way. I promise,' she said.

'But the client could find out? Who he really is, I mean.'

'I couldn't care less. Do I know? Do you know? We must live, Nina, we must live,' she said, raising both arms in the air as though a great wind was blowing. A high wind. For Jamaica. I loved her.

For the first time in our married life I told Bertrand I wasn't

in the mood to make love that night. I really couldn't. I was
heading for dangerous waters. I no longer felt like we really
belonged together. Already. I only kissed this other man.
Graham. Graham. Whatever his name is. Oh, you silly, silly
girl I thought to myself as I went to sleep, you silly, silly girl.

The next day I went to the video store again. I felt guilty
but I told myself, I could be in here renting *Gone With The
Wind*, couldn't I? They had three videos I hadn't seen yet.
Trouble With Strangers, *Mounting Mounties*, which from the
cover took place in Canada, and *Giants* in which he seemed
to be one among many men.

A passing clerk glanced at my selection and said, 'There's
another one with him over there. *King Size*. His name was
Luke Grate then, I think.' 'Oh, I think I have enough,' I said.
'Enough is never enough,' he murmured under his breath.

I paid for my rentals, put them in my carryall and was very
careful not to look around to see who might be looking when
I came out of the store. I could be taking a course. The films
of John Ford. Maybe I was planning to watch *Stagecoach*.
Right? Right. I wondered if Edwina ever had thoughts like
these.

I stowed the videos away in my armoire and the next day
asked Edwina if I might stop by her apartment on my lunch
hour. She handed me her key saying, 'The doorman knows
you. Tell him you're dropping something off.' Like my mind.

Trouble With Strangers was very strange. I think someone
had seen *Teorema*. It took place in a motel where Graham was
staying in the next room to a family. He saw them going in,
mother, father, two teenagers. I had to admit that the kids
looked pretty adult, even with the braids and the baseball
cap. The plot line was simple. The family was playing their
television loudly. Graham raps on the door. The son answers
the door in tiny shorts, comes into the hall and rather illogi-
cally goes to Graham's room. You don't need to know the
details. Well, there was mutual masturbation. A rap on

the door. Sister enters. Then Mom. Then Dad. Fairly
amazing. Only really bearable when you repeat to yourself,
these people are not really related. Graham seemed to be
enjoying himself. The others were deadly serious, but his
expression was one of good fun. And he delivered the few
lines he had rather well, I thought. And displayed absolutely
beautiful abdominal muscles. I had spent my life pursuing
glamour and beauty and this was where it had brought me.
Abdominal muscles.

I decided against looking at the others. I'd come back I
decided. I looked around Edwina's apartment before I left.
Dark green is a favorite color for Edwina. Dark green walls
in the living room. Large flowered wall-to-wall carpet. Very
Dorothy Draper. Dark furniture. I had only been here once
before at a party and hardly remembered it. I did remember
Edwina showing us around and seeing her pale blue bedroom
with the dotted Swiss curtains. George Campanella was with
us and said, 'Very virginal.' 'And why not?' Edwina replied.
No one said anything.

I don't pry, but I did look in the fridge. There was nothing
in it but a couple of bottles of cologne. Ma Griffe by Carven.
And Tuvache. I smelled it. Just like Jungle Gardenia. Nothing
American, of course, although Nixtrix makes some of the
biggest sellers. Ma Nuit de Folie, for one. What a nightmare.

Back at the office I saw that a meeting was scheduled for
the next day to discuss Jamaica Wind with the client. Not
really pre-production, but pre-pre. I also had a message from
Mr Grant. With a number. I called. He was not there, of
course. I left a message, saying I'd be in the office until six.
Three in LA. I always point that out to people. Amazing;
people still think the time goes the other way. And *forget* what
time it is in Europe. They'll never get it.

He called back right away. He was in his Porsche evidently.
'When will I see you again?' he wanted to know. I told him
that curiously the commercial we had auditioned him for

seemed to be raging forward. 'What if I came to New York?' he wanted to know. I said that was a fairly poor idea.

What was I doing? Married women don't do this kind of stuff. Not married women like me. Was this what having an affair was like? I knew I wasn't constitutionally cut out for this kind of thing. Bertrand and I might not be exactly chummy, but I wasn't going to run around behind his back. At least I didn't think so.

I told him we were having a meeting and he was our first choice for talent for the commercial. And I'd call him back Monday to tell him what was cooking. He said, 'I'm not all that interested in the commercial. I'm more interested in seeing you. I might just show up.'

I said, 'I saw *Trouble With Strangers* today.' He didn't miss a beat. 'Yeah. How'd you like it. One of my best I think.' 'Well . . . it was kind of fun. You were kind of fun. More than the others,' I said. 'I can be a lot more fun than that actually,' he answered. 'This conversation is getting a little reckless,' I said. 'We should talk again Monday.' I was getting a little short of breath to tell you the truth. 'Okay. I'll call you. I think I love you,' he said. 'Oh, not yet, not yet,' I called into the phone, thinking of him whizzing along some freeway on his way to have intercourse with someone. And hung up.

Whooo. I got out of there fast. Going home to fix a spaghetti dinner was kind of a letdown after that. More of a letdown, there was nobody home when I got there. Freddy left a note, he was at Jason's. A message on the machine from Bertrand; they were having trouble with the Raquel Welch shoot and he'd be late. So I took a bath, ate an apple and a yogurt and went to bed to read more *Cousin Pons*. Finished it. So sad. So tough. Is life really like that and I just don't get it?

'Well, if I don't get it I don't,' I thought and rolled over and went to sleep. I didn't even hear Bertrand when he came to bed. Must have been late as he didn't get up when I did and was still in bed when I left for work.

I went to the gym again and Mr Fitzgerald said I was looking good. 'Are you dieting?' he asked me. 'For one day,' I told him. 'You get great results,' he said. I determined to plunge on with it and took a yogurt to the Jamaica Wind meeting at Nixtrix. Mr Carlson was rather calm for a Friday. 'How'd it go?' he asked me. 'Merida was great,' I told him. 'Looked great, did her lines great, stayed great and left great,' I told him.

'Yeah, I know. She called me this afternoon. Thinks you're terrific.'

'Me? She doesn't even know my name. But she did a great job. She really did,' I said.

Mr Carlson said, 'She knows your name is Nina. Said she always wants you there on her commercials. Said you have a calming effect.' And he sort of snickered.

'Like a gas leak I suppose you mean?' Edwina said. 'Who wouldn't love to hear that they have a calming effect? Go sit next to Mr Carlson, Nina. We're going to need a calming effect when he hears the budget for the new Jamaica Wind commercial.'

She put it in front of him. He said, 'Jesus Christ.' He does sort of nice, old-fashioned swearing. There are certain things he'd never say in front of a lady. He probably doesn't say 'Boo' to Mrs Carlson. But he didn't really turn it down. He liked the board. He liked the talent. Wanted to see some other guys on the video but agreed with Edwina that Graham Grant was the best guy. Didn't really pay much attention. Edwina didn't argue about Bernice as the lead girl. She was cutting a deal. For me I think. And we left. A piece of cake.

'Happy?' she asked in the cab on the way back to the office. 'I think it's going to be a great commercial,' I said. 'You are really quite a piece of work, you know. I pity that poor Graham Grant. He doesn't have a Chinaman's chance at a Japanese gang-bang.' She always has a lovely choice of similes. And we both laughed and laughed until the cab got back to the office.

About 10.30 Monday morning Graham was on the telephone. 'You're up early,' I said.

'Why? It's about 10.30 isn't it?' And I knew.

'Graham, you're here, aren't you?'

'Actually, I'm about 200 yards from you,' he said. 'I'm at the Intercontinental, over on Lex.' I didn't say anything. I couldn't think of anything to say. 'Are you there? Don't hang up. I'm coming over to take you to lunch,' he said.

'Don't do that.' My brain finally kicked in. 'It looks like you're going to be doing this commercial and I don't want people seeing me having lunch with you before we even shoot it. It'll look like you slept your way into the job.'

'Haven't I?'

'In my dreams, I think. In my dreams.'

I had him meet me for lunch at Un-Deux-Trois way over on the West Side. At least if I ran into someone I knew they probably wouldn't be from the agency. He was already at the table when I got there. In a blazer and tie. I thought, who would think such a beautiful body lurked inside those duds?

I sat down and said, 'Have you ever had a dish slip out of your hands and you see it in the air? It isn't broken yet but there isn't any way in the world it isn't going to be. You just have to stand by and let it break. One second it's perfect. The next second it's in smithereens.'

'That's how I feel when I see pictures of someone jumping out of a hotel window during a fire. Or someone leaping off a roof committing suicide. There they are. Every bone is intact. The blood is pumping through their veins. Nothing is wrong. But nothing can save them,' he said.

'Sometimes babies survive plane crashes,' I told him. And added, 'Once I knocked a bottle off a shelf, saw it falling, and caught it between my feet before it hit the floor. Honestly. Accidents aren't always catastrophes.'

'Let's order,' he said.

I didn't even mention that I was surprised he was in New

York. Later he told me he thought that it was so cool that I didn't babble on about what a surprise, etc. But it didn't really occur to me. He was there. He was supposed to be there. And so on. Whatever was happening between us obviously couldn't take place if we weren't in the same place at the same time.

We ate something, and as we looked at each other we talked about nothing. I said, 'I just read an excerpt from Dawn Powell's journals last night.'

'Dawn Powell?'

'You're excused for not knowing who she is. Was. A New York writer. Not very well known. When her husband died after forty-two years she wrote that she was sure he would have thought the same thing when she said, "We have been through worse things than that." And she could honestly say that he was the person she most enjoyed running into on the street. That's what I want. Someone I would still enjoy running into on the street, more than anyone else, after forty-two years.'

'They probably got along so badly they never got bored with each other,' Graham said.

'I hate the acceptance. The "This is what it is." It isn't good enough.' I was opening my mouth and hearing things come out I didn't even know I'd been thinking.

I said, 'I think women are awfully disappointed by men. We're full of all these emotions and enthrallment and obsessions about men in general, and then we get one specific one for the roller coaster ride to adventure and it turns out to be a long drive across Kansas.'

'I suppose a lot of things get in the way. Children. Bills.'

'How about lack of imagination? How about not caring that somebody loves you a lot? How about wanting to get lost in the repetition so you don't have to think about anything? How about thinking some stupid magazine is *very* important?' Whew!

'I assume your husband works on a magazine,' he said politely.

'Dumping. This is called dumping I believe,' I said. 'But let us not complain. It only makes us unattractive. That's what my boss always says.'

'I rather like complaining. I like *you* complaining. It brings you down to the level of being a human being instead of some sort of goddess.'

'So let's take you to meet Edwina. My boss. You'll like her,' I said.

'The guarantee for instant hatred,' he said.

'No, honestly. I think you two are on the same wavelength.'

In the cab he said, 'This is pretty funny. You travel all the way across Manhattan so no one will see us, and then you take me right up to your office.'

'The will to fail or something?' I asked. I knew I was doing this more for myself than for Graham or Edwina.

Edwina wasn't in. I took Graham into my office. He was gathering looks from the squads of secretaries. Male and female. He certainly had that 'somebody' charisma. I could only hope that these were not regular watchers of Mr Bigge and his cohorts. I mustn't let myself get paranoid about this, I told myself.

Graham looked around my office. The French Provincial desk. The huge painting of roses I'd found in the Marché aux Puces in Paris with its battered frame. 'I guess this is exactly what I thought your office would be like,' he said. 'How, exactly?' I started to sit down behind my desk and then came out again to perch on the window seat near his chair. 'Female. Not too pretty. Something like a home.'

Edwina put her head in the door. 'Aha. There you are. My secretary said you were looking for me.' She saw Graham and crossed the room holding out her hand. 'Edwina Gray. You must be Mr Grant.' She was remarkable with names. 'I saw your casting. Excellent. We all thought you'd be great for the commercial.'

Graham stood up and shook her hand. He said, 'Do they require that everyone who works here be beautiful?' Edwina didn't act flattered. She settled on the edge of my desk. Graham sat back down again. Edwina was studying his face to see what he *really* looked like, as she puts it. 'Yeah, I think you're great looking. Very heart-throbby. You could move a lot of merch for us.'

Graham said, 'I'd be delighted to move a lot of merch for you.'

'Where are you from?' Edwina asked. She began her interrogation techniques. Next was the inquiry as to where you went to school. Then what you'd been doing since then. Ending with wanting to know what you were reading. She says usually you don't have to ask *all* these questions to elicit an entire evening of one-sided conversation, which she finds very restful.

Graham told her that he had graduated from St John's in Annapolis and as to what he had been doing since then, he said, 'I've been seeking purpose.' Edwina said, 'And it has come to this?'

He agreed, 'It has come to this.'

'Well, now you have fallen into our hands we'll see what we can do with you,' Edwina said.

Graham said, 'This sounds like so much more than a television commercial.' 'Oh, it is, it is, it is,' she sang, leaving with her usual air that she was going somewhere more interesting.

We then had a long and rather embarrassing argument about why I wasn't going to come over to his hotel right then and there. And why I couldn't spend the night with him. And why I couldn't even come over at the end of the afternoon and go home and say I had to work late.

'I just can't, Graham. I'm no good at lying. And if I sleep with you it's not just going to be for the fun of it.'

'So I came here for nothing. I don't give a damn about this commercial. I came here to see you. To pursue you. You said you were obsessed with me. So what gives?'

Like Edwina, I never close the door to my office. If you do people just think something even more flamboyant is going on inside. But this was getting pretty flamboyant. There was increasing foot traffic outside trying to get an earful.

'Why don't I walk you out to the elevators?' I asked calmly. 'Then maybe we can have a drink at the Intercontinental about 5.30?' I went down in the elevator with him and we did manage a pretty smoochy kiss between the 14th and the 9th floors while the elevator was empty. I stayed in the elevator and went back up.

I worked on the Jamaica Wind script some more and then went to the production department to talk about where and when we might shoot it. I of course wanted to go to Jean Rhys' native island, Dominica, where the original imagining for *Wide Sargasso Sea* had taken place. Millie Augustine, our producer, soon woke me up to reality. 'It's too far away and too hard to get to. We've got to go to St Thomas or Guadaloupe or one of those islands you can fly to directly. Maybe even Puerto Rico. What do we need? Beaches. A horse and carriage. Winding cliffside roads.'

'Crumbling mansion houses and Spanish moss?' I inquired timidly.

'I don't see any Spanish moss,' she said, peering intently at the board. 'Mansion house, maybe. Frame three.'

'I was just thinking about the magic,' I said.

'It's too late for magic, Nina,' Millie answered me. 'Magic was when you were writing this. Magic ended the minute the client okayed the board.'

I ran into Edwina in the hall on my way back to my office. 'Pretty cute,' she said. 'Oh, Edwina,' I said, following her into her office. 'Oh, Edwina, what am I getting myself into?'

'Could be nothing,' she said, rapidly scanning the memos

on her desk. She is great at reading and carrying on a conversation at the same time. 'Could be something. It all depends on you.' She looked up. 'The only reason not to have an affair is that it irrevocably alters the intimacy between you and your husband. It can never be the same again once you conceal something from him. My reading of your marriage is that it is already irrevocably altered. Which in my book leaves you free to enter phase two of your relationship with him, your hubby. Friendly but not completely intimate. Or jump directly to phase three, not friendly, not intimate and maybe kaput.'

'You know what I'm like, Edwina. I'm too romantic for that.'

'D. H. Lawrence called it cold-hearted fucking,' she said.

'Exactly,' I said.

'Well, darling, I leave it in your capable hands. I have two rules about conducting an affair and I'd suggest you follow them. One, never go in the bathroom together. Two, never eat in. One guy I knew would never let me make a meal. Not even breakfast. And he was right. There's something about cooking that takes away the sexual edge.'

I said nothing. Her eyes were steady on me. Then she smiled and tilted her head and went back to her memos. I went back to my office.

I freshened up. Sprayed some 'Paris' into the room and walked through it. Twice. So it would infiltrate everywhere. I am Edwina's pawn. Everything I know about being a female I learned from her. Put on too much lipstick. Then blotted it and rubbed my lips together. I didn't look bad. Thank God I have good hair.

He was waiting for me by the birdcage in the lobby. He's not awfully big but he has presence. And one might imagine that when you've made a number of films where you have done unspeakable things to all genders you could be expected to be a little gun-shy of public recognition. But not our Graham. He couldn't have been more at ease if he made a living shining shoes.

When we sat down in the bar he said, 'Are you just playing hard to get so I'll really fall in love with you?' I said, 'Oh, gosh, Graham, I wouldn't even know how to do that.'

'What a perfect answer,' he said. He ordered a scotch. I ordered a white wine and decided it would be the last time I did that. I can order scotch, too. I don't mind drinking. I can handle it.

'So. What are we going to do?' Graham said.

'Well, I think we're going to do this commercial together. We're going to the Caribbean for a week or so. Maybe you'll find out that you don't like me at all. And then we'll have saved ourselves the awkwardness of having slept together,' I told him.

'Yeah. And maybe I'll get completely bonkers about you and then you'll have to explain to me about your being married and having a child and all that.'

'I promise I'll never ever do that. That much I know I can promise.'

'I wonder if I can get laid around here,' he said, lifting his glass to his mouth.

'I'd expect you can get laid just about anywhere,' I said. I was beginning to get a little short of breath. Have you ever had that feeling when you're sitting right across from someone that suddenly your whole insides were melting away. Right towards your crotch, of course. It's not really romantic. It's purely sexual. Like a big bell ringing, 'This person can have me.' But then I wonder if it is really Graham that makes me feel that way or do I need to feel that way and someone else would be sitting in that chair opposite me if it wasn't Graham.

'I have to go now,' I said. Graham stood and walked to the curb where the doorman had a taxi. 'Don't kiss me,' I said.

'Soon. Soon,' he muttered into my ear as I got into the cab. I didn't look back. This was getting rugged.

In the cab I thought of how Graham had said I could have stayed at the hotel and told Bertrand I had to work late. If he by some chance had gotten home before me. And then, like a bell, it rang. Bertrand always had to work late.

When I walked in the door he was there, watching the news. I walked up to his chair and said, 'Bertrand, are you having an affair?' He looked up at me. 'I thought you'd never ask,' he said.

chapter 6

on location

What can I tell you? The glamour of location. The nightmare. I was so disheveled with Graham being there I hardly knew what was happening.

We were on St Thomas, because it's easiest to get to, but working nearby on St Johns because it's more beautiful. Go figure.

We stayed at Bluebeard's Castle. Nice. Windy. Location shoots are always plagued with problems, but this one was a lulu. Our girl model was Lala. They'd decided against Bernice, the contract model, for some reason. Not brunette enough? Lala was a last minute choice by the client. Anyway, Lala is Russian. I think Carlton Carlson felt he was being terribly avante garde and with it in choosing her. It wasn't because he planned or hoped to sleep with her. The clients never come on shoots. One of Edwina's rules that makes life a hell of a lot easier.

What was Lala like? What is Siberian for brainless slut? The Russians have learned the ways of the West very rapidly. Ten years ago she would have been on a collective collecting turnips. Now she was wearing a bikini in Charlotte-Amalie and hey, no problem. I hate to think poorly of another female but her first day there she stretched out in the sun for four hours. Such a change from Archangel. Soon she was bright red. And complaining from under her layers of Noxema. Roland Petitfour assured me he can cover her with dark makeup so no one will ever notice.

Did I mention that the local production team were drug addicts? A couple. Of creeps. They flew in ahead of us from Miami and managed to get into their hotel room and into some cocaine *tout de suite*. They prepared nothing and when we arrived I went to their room several times to ask questions before I figured out that the smiling, stunned, speechless wife didn't know if she was on St Thomas or the moon. The husband never surfaced at all. I left them for the producer, Millie Augustine to ship back to Miami. It wasn't her fault but someone has to be punished. That's the kind of mood I was in.

It was even harder than when Graham was in New York because here we were within touching distance and there couldn't be a hint of any kind of relationship. I know these crews too well. If they had the slightest inkling anything was up it would be all over the television production world and into the advertising agencies the second their feet hit the ground at Kennedy. I'm not famous but I'm known. Edwina wouldn't mind if I behaved dramatically, but she wouldn't like someone on her staff having the reputation of a sleeparound. Anyone in this business who thinks that everyone doesn't know everything is only kidding themselves.

And as Edwina is fond of saying, 'I would never sleep with a member of my own staff . . . the night before a shooting.'

So we sat at the big tables for lunch and dinner and chatted aimlessly with whoever was seated next to us. Grips, electricians, stylist, whoever. I was always careful to leave the table and go to my room while Graham was still there. He got the picture. He maybe even liked torturing me by paying not the slightest attention.

We went to look at the manor house we were using in the commercial. Went to see the horse and carriage. Went to see the winding mountain road. Lala assured us she could drive the horse while seated in the carriage. In fact we'd probably have to do long shots with the carriage's burly owner wearing Lala's dress in the carriage.

Thank God Rad Radomir was the director. Always in good temper and I think Lala had rather captured his attention, sunburned or not.

We had fittings yesterday. We'd already done them once in New York. I always double-checked. Lala would wear a big pink ruffled dress. Galliano. I talked the client out of the big hat that went with it. And the usual mandatory Bulgari jewels. I convinced them that sending an armed guard along just for the jewels was a needless expense. The Nixtrix people always keep reminding you, 'We are not sandwich people.' But even three-course luncheon people like to save a little money from time to time. Graham wasn't in New York when we did the fittings so we had to see him in his Speedo trunks. White. Pretty dreamy. Adrian the stylist said, 'Graham, can you push that bulge down a little?' He tried ruefully and asked, 'Is that any better?' I said, 'I think we'll cut before he's that far out of the water.' 'Pity,' said Adrian. 'I can make it bigger,' Graham said. 'Oh, I imagine you can,' Adrian said. She used to be a model and liked coming away on these location trips to get away from her millionaire husband. She was flirty but I don't think she fools around.

Rad Radomir poked his head in the door and nodding his head towards Graham said, 'He's great, where did you find him?' 'In Hollywood,' I told him. 'Excellent choice. And,' he said, looking at Lala wandering around in her bikini panties with her arms crossed over her chest, 'that is a superb choice.' Lala, who had been getting a little sulky with the attention being directed to Graham, perked up. She gave Rad a burning Slavic glance. One of about four expressions she has. He gave her one back. Who was it said, 'The Slavs. Always up to *here* with their emotions.'

Did I mention that it was very romantic on St Thomas? The trade winds blowing, the bougainvillea looping in purple festoons everywhere, the sea glittering below in the moonlight. I decided to go to the pool and swim a little before dinner. We were shooting the next day and I hadn't been in yet. Graham was in the pool when I got there. I always wear a one-piece. The classic black *maillot de bain*. I wasn't brought up to make a statement with my body.

Graham swam over to the edge of the pool. 'Nice legs,' he said, his hair slicked back from the water. Pretty cute. No one else was there. I dove in over his head.

I swam ten lengths and thought I had shown off enough for him. I do swim pretty well.

'You swim pretty well,' Graham said from a flowered chaise longue. I climbed out of the pool. I took my towel and went over to sit on the chaise beside him. This is perfectly normal behavior for two people of the opposite sex on a location shoot. It would be rude not to be friendly. If anyone saw us together they'd note it, but they wouldn't think anything was going on unless you gave them a clue. And a tiny one would do.

'I'm also a good shot,' I told him. 'My two skills. Otherwise I'm pretty maladroit.'

'A woman who can swim her way out or shoot her way out of any situation,' he said.

'Never had to yet,' I said.

'Where'd you learn to shoot?' Graham asked.

'My father taught me. He loved to hunt and wanted me to go with him. My Uncle Fred refused point-blank to shoot with him. He always referred to hunting clothes as "clothes to kill in".

'I loved my father very much and I would have gone over Niagara Falls with him if he had wanted me to. He used to throw up tin cans and I was pretty good at hitting them. You have to lead with your aim.'

'And animals?' he asked.

'I never actually went hunting with him. We'd go out in the woods looking for squirrels and rabbits but they always ran away. We lived in Darien then. He taught me about never walking with a loaded gun and leaving it open so no accidents could happen. And then he died so we never went on safari or to Canada or anything like that. But I would never kill an animal. There are some people I might shoot. But not an animal.'

'Exactly,' he said.

'Why don't you and I go to visit my uncle on Saba when the shoot is over?' I said. Where did that come from? I hadn't even thought about it. Blah! It was there.

'The one who didn't want to wear clothes to kill in?' Graham asked. 'Is he gay?' 'Yes and yes,' I said. 'But I don't think of him that way.'

'Where's Saba?' Graham asked. 'Just over the other side of St Martin's. We could fly from here to St Martin's I imagine. We might have to go back to San Juan and down to St Martin's. Then change for Saba. Some people pronounce it to rhyme with Abba, you know that Swedish group? But actually it's like the "a" in Mable. Saba,' I told him. 'It's a volcanic cone. No beaches. I've never been there. I'd like to see it and I need to see my Uncle Fred.'

'Sounds cool,' he said. 'Would I be presumptuous to ask what our going to Saba together means?'

'My husband is having an affair,' I told him. 'You turned me on to it when you suggested I go home and say I had to work late. Which he says all the time. So I asked him.'

'Pissed-off?'

'Not really. Kind of relieved. I can't imagine why I didn't think of it before.'

'When you and I go to Saba together everyone here is going to know.'

'I know. Even if there's nothing to know.'

'Well, what do you think of that?'

'I'm not a subterfuge kind of person. I guess it's a kind of decision.'

'One I'm proud you're making,' he said, jumping up and striding off, wrapping his towel around him.

chapter 7

....

departing for saba

This is how it worked out. It's possible that Graham and I went to Saba without being a *cause célèbre*. I told Millie Augustine, our producer, I wasn't going straight back to New York, I was going to visit my uncle on Saba. What Graham said I have no idea. The New York flight with the crew and talent left early. So they were out of the way when our flight left for St Martin's where we would transfer for Saba.

Maybe yes, maybe no as far as any talk goes, but at least we weren't seen boarding the flight together.

'Well?' I asked Graham after we got into the air. 'I told them I was going back to the Coast,' he said. 'I never was going back to New York with them.'

'That makes sense,' I said, feeling dumb. And overly nervous, now our escapade was underway.

Graham was the hero of our last day of shooting. We had planned a helicopter shot of the horse and carriage on the road on the nearby island, St John's. And only learned the same morning that the helicopter didn't have permission to land on St John's. So once our director was in the air he would have to go back to St Thomas and come over by boat to finish the shoot. Which would get him there too late to finish the shooting in the same day. And one additional day of shooting puts you over budget by fifty to a hundred thousand dollars.

Good old Millie figured it out. 'We'll send the rest of you by boat early and you can rendezvous on that little spit just off St John's. The helicopter can land there, you'll take Rad and the cameraman on board and we'll stay on schedule.'

Great. Except nobody knew there was a lot of current off that little spit. And the boat couldn't be nosed up to the beach. Once the helicopter dropped them off Rad was okay. He just plunged in and swam out. But the poor cameraman was in his fifties and no swimmer. I was in the bow and it was just dawning on me that this guy was drowning when Graham dove off right beside me. He was with the cameraman and was holding him on his back with one arm and swimming to the boat with the other before the rest of us could say squat. We pulled the dripping, embarrassed cameraman aboard, Graham holding him from the water. Then we gave Graham a hand up. He still had his wet sneakers on, squishing as he stood on the deck. None of us knew what to say. He said, 'I used to be a lifeguard.' 'Lucky for Larry,' Rad said, 'or he might be on his way to St John's by himself.' He didn't add the fact that he would have been on his way underwater.

Well, it impressed me. My hero. He dismissed it as nothing, which I'm sure it was to him. But the crew had never seen a male model save a life before. It made this very handsome person more real to them. And to me.

They did the final meeting scene on the beach when we got to St John's. Graham's apparition scene coming out of the water. Rad wanted true sunset behind him.

Petitfour had to keep pouring water over Graham as he dried out so he looked fresh from the sea, take after take. Close-ups in profile, leaving space to put the Jamaica Wind bottle in for the final freeze frame. Rad also did three-quarters shots of Graham walking toward the camera, framed so you couldn't see if he was wearing trunks or not. That would be our big daring new thing. Is the male model naked? Rad had me look through the camera. Graham looked great and he knew how to work. His face was doing things for every take, and not the same things.

But the final shot of him emerging from the water was really wonderful. The sun was setting behind an empty sea and suddenly up from the water like a sea god came our Graham. There are people who at certain times of their lives exude a kind of superhuman beauty and glamour. You see it in models and then they learn to recreate it for the camera after it has fled, with the help of the hair and makeup men. Graham was in this period of his life. It was like electric rays shooting out of him. Wow. Everybody saw it but Petitfour and I were the most overwhelmed. 'I didn't do anything but comb his hair back and look at that,' he wheezed into my ear.

'It's going to make this commercial,' I said. 'They're not going to be able to keep Jamaica Wind on the shelves.'

Even Rad was pretty taken with this scene and was still shooting it when the light was really gone. The God emerged, head back to make sure the hair fell into place and strode towards us, pushing the waters apart with the strength of his body. Water drops still flying from the curved muscles of his shoulders. The abdominal muscles pulling to keep the body upright against the solidity of the water. The face inscrutable except for the eyes that seemed to promise some new kind of mystery. This was certainly Graham's best moment on film, even with all the naked, naked stuff he'd already done. Or was I going overboard?

On the fourth take, as Graham came hurtling up, drops splashing into the sun, a flock of gulls that had settled in the distance flew upwards like a curtain rising. That would have to be the take. We wouldn't see the rushes until we got back to New York, but this was a scene that was going to move the merchandise or I knew nothing about advertising.

'You were great,' I told Graham when they finally let him

come out of the ocean into the darkness on the beach. 'It's just like the opening scene in *Boys in the Sand*,' he said. 'I didn't do that one. It was before my time.'

So we got it all. The close-ups of Lala awakening in her four-poster island bed swathed in netting. I would definitely like a bed like that in my next life. The pink dress going over her head, never mind that in reality it took three people to get her into it. And two people four hours to get her to look like that.

And down the plantation stairs. Longshot on the winding road through the palms. Floating out of the carriage on the beach. To meet Graham. Thirty seconds on the screen and thousands of man hours in the making. Now I had to think what the music would be like. I'd like Rachmaninoff but I always get shouted down. Maybe not this time.

chapter 8

....

visiting saba

Saba was a strange little island. Like a bit of Scotland that
had got loose and drifted off into the Caribbean. All up hill
and down dale. A green volcanic cone with no beaches. The
landing strip is a flat little outcrop. Our plane's wheels hit the
crumbling edge of earth as we landed and stopped abruptly
with the propellers whirring over a cliff's edge at the other
end. The little caddy-shack of an airport had locals sitting on
the front porch. They didn't want to miss that day when the
plane plunged over the cliff.

I could see Uncle Fred sitting on the porch in a straw hat.
Beside him his pal Gurney. What should one call Gurney?
Longtime companion? Mate? A bit long in the tooth for 'boyfriend'. Freddy and Gurney as they are known here on the
island. Or Fred 'n' Gurn, like Shake 'n' Bake. They'd been
together more than thirty years. Once I guess you could have
called them lovers. They were sort of like the Duke and
Duchess of Windsor. Legendary lovers.

Uncle Fred looks like Mom. The remains of being blond.
A little overweight. Piercing blue eyes. Prominent nose. He
broke his nose in a fall a few years ago and said, 'When a
Morton falls down it's their nose that hits first.' Five ten or
thereabouts. Not big. But with aura.

Gurney is taller, blonder. Dutch. Drinks too much. But

good spirited. He can be biting but never mean. They looked
something like brothers at the airport. Blonds in white pants
and T-shirts.

When I was little I thought they were the epitome of
elegance. So swell, so dashing. When they left you always had
the feeling you wanted to go with them. I wanted to grow up
to be Uncle Fred. I remember Mother saying, 'But you can't.
You're a girl.' And my father saying, 'So is Fred.' My mother
turned and glared at him. I didn't say anything. I knew what
he meant. But I still wanted to grow up and be him.

I think Uncle Fred began working at Arnold Constable.
Then went on to Best and Co. I always had all those little
tweed outfits. And the velvet dress with the Peter Pan collar
trimmed in lace. And Mary Janes. I was a sight.

Thankfully he went on to Saks. So I had some decent
clothes when I was a teenager. He used to take me shopping
and buy me the things that looked good on me, while I
actually longed to have the outfit with sunflowers all over it.
But then he always bought me one dream thing. Three-inch
heels when I was fourteen. A silver mini. A sequin beret. With
big sequins in all different colors. I was too much of a wuss
to wear anything like that to school but I paraded around my
bedroom to the astonishment of the cat.

I think that's why he did so well at Saks. He always understood what a woman's heart needs. Like handsome Gurney
Hollander. He was quite a dish in his day.

While I'm thinking this we were sailing straight up one hill
and straight down the next incline. Even the little town of
Windward Side doesn't have any flat streets. All the little
houses are ten feet above their neighbor on one side, fifteen
feet below another neighbor on the other. In the distance the
glittering Caribbean stretches off under clouds that leave dark
shadows on the sea. In a boat you pass in and out of their
shade with the glittering water all about you.

I wondered if I was going to sleep with Graham that night.

And decided I wasn't. It's not as though I felt guilty about
cheating on Bertrand, more that I wanted to turn my full
attention on Graham. I wanted to be out of the old situation
completely before I started the new one. Was I setting myself
up for the disappointment of the century? With Graham
walking out on me after we slept together once, or a couple
of times?

It was all over with Bertrand and me anyway. All the town-
houses on the upper East Side couldn't have kept our little
ménage together. He was thoroughly and finally bored with
me but liked the nice rhythm of his life. He didn't want to
rock the boat, he just wanted to drag someone else into the
boat with us.

Whatever I felt for Graham I never felt for Bertrand and I
needed to do this. I needed to find out what the hell I was
all about. Actually I was kind of proud that dull little dish-
water-blonde me was capable of having these emotions. I just
had to find out what they all added up to.

Uncle Fred had booked us rooms, or should I say a room,
at the Captain's Rest. He actually had room for us at his
house but I didn't know what was going to be going on in
the night. There might be screams and oaths or groans or
God knows. I opted for a little caravansary nearby. It *was*
like Scotland there. Green grassy knolls and a kind of stout
yeomanry look to the people. Blacks and whites all had the
same family names Fred told me and seemed to regard each
other as cousins. This was not an island of beach cabanas
and bikinis with gold chains. Nary a sight of what one might
call a tourist.

Uncle Fred and Gurney took to Graham right away. Why
shouldn't they? And I could count on Uncle Fred not to say
a word about Bertrand or little Freddy. If I wanted to come
visit with the handsomest man in the world in tow, so be it.

Uncle Fred's house hovers on a hillside with a spectacular
view all the way to St Martin's. One could see why people

chose to live here. It's not to run around but to sit and look. They had a big terrace in front of the house with trees that created shade. It had a feeling of Provence. Lunch was served with gin and tonics. I thought what the hell and decided to drink. Which I never do, but I'd come this far.

'What do you do?' Uncle Fred asked Graham, after the tomatoes were served. 'I'm an actor. An aspiring actor. I guess you could say that, couldn't you?' he said, turning to me.

'He's an actor,' I said.

'Who would have guessed?' Gurney said.

'I've just done a small part in a commercial for Nina,' Graham added.

'Jamaica Wind,' I said, 'an old fragrance to be made new again.'

'Is it going to be called Second Wind?' Gurney asked. Not bad for a Dutchman.

'I wanted Broken Wind,' Graham said.

'Bea Lillie used to do a number called *Wind Round My Heart*,' Uncle Fred said. 'You've probably never heard of Bea Lillie.'

'Didn't she also do *There Are Fairies At The Bottom Of My Garden*?' Graham said. That got my attention. I poured myself a glass of iced tea and bailed out on the gin and tonic.

'Yes, but I can't sing it,' Uncle Fred said. 'There are goats at the bottom of my garden,' Gurney said and got up to throw a stone over the railing down the hill. I heard a distant baaa.

'Are you living in Los Angeles or New York?' Uncle Fred inquired. 'She found me in Los Angeles,' Graham said. 'But I used to live in New York. That's where I heard of Bea Lillie.'

'She was very small you know. Television rescued her. It made her look twenty years younger and the same size as everyone else.'

'I remember passing her on the street once in New York,' I said. 'She was wearing a kind of embroidered pillbox. I don't remember that she was so amazingly small.'

'Perhaps she wasn't. I never saw her. I'm just passing on her legend,' Uncle Fred said, lighting a cigarette. I had one, too under the spell of the tropics.

'So what's the plan?' Uncle Fred asked.

'I don't know exactly. I know I'm going to leave Bertrand. He's been having an affair for years with some woman at his office.'

'Lucky me,' Graham said.

'And I'm obsessed with this person you see before you,' I said.

'He's definitely obsession material,' Gurney said. 'I'd guess there must be thousands who have been or currently are obsessed with him.'

I looked up. 'We do have television here,' Uncle Fred said. 'And we do have videocassettes. We've seen Graham. But that's not your name in the films you do, is it?'

Graham said, 'They change it around. I don't really have control over that.'

'I don't really want to talk about that. I'm sure it's a metier like any other. And as my friend Clive Arrowsmith always says, "Having made love with five black men on television doesn't make you a bad person",' Uncle Fred said.

'I think it's a dangerous profession,' I said. 'Oh, probably no more than working in the circus,' Uncle Fred said. 'Similar probably. You're never really sure when something will happen. I don't think you really know anything about people until you know what they're about sexually, and in your case, you already know so you can skip right to getting to know each other intellectually.'

'That's nicely put,' Graham said. 'Your friend Clive wasn't talking about me when he mentioned the person who made love with five black men on television was he?'

'Have you?' Gurney wanted to know. No one bothered to answer him.

'It's sort of the final barrier, isn't it?' said Uncle Fred.

'Once you've been seen making love there isn't much more for people to know about you, is there? I mean, of course, there's much more for people to know about you but you don't have to hide anything from them. Must be quite refreshing.'

'Most people wouldn't want to be seen making love because they feel they don't look good enough,' Gurney said. 'They're afraid people would say "Ugh, look at that sagging stomach. Or those skinny thighs. Or that teeny penis". If no one ever sees you there's always the delusion that you're beautiful and powerfully hung. I once was both. I wish I had some movies of myself to look at.'

Graham said, 'I read this interesting theory that our bodies are just space ships for our genes, and our genes run everything. When they see breasts and hips and hair and lips, it's like they know this is good breeding material for the continuation of their genes. Assuming you're a man. I imagine women's genes do the same thing. Guide them towards the strong muscles that look good for survival.'

'And us?' Gurney said. 'On our *Mission Impossible?*'

'Well, obviously genes still think they're in the caveman era, so I don't think I'd worry too much that *your* genes have their own little quest. Do your genes feel fulfilled?' Graham asked Gurney.

'Look at him,' Gurney pointed at Uncle Fred. 'One of the great catches of the day.' Uncle Fred tapped his cigarette on the edge of the ashtray and looked out over the sea as though they were talking about someone else. I could tell Gurney meant it, he wasn't kidding around. Funny to think of Uncle Fred having been admired for his beauty. And perhaps the size of his penis. We keep trying to force our relatives into the molds of 'dear' and 'old' but they do keep resisting us.

'With the green flash at the edge of the ocean at sundown for dessert,' said Graham.

Gurney took us back to the Captain's Rest so we could get

some rest before dinner, which was to be in the Chinese restaurant at the top of the hill.

And there was our room. With two large beds. Uncle Fred is so knowledgeable. He probably has had plenty of occasions in his life when two beds would have been welcome.

These little Caribbean hotel rooms, all cement and limp bedspreads and shower stalls that never dry. Foliage pressing in all around. Damp wind blowing through the screens. The uncharming part of a world where everything is fundamentally rotting.

'Alone at last,' I said, nervously putting my bag down on the bed nearest the door.

'Lets's neck,' Graham said. 'I've been wanting to hug you all day long.'

He pulled me down on the other bed and held me very tightly, his face in my hair. I wondered why I had decided to wear a skirt. If I had jeans on it would help me to not lose my resolve. That treacherous sub-conscious, always trying to get me in trouble.

'Maybe I should take all my clothes off and you can keep all of yours on,' Graham said, sitting up and pulling off his T-shirt.

'Let's just lie here like this,' I said. 'It's so nice. And nobody ever does this with me.'

'You're just a little cuddle bug, aren't you?' he said. I said, 'Mmmm.' And fell asleep. I think we were both tired and kind of worn out from the strain. And we really never had been alone together in a room with the door shut before.

I woke up occasionally and moved around a little and kissed him on the cheek and he'd kiss me a little bit and we'd drowse some more. It was really sweet. The perfect argument for people who think women are only interested in sex until the penis goes in and that men are only interested after it goes in.

'We have to get up,' Graham mumbled in my ear. 'They're going to be here in half an hour.'

I sat up beside him, messy and bleary-eyed. He rolled back and put his arms behind his head. A beautiful chest. Beautiful biceps. Some underarm hair kind of buried in the crevices of his armpits. Light brown.

'I have a hard-on,' he said.

'Oh, Graham, you make me feel like such a shit,' I said. 'I want to sleep with you so much. But not as a married woman. At least a married woman still living with her husband. Can you understand that?'

'Yes,' he said, pushing down on his crotch. 'I can. I do. You don't have to apologize because you don't just hand it around. I think that's admirable. Not that I don't want to screw the daylights out of you. If . . . when . . . you *are* with me I won't have to concern myself about you slipping around behind my back.'

It occurred to me that I wouldn't have that worry either. I would know where he was. In studio. Screwing an assortment of beauties of many different kinds. I fell on top of him and kissed him very hard.

He said, 'Whoa, let me up. I'm taking a shower before I burst my shorts.'

He jumped up and pulled off his shorts. He wasn't wearing any underwear. All those curvy muscles and tan all over. No white bathing suit disfigurations for our boy. And very studly. No foreskin. Long and getting firm but not all the way there. He was quite a sight. More beautiful than in his movies. Sort of perfect and ideal. He said, 'Not fair looking. I've never seen you with your clothes off.' And dashed for the shower.

I felt like I was sliding off into space. Out of my world into nowhere. Walking out of a theater where the movie of my life was playing. It was going on back in there, I could hear the voices and knew what they were saying and doing. Soon it would be time for me to walk back in and play my part. Except I wasn't going to. And the movie would have to go on without me and I wouldn't have any part in it. I would be in a new movie.

I didn't know if Graham and I were in love. Or if this was just a few dizzy moments of unreality. But I knew it was too late to go back. It was already too late after he came to New York. Even the little that had happened was too much to just forget and go on as though nothing had happened at all. I didn't want to become the kind of person who goes back to her husband, forgets he's been cheating on her, keeps on with her job. Sends her child off to college, starts seriously sagging and then what? Emptiness. 'I can't go that way,' I said, getting off the bed.

'What?' Graham called from the bathroom where he was out of the shower. That was quick.

'Oh, nothing. Everything. You know,' I said, being funny.

'Really heavy,' he said, putting his head in the bedroom door. 'Let's just wing it for awhile. Just enjoy the fact that we're together. I can hardly believe it, speaking for myself.'

'Right,' I said. 'Let me just change. I'll go out with dirty hair and no makeup. Like a model. I think I hear their car.'

The Chinese restaurant was terrible. I guess the wonderful thing was that on an island like Saba it was there at all. I hate Chinese. Probably everyone at the table did.

I said to Uncle Fred, 'So how did you happen to come to Saba?' He said, 'Blondes when they get older should go south.' Gurney said, 'It's true. I had a friend with wonderful long blonde hair who was confined to a wheelchair with arthritis. So she went to Ecuador. Very popular. A real hit actually. I guess they figured you can't have everything.'

'Am I at that point where I should be thinking of heading south?' I asked.

'Well, heading somewhere,' Uncle Fred said.

'Were you always heading somewhere?' I asked him. The spring rolls arrived. 'Yes, I was always heading somewhere but it was largely internal. I was always heading in my dreamscape

towards true love. And I found it.' He looked at Gurney.
Gurney looked at the table.

Uncle Fred added, 'I've always gotten everything I wanted.
And I've tried to be a good sport about it.' I said, 'Someone
in Hollywood said much the same thing to me. I hope I can
be.'

He went on, 'You know, Nina. In every relationship there's
the lover and the lovee. Or loved one. Even if it's 49 per cent
and 51 per cent, there's always one who has a slight edge.
Usually it's more than slight. You've read *Ballad of the Sad
Café*. That's all about this. But finally, even though the lover
may be the vulnerable, the mistreated one, it's the lover who
is the lucky one. Because the lover is the one who has the
experience. The one who has felt something.'

'I don't think I've ever been in love. I've been in lust,'
Graham said.

'Same thing,' Uncle Fred said.

Some horrible duck thing arrived. And some shrimp from
the same far-off frozen place. Luckily we were talking about
love and I could sort of ignore it. I wasn't really hungry
wondering what was going to happen when we got back to
the room. I dreaded it and I couldn't wait to get there.

'Do you think you can love someone for a long time. Your
whole life?' Graham said, messing about in his noodles. He
looked so adorable, like a little blond boy being polite. How
was it that I was here with him on this island in the middle
of nowhere? Thank God my uncle was with me.

'Yes, but you both have to keep busy with other things so
it's not all you have to think about. But really, there is some
sort of destined chemistry at play in a great love affair. I've
been sleeping with Gurney for over thirty years and I never
once didn't feel like it.'

'We're really saying everything that's on our minds tonight
aren't we?' said Gurney, spearing a gray shrimp from a heap
of exhausted vegetables in the middle of the table.

'This is my niece. I feel no compunction in expressing myself in front of her,' Uncle Fred said a little sharply.

'I hope in thirty years I can be saying some of this kind of stuff,' Graham said.

We drove sharply downhill from the restaurant, and even more sharply downhill around the slope of dark fields rising toward the old volcano's edge. There was a moon, full, the color of Edam cheese, hanging above the edge of another slope, across the valley from the road's edge. It was wrapped in stringy dark gray veils of cloud. Like smoke rising from the sea, shining under it far below. It was romantic but in a kind of seasoned way. As though it had done its job shining down on lovers for a very long, long time and it wasn't feeling really very fresh at this romance thing anymore. But it was still in there doing its job.

Byronesque, that was what the moon was like. Not for teenaged lovers. But lovers like Graham and myself. Not fresh, not for the first time, but lovers all the same.

When we got back Graham said that he wanted to see me nude. I had seen him nude that afternoon and now he wanted to see me. He lay down on his bed and I went into the bathroom and dutifully took off all my clothes and hung them on the hooks by the door.

I came to the door and just stood there, my arms hanging down by my sides. Ungainly. He looked at me and said, 'Everybody must fall in love with you.'

The next day I told Uncle Fred about it. Graham and Gurney had gone for a hike. Down to the water. No beaches on Saba but you can get to a pier, walk out on it and jump in.

I told Uncle Fred what Graham had said and how I felt in fact that no one had ever really fallen in love with me. And that I had put on my little white nightgown and we sat and talked into the night.

Graham said people always say you can't fuck brains, but in my case my brains actually gave him an erection. Finally somebody to talk to, he said. After you fucked. Or before if you prefer.

He told me how he thought about AIDS a lot of the time. He thinks that every one of his friends who died of AIDS gave him the clue as to who it was that gave it to them, even if they didn't realize it themselves at the time.

His friend Guy, the hairdresser, told him about making love in the men's room at a gay bar with a handsome South American who hardly spoke English.

Another friend, Leonard the designer, told him about picking up a man at a steam room and taking him home. 'I just couldn't get enough,' he told Graham.

He passed one friend, John, a TV producer, in a crowded Pennsylvania Station in New York. John was with a younger, very handsome man and avoided Graham's eyes.

Another friend, Mort, whom he'd met in an advertising agency, he saw for the last time in Paris. Mort was all in black leather with some Frenchman at an art exhibit at the Petit Palais. And recently he had heard that Mort was dead.

I told my dear sweet uncle all these things as though they had happened to me. It had really pierced me, Graham lying on the bed looking at the ceiling telling me all those stories, holding my hand.

The list went on and on, so many dead. Graham told me he'd never slept with any of them. He only makes love to men in his movies. For the most part. He gets tested every six months and is seronegative. But it haunts him that he may have seen the avenging angels before his friends died. Not that there was anything to be done. But he was a witness.

And then I went to my own bed and we turned out the lights. It was really no time to be thinking about sex. I was grateful for that.

'This is fairly major,' Uncle Fred said. 'What you've cut out for yourself here. The love of a lifetime. The love affair of the century. Didn't you feel that way about Bertrand?'

I told him, 'Honestly, no. Unless I forget. Bertrand excited
me and I wanted to be with him so I married him when he
asked me. But I think if he hadn't asked me I wouldn't have
pursued him until he did. I had nothing to compare it with.
It certainly wasn't like this. I wasn't obsessed with Bertrand.
Maybe I'm not even in love with Graham. Just obsessed.'

'It's the same thing,' Uncle Fred said.

'I can't imagine him being somewhere in the world and I'm
not with him. And I haven't even slept with him. I'm not
going to do that until I move out.'

'You're right. It's one thing to be sexually driven. It's something else to be a slut. People confuse them. They start out
one way and before they know it they're the other.'

I looked over at my uncle, so trim and neat in his white
shorts and navy blue T-shirt. And sandals. Sitting back in a
chaise longue in the shade of the awning. Thank God somebody knows something.

'You've got to go for it, honey,' he said. 'You've got to find
out what's cooking with this guy and you. Or you'll wonder
all your life.'

'It isn't as though I'm going to be breaking Bertrand's
heart. He has some floozie at the office who is giving him
blow jobs behind the door.' I surprised myself at how angry
I sounded. I guess you don't have to love somebody to be
jealous.

'She's probably not a floozie. Probably someone very
correct who would be more Bertrand's type. He's going to be
upset that you're leaving him because it will be bad for his
image. You were such a perfect wife for him. But he's French.
They're always into the way things look,' Uncle Fred said.

'Mother is going to be very unhappy. And I don't know
how I'm going to explain it to my son.'

'You can't not go through with it just because you're too
embarrassed to tell people. And I'm not so sure that Alicia
will be so shocked. She's got more mileage than you think. If

I had been a woman I would have had her life no doubt. Handsome, nice husband. Beautiful child. We're both quite conservative you know. That good upbringing in Wisconsin.

'And if she had been me she would very likely have had my life. She's quite man-crazy, you know, underneath it all. And very willful. It's just that what she wanted many people want, so it wasn't so noticeable.

'As for Freddy your son, sometimes you just have to be guilty of things. You can't have a guilt-free life. The only people who feel no guilt are people who are lying to themselves.'

'Are you guilty of things?' I asked him.

'Many things. But they haven't driven me to my knees yet. Maybe I'll have one of those awful deathbed experiences, where all my guilt will sweep over me. It hasn't so far.' He laughed.

'Like what,' I wanted to know.

'I took Gurney away from his fiancée. I often wonder if he wouldn't have been happier married and with kids and all that stuff. But then I know better. He would have been fooling around on the side and sooner or later would have left the wife and kids for some guy. And one of the children could write their memoirs and entitle them, "Father Was A Faggot".' He laughed again and got up. 'And he does have fabulous me. That's nothing to sniff at. Do you want another iced tea?' And he went into the house to get us something to drink.

I knew he was only kidding about Gurney being lucky to have him. But he's not so wrong. When he came out he said, putting my tea on the table beside me. 'I gave you two spoonfuls of sugar. Nina, Nina, Nina. The world is like a classroom of obedient children with their heads down on their desks. Those who are brave enough to raise their heads are surprised to find there isn't any teacher.

'Nobody really cares what you do, Nina. They're so

absorbed in their own lives they don't have time to feel anything for you. Even Freddy. I do. I care and I love you, but
only you can live it.'

Uncle Fred got up and came over and hugged me and gave
me a kiss on the cheek. He's quite demonstrative. Much more
than my mother.

Looking off the terrace he said, 'My rule is that if someone
hasn't seen you for a day and calls you to see how you are,
they are involved in your life. If they haven't seen or heard
from you in a week and they call, they're involved in your life.
I'll even give you people who if they haven't heard from you
in a month will call and check on you. But more than one
month? Can we honestly say we are involved with people who
wouldn't know you were dead for at least a month afterwards?
Those people really don't figure in your life, Nina. And this
is most people we know, discounting those we work with.
Who aren't really friends, but people who will immediately
hire someone else if you've gone to the great beyond. So
figure who you know who will really miss you if you go on to
a completely new life. Not many. You're entitled, Nina.'

Gurney and Graham's heads emerged over the end of the
terrace. They had climbed the hill directly from the ocean
instead of coming up the road.

'Do what you feel like doing, Nina. Not what you think
you should do. You'll be doing what you want to do and be
able to carry it off. Otherwise you're just hanging around,
killing time.'

We had run out of time. Uncle Fred and Gurney dashed
with us to the caddy-shack airport, we skittered off the edge
of the cliff, changed planes in St Martin's and then had to
say goodbye in Miami, my lover and I. He to go back to Los
Angeles, me to New York.

I hung on to him at my gate. I was leaving first. Graham
said, 'You can have me. You can completely control me. I'm
yours. You don't have to break up your life for me.'

And I said, 'No, that's all over. That life is over. You're it for me, Graham.'

He let me go. 'I make a living doing dirty movies.'

'You have to start somewhere,' I told him. 'Maybe I will, too.' And I laughed and ran down the corridor to the plane.

I had almost stopped crying by the time I found my seat. The stewardesses were nice to me. Who understands crying when you say goodbye better than a stewardess? They've seen it. They've done it.

As soon as we took off I felt much better. Even chipper. That's done, I thought. And went to sleep.

chapter 9

....

my mother and the news

We had lunch, the three of us, sometime after I got back to New York. My mother, Freddy and I. Now that I'd moved out I was trying to set regular engagements to keep in contact.

When I first told Mother about Graham and that I wasn't going to stay married to Bertrand and well, there you have it, she said something like 'Oh dear.' But didn't seem to want to know any details, that usual WASP thing of not wanting to add any of your burdens to their own. But she did say, 'I'm sure you know what you're doing,' which surprised me.

We hadn't seen each other since I broke the news, when I asked her to come to have lunch with Freddy and me at Bice. I know, I know. But Bice is where I go to lunch. I felt I could hold up my end in that kind of blonde, impersonal, no-real-nationality atmosphere at Bice. Really just another business lunch.

Freddy didn't want me to pick him up. He said he'd come over by himself, and he did; sulky and pissed-off but not really upset. Like his father, he has his own inner program and the rest of us are never going to know about it.

He and I were at our table when Mother came in. As always, I realized that she is taller than I am. That's wrong, don't you think? No child should be permanently shorter than their mother. I looked at her as other people must have looked at her as she crossed the room. The gray suit. The gray blonde hair parted on the side and turned under, like always. The good shoes and bag. No jewelry really. Her ears aren't pierced and she doesn't like bracelets. She doesn't as she says, 'like things slipping around on me.' I suppose that cuts out silk underwear. Isn't it bizarre, I really don't know what her underwear is like. Some daughter, me.

I wondered if the older men in the room found her attractive. Or the younger men. She gives off no sexual clues. A real lady wouldn't and that she certainly is. She's prettier than I am, too. Nicer features but with that 'out of the running' look. I wonder why?

She kissed me once, lightly on the cheek. Both Freddy and I stood. She kissed Freddy with a little more enthusiasm. She has never doted on him per se, and would never babysit him when he was little. But has always been good about taking him to museums and the theater. Things she wants to do herself.

We chatted about this and that. Ordered. She and I had pasta and a salad. Freddy some kind of steak smothered in tomato sauce.

I thought we would sit through the whole meal and never bring up the subject of my bizarre behavior. She said she was replacing the refrigerator in her apartment, asked Freddy how he was doing at school. I hadn't.

Freddy brought it up. 'Mom's leaving us,' he said. In a kind of defiant way. 'I know,' my mother said, 'I know. I'm sorry. I guess. But your mother has her life to live.' I sat up straight in my chair. Never in my life has my mother taken my side in anything. Not that she's taken the opposing side, it's as though she never felt she had to reassure me about anything. Her timidity? Her lack of interest?

Freddy was complaining about having to fix his own meals. And taking the laundry to the laundromat. I've only been gone one week. How many meals could that have been? Of course I feel guilt. But somehow that guilt is in another room inside me somewhere. An empty room with lots of light coming in the windows. A room where the silence of Sunday will always reign. And I'll go in there from time to time. But I'm not going to live in there.

Freddy said, 'But I'm only fifteen.' And my mother said, in a conversational tone while she picked at her penne, 'Fifteen isn't so young.'

I said nothing. Freddy said nothing. She went on, 'When I was fifteen my father had already been dead for four years. My mother worked. The war was on. I don't want this to sound like delivering newspapers in the snow, Freddy, but when I was fifteen I had been making my meals, making my bed, doing the laundry for a long time already. My brother and I lived as though we were in our twenties. Nobody paid the slightest attention to us. And we loved it.'

She looked up at me and I saw what I hadn't seen before. My mother was really grown-up and had been a lot longer than I have. I was sitting at the table with a grown-up person who did not complain, who did not ask any special attention from me, and if she didn't make any great effort to be especially amusing, why should she?

'What happened to your father?' Freddy asked her. Good question. One I must have asked years ago. But I only vaguely remember he had sickened and died. He hadn't been lost in the war.

'He died of cancer. Over a long period of time. I think he was pretty well crushed by the Depression. He couldn't cope and he died. I can remember one of my aunts telling me years later that he had told her that he felt terrible that he was dying and wasn't able to take care of his children. And that certainly was true. He didn't take care of his children. We had to take care of ourselves. Of course, I had my brother. And he had me.'

I felt a big pang of sadness. Probably the most like love for my mother I've really felt. I thought of her brother Frederick and her, rather like Hansel and Gretel. *The Orphans of the Storm* kind of thing. She looked at me across the table. Her eyes are gray, too. 'Actually we rather liked it. At least I don't ever remember either of us complaining about not having enough attention.'

'But what did you do?' I asked her, about twenty years too late. 'We got up in the morning. Our mother had already left for work. We ate our cereal. Drank our juice and our milk. And left for school.

'There was a war on. No one ever asked where we were or what we were doing. There was a coastguard station not far away. We ran around with sailors. We drank. We smoked. We hardly ever studied. The teachers were terrible. The dregs. Suddenly we were free. And we loved it. And I remember we paid a lot of attention to our clothes.

'I think we liked being on our own with our own money because we could pick out our own clothes. Fred worked as a check-out clerk in a grocery store and I was a waitress in a coffee shop. We did all right. We went to dances. We went out on dates. We could both drive. Sometimes Freddy drove. Sometimes I drove. It was fun.'

I imagined my mother with her long blonde hair flying, wearing a plaid skirt and saddle shoes and white anklets, turned down. She went on, 'Sweaters were so important then. You had to have a good selection. All cardigans, with matching ribbon binding down the front. Sometimes you wore them over a white blouse, and sometimes you wore them backwards, buttoned up the back. With a dicky.' She laughed. In a way I can only remember her laughing a few times. Thinking about being fifteen and on her own.

'Who buttoned you up?' I asked. 'Fred?' 'No, as I remember you laid the sweater on the bed and buttoned it and pulled it over your head,' she said.

'What's a dicky?' Freddy said, taking a second roll from the

waiter who was passing by and putting half the butter dish
on it. He was sort of getting into it. Poor kid. He didn't
realize how my mother was setting him up never to be able
to complain again. I wanted to get up and give her a hug. So
manipulative. Who would have thought it?

'It was just a little Peter Pan collar. There was a little front
to it as I remember, with little strings that went under your
arms to hold it in place. It was much easier to wash than a
whole blouse. I suppose no one wears such a thing anymore,'
she said.

'Not since the T-shirt,' I told her.

'And loafers. Loafers came in then. Penny loafers. You put
a new penny in that opening across the front. Where could
they have come from? Scotland? As a little girl I wore Oxfords
I remember. They were hell to lace up and tie I remember.'
My mother never swears. Never. I guess using the word 'hell'
in front of us indicates that Freddy and I were being admitted
simultaneously to the world of grown-ups.

'Where are all those clothes, do you suppose?' she asked,
turning towards me. 'Sometimes I imagine all the clothes I've
ever worn in one huge pile in front of me. It would probably
be as high as this building. And what fun it would be. Excava-
ting down to that pale-green organdy strapless my mother
made for me to wear to my first formal dance. With Jimmy
DeWeir.'

I checked my mother's glass. We had each ordered a glass
of white wine. Hers was still half full. She wasn't drunk. Or
maybe she'd been drinking at home before she came to lunch.
Unlikely. I could never find even a smidgen of wine, let alone
booze, when I was 'watering the plants' so to speak.

She went on, 'My mother sewed very well. She could even
make suits. But never for me. Dance dresses, yes. She loved
seeing me go out. I had a very sexy fitted gray evening dress
with long sleeves when I first went to college.' Sexy! I had
never heard my mother use that word in my whole life.

Freddy was really concentrating on her. He had never seen her this animated and this confidential before either. We were a real family, now that I was breaking it up.

'And my first cashmere sweater. I was still in high school. Fred got it for me for Christmas. You know he worked his way through college, and made enough money to get me expensive gifts, too. He was such a hard worker. But always fun. And always had wonderful clothes. We were always just one step ahead of getting our dorm bills paid, but we had our camel hair coats and cashmere scarves.'

She focused on Freddy. 'My brother never wanted us to go without anything. He always said that the worst thing in the world was for a woman not to be properly dressed. A man can rise above it, but no woman should have to go out into the world wearing clothes another woman might make fun of her for. How does that song go? "She may be weary . . . dum-tum-dum . . . wearing the same funny dress." ' Now my mother was singing at the luncheon table. She was really letting it all hang out. 'We were talking on the phone only the other day and he said that he hates to go without something he wants. It makes him feel like a deprived child. Well, goodness knows we both knew what it was like being a deprived child well enough.' They had both made up for it.

I remember Uncle Fred taking Bertrand and me to the Five Oaks shortly after we were married. With Gurney. And while the music was playing loudly Uncle Fred said to no one in particular, 'I wonder if they know "He May Be Good Fucking But He's No Fucking Good".' I always thought he was referring to good-looking Gurney, which only made Gurney even more attractive as far as I was concerned.

He also said, 'If they arrested everyone in this place they'd do a lot to help clean up New York.' I love the Five Oaks. You can't go to the bar, of course, without being accosted but the dining room is so much fun. The last time I was there I saw a whole table of people on their way to Cindy Crawford's birthday party and they were all dressed as Cindy Crawford. Men and women alike. And they all did look very much like her. One of the men especially.

Come to think of it, my uncle and my mother do have many things in common. He is a gentleman, albeit a pretty flighty, feisty and flamboyant one. As she is a lady. And neither of them seem to have the emotions you'd expect from them. Certainly not very sentimental.

Now Freddy had to go. He had promised to meet his friend Eric in Central Park to watch the skateboarders. And so he had to leave, doing it all very correctly, kissing us both, walking away straight and tall through the tables. He has Bertrand's personality but Thank God he looks like us. Blond and nice bearing.

My mother said, 'He has something of Fred, big Fred, about him. But it doesn't appear that he will be homosexual. Which is a blessing.' I said, 'Mother, don't be a bigot.' She said, 'You have no idea. I do. After all, Fred is my brother. It's a burden for him. I wouldn't change my brother for the world but it's been hard for him. Hard, hard, hard.' And she closed her purse, and her mouth and didn't want to continue with that subject.

'You were wonderful to me today, Mother dear,' I said. 'Just wonderful. To come to my defense that way. I know you would never have done what I'm doing, which makes it an even greater thing to do.'

'Don't be so sure of that, Nina,' she said. 'I never really had the opportunity. We lived in the suburbs. I only saw the men who were your father's friends. I certainly wasn't going to humiliate him by getting involved with one of them. And I really loved your father. He wasn't my first lover, and I really valued him. He was very much in love with me when we first met but he didn't have the temperament to be really interested in sex over a long time period. I did. But I always had to provoke him.'

Am I unimaginative? Or have I just avoided thinking about my mother and father in bed. Just as Edwina said when we were talking about pornography, 'I don't mind doing it, but I don't want to look at it.' I guess I have always averted my interior eye from observing these things.

'I guess that's the main reason I'm leaving Bertrand,' I said to my mother. 'It isn't that I love Graham. It's that I'm obsessed with him. I don't think I can find out who I am without him. If I don't know who I am sexually do I really know who I am?' I was talking to my mother as if I was talking to Edwina, and even talking to *her* so openly was of very recent date. I had gone too far. She looked down at her dessert plate. *Iles Flottantes.* Or *Oeufs à la Neige.* Depends on the restaurant and what they decide to call it.

'Anyway,' I said. 'You were wonderful to take my side.'

She looked up. 'I'm not taking your side, darling. I think you probably are making a mistake. I think you would have been better off to have tracked this new lover of yours down and said nothing to Bertrand.'

'But I discovered Bertrand's been having an affair with this woman at his office for years. Since before our marriage,' I said.

'And how did that impair your marriage? Were you unhappy? If you had never found out would it have mattered? I mean Bertrand did choose you and was certainly not planning to leave you. Now you've rather lumbered him with his aging what's-her-name.' I felt a little dizzy. My mother never speaks this plainly. I didn't even know she thought this plainly.

'Claire,' I said.

'Claire,' she replied. 'A nice name for someone who certainly can't be a very nice person.'

'She's always been in love with him I guess,' I said.

'What nonsense. Can you imagine a woman sitting around letting her looks collapse waiting for some man? She's just one of those women who don't want to get really involved. A part-time lover is right up their alley. Of course they dress it all up as unrequited love. They can't be bothered or they're too selfish to take someone on full-time. This town is full of those women. They can't go to bed with anyone on Thursday because that's the day they get their hair done.'

'I promise you I'm not going to worry about Claire,' I told her.

'Good,' she said shortly. 'Look,' she went on, 'I'm not very concerned about Bertrand or Freddy. They'll be fine. And I'm not going to let myself be overly concerned about you. I think you're acting like a teenager. Even worse, I think you're acting like a man. You're getting a little older, you think you're not as attractive as you were, you think you haven't experienced romance sufficiently so you're running off to start all over again. Thank God, your looks are holding up or you'd really look ridiculous. How much younger is this man than you are?' she finished, looking at me suspiciously.

'Ten years,' I told her.

'That's not so bad. But even so, you're probably not going to end up with him.'

'I don't know, Mom. I don't know. This seems pretty profound. He might not stay with me, but I can't imagine getting over this very quickly.' I never call her Mom. This whole thing was beginning to sound like one of those conversations you hear on an afternoon soap.

'Well, look,' she said, pulling on her gloves, 'I talked to Fred about this and he said, "Loyalty and support, Alicia. Loyalty and support." You know you'll always get that from me. You're my daughter. Flesh of my flesh.' She flashed me a smile from her war-time youth. One kid to another. 'I've never made a major decision except out of fear. So maybe I really don't understand this. Maybe I wish it was me running off with some sex god. And actually, to your credit and to mine I guess, you didn't lie.'

We had been standing talking at each other from each side

of the table too long. Neither of us are much on dramatic confrontations. I said, 'I think we should get out of here.' And we did.

But when I got back to the office I called her. 'It's me,' I said. 'What kind of underwear are you wearing?' She didn't miss a beat. 'Actually what I always wear. White cotton panties and a good bra. A French one. But not the kind that pushes you together. *And* a slip. A silk one. I don't like synthetics on my body.'

'I thought you don't like things slipping around on you.' She laughed and said, 'I don't mind a slip. I wouldn't want to feel the wool of my skirt on my legs.'

'You wouldn't feel that through your tights,' I said. She said, 'Isn't it pathetic, I wear hose. And a garter belt. I'm from another planet.'

'Or very avant garde. I don't suppose you wear a Merry Widow?' This made her really laugh. 'No, but I've got a waist cincher from a hundred years ago around here someplace. The elastic is probably shot by now.' Girl-talk. But you understand that we never did it before; me and that wild little blonde from the 1940s.

chapter 10

....

over her head

It must be the sunspots. Your life goes along. Nice job. Nice husband. Nice child. Nice house. Then suddenly gears shift. You're not unhappy. You have no real reason to want your life to change. But bang! You're in another gear . . . another life . . . altogether.

It could be sunspots or maybe there's something churning along inside you, like a computer disc you know nothing about, and then the moment has come. The gear meshes, and everything changes.

Grinding me forward into my own dreary little studio in the East Seventies near 3rd Avenue. Nothing on the walls. Just a little bed, a little bureau and me. I didn't move in with mother. She was perfectly game but interim is interim. Better to wait until the next stage comes into view all by myself. And I figured if Graham came roaring into my life, I didn't want him roaring into mother's guest room. I didn't want to imagine her making love to someone and I didn't want her to imagine me. I felt I'd asked enough of her.

I left the house without a murmur to Bertrand and Freddy. It was less disrupting for their lives. Bertrand betrayed me, but I really betrayed him more. He had no desire to leave me. And I had big desire to leave him. Bertrand and Freddy are really two of a kind. Self-centered. Wanting good service.

They could get all that with a good housekeeper. I heard Bertrand has plans to marry Claire. Now she'll be the manager. He really made no objection to my wanting a divorce.

Graham was very attentive. That was the word my mother would use. Certainly we were still in our 'going somewhere' phase. We talked on the phone most days and we always had something to talk about.

It was bizarre. He'd done two more porn films since we worked together in the islands. He said he was definitely in the 'A' category. The films were getting more elaborate. Three or four days of shooting. Excellent locations. Hair and makeup for the women. Even so, less expensive than the average television commercial. And supposedly someone makes millions with them. Thousands? Many thousands? Who is to say? And who makes that money exactly?

In the last video he was an android that has come to earth. Sort of like *Blade Runner*. He slept with everyone until they were exhausted. He said it's all done with editing, he doesn't *really* screw them until they're exhausted. He says. Was I living in a strange new world or what?

He said actually it was pretty funny. He didn't get to act but his friends in the film did. They staggered around holding their heads and their crotches, groaning. One of his friends, a big fat hairy man, came out of retirement just to be in the film and agreed to be a 'bottom', which he had never been before, just because he thought it was funny. When you're a 'bottom' or a 'top' it makes things pretty clear, doesn't it. Women are all bottoms, even when they are on top it seems. It has to do with who was penetrating whom.

Graham was an android encyclopedia salesman going door to door. In the original script he was handing out *The Watchtower* but they thought that was going too far. I could see one had to really get into it to make these discriminations as to what too far was. Actually, I would have loved that.

Anyway, Graham and I did make it. Right after I moved out. He came to New York just for the event. We had dinner at La Metairie in the Village. And then walked around. Greenwich Ave. Bleecker St. We didn't drink very much. I did want to remember what went on. We shop windowed. He wanted to buy me a wonderful kind of coral and turquoise belt . . . or was it a headdress? Tibetan at any rate. At Mr Nusraty's shop. Mr Nusraty didn't know himself what it was for. But it was *cher. Très cher.* So I said no. It was quite an object, certainly. Graham is drawn to the best quality. Which reassures me.

It's so silly and strange to be sexually obsessed with someone. You want to go rushing home, loosening their clothes in the taxi, and you're terrified at the same time. Maybe you're afraid of waking up from the dream that is your obsession and going on to the next stage. The reality stage. An obsession can be pretty sustaining.

Graham said, 'Ready?' in Sheridan Square and we got in a taxi and went uptown to my apartment. I felt very shaky. We sat on my little stupid mattress bed and he held me and kissed me very nicely. Kindly. I think he felt I wasn't very responsive. It wasn't that I didn't *want* to do, I didn't know *what* to do.

'Let me give you a massage,' he said. 'Would you like that?' 'Sounds like fun,' I mumbled as he pulled my T-shirt over my head. Who wears a T-shirt in anticipation of a night of love? Me. At least I wasn't wearing sweatpants and hiking boots.

He was really sweet. Sort of like a nanny. He unbuttoned my skirt and took it off and hung it over a chair, and took off my shoes and stood them neatly side by side in the closet. My little studio looked more and more like a nun's cell in a convent to me as I watched him.

He rolled down my pantyhose and shook them out and took them into the bathroom. He knew how to take them off. He's a neat, precise kind of guy.

He rolled me over face down on the bed and put a pillow under my chest. Sort of like a nurse. I still had on my bra.

Not one of those push-together jobs either. I really have no idea what kind of bosom I have. It doesn't sag particularly. I was never one of those girls who went around pushing them out. Nor did I slump. They were just there. Bertrand never really paid a lot of attention to them.

'Just a minute,' Graham said, and kicked off his loafers and took off his shirt and stepped out of his trousers. I peeked. My head was turned to the side on the pillow and I could just see him. He didn't look at me. It was unreal, that beautiful golden body. Those strong muscles in his thighs as his knees lifted out of his trousers. The ridges in his stomach that flattened out tightly when he pulled his undershirt off. He wears an undershirt. With straps over the shoulders. Is that kind of working class? My father always wore them, they came from Brooks Brothers. Graham was not showing off his body, he was just stripping down. Very unself-consciously. Only the lamp on the table was on so it was all dim and shadowy. It was like being at a great art exhibit of pictures you've seen in books all your life. You keep thinking, it must be a copy, this beauty. It can't be the real thing, really here. He kept on his underpants. Jockey shorts. I could have handled it if he had been wearing bikini underpants, but it was kind of comforting to see those familiar old Jockey shorts. He didn't have an erection.

He sat beside me and rubbed my shoulders, squeezing the muscles at the top between his fingers. It hurt. I groaned. 'Good, huh?' he said.

Slowly he worked his way down my spine, pushing the muscles with his thumbs. As though he was pushing something out. What? The ability to stand up, I guess. He undid my bra and said, 'Lift up.' I pushed up on my elbows and one arm at a time he pulled it off.

He straddled my body below my buttocks and squeezed them like kneading bread. Then pushed his thumbs into the sockets. 'Nice,' he said. 'Solid.' It hurt. 'It must be all those stairs at home,' I mumbled into the pillow.

Strange. Sort of like your mother putting you to bed. He rubbed my feet and pulled each of the toes separately and then squeezed my calf muscles and my thighs. With that kneading bread motion. I felt more and more that my muscles would not respond normally ever again.

'Now you do that to me,' Graham said and flopped down beside me. 'Here, let me get these off,' he said and turned on his side and pulled his shorts off. He threw them at the ceiling fixture, a kind of weak-kneed three-pronged attempt at Louis Quinze. They caught. 'I always like to do that so I know if I had a good time the next morning,' he said.

He flopped back laughing, pulling the pillow from under me and stuffing it under his own chest. 'Harder,' he said as I started rubbing his shoulders. 'Really squeeze them.' I did. It wasn't easy. His muscles are hard. 'Dig in with your thumbs,' he mumbled. I tried. 'Just run your nails lightly over my back,' he said. 'Mmm, mmm, mmm.' He wriggled and got goose bumps.

I massaged his head, too. That I knew how to do because Bertrand liked me to do that while he was watching TV. Graham has beautiful hair. Curly, but not too. Light brown I suppose it would be if it wasn't streaked by the sun.

I got on him horseback style and rubbed and pushed down the spine towards his butt, like he had done to me. And then I slid down and kneaded that smooth bottom. So sexy, that unblemished skin over those strong muscles. I wondered if he was getting an erection yet. I just smoothed that beautiful butt in my two hands. I sort of got the idea of how men must enjoy feeling a beautiful pair of breasts. So complete, somehow.

I turned around, sitting on his bare bottom with mine. Erotic and exciting and innocent. I don't think I have ever pressed my bare bottom against someone else's. It doesn't even come into the category of foreplay. Gee, there must be tons of things to do I haven't done yet, occurred to me. I massaged down his thighs, and then bent his leg up towards me so I wouldn't have to give up my seat on his seat. This was fun. I could get good at this, I thought. Such a pleasure to touch every square inch of the one you love like this. Your dream lover. Your obsession. At least if you touch every inch of your lover you can be sure they are there, can't you?

I did get up and turned around to kneel between his legs, pushing his thighs apart so I could really squeeze each one separately. Two giant loaves of bread. His leg hair isn't very thick but dark. Darker than you'd imagine.

I reached between his legs to find his cock. He didn't wince but lifted himself up slightly. It wasn't soft or hard. Sort of spongy and limber, like some kind of vegetable. I pulled it out upside down and let it lie in the palm of my hand, the head of it on my wrist. I ran a finger up and down it. It stirred and lengthened. It would be fun to have something like this that changes shape. The head of it upside down was like some sort of pink marble carving. So precise.

I never had done this for Bertrand. He wasn't circumcised and it always seemed sort of messy. Like eating endive.

I had to push my forehead down into the mattress strongly to get it in my mouth. Graham opened his legs further and pushed so it kind of blossomed in there. I could feel the blood pulsing into it. I just held it in there, warm and safe.

I pulled my mouth off it and said, 'Time to turn over and do the other side.' I was running the show. A kind of genius this guy.

When he turned over there was that beautiful thing. Graham looked down at me as I knelt beside him as though he was almost asleep and smiled. He reached down and pulled me up, holding me under the arms. As he folded his arms around me he sort of settled me down on it. It was entering my body, sort of filling up a space that was waiting for it. And we just lay there. Two people becoming one person. For awhile. I started moving first.

chapter 11

·······························

the fan is hit

Here's my theory. You can't just step outside the line of correct bourgeois behavior and then step back inside again. Once out you start a trajectory and you just keep going further out all the time. Isn't Gurdjieff's theory like this? That everybody is behaving in a repetitive way so their lives go in long oval circles. And one must try to be aware of every action so that life goes in a straight line, instead of circling back upon itself.

Well, mine could hardly be said to be circling back upon itself. Nixtrix had got the story on Graham. And Carlton Carlson went into orbit. Wanted to pull the Jamaica Wind commercial, even though December sales were through the roof. They were evidently getting mail by the armload, most of it about the Jamaica Wind man.

Edwina thought Ron Barricade tipped them off. Ron Barricade was the head creative director of the agency. The only time Edwina sounds at all French is when she mentions him. 'He looks like a raaat,' she said. It sort of rhymed with 'hot'. He *was* sort of a little rat. As Edwina says, 'No one is short by chance.' Ron hated Edwina because she had a contract that said no one could supervise the Nixtrix work. And she was tall. And she was blonde. She was probably everything he longed to be. Now I'm getting bitchy. I had no bones to pick with Ron actually. We'd never exchanged ten words. But as Edwina said to me, 'Who is there in the agency most likely to recognize porn stars? He probably has a huge video library. Huge!' She was very live and let live, but when someone gets in her way, watch out for Hurricane Edwina.

She was great in the meeting with Carlton Carlson. He loved nothing better than staging a huge scene. He came storming in screaming, 'We've got a goddam porn star in the Jamaica Wind commercial.' Edwina was so cool. She said without blinking an eye, 'The girl or the boy?' He said, 'Oh God, do you suppose the girl is too?'

Edwina said, 'How do you know this, Carlton? He's a nice-looking guy. Where did you hear this?' Carlton said, 'My secretary told me.' 'Your secretary?' 'She heard it on some radio station. Who's that awful woman. That friend of Imelda Marcos? Cindy whatever?'

'Where would she hear something like that?' Edwina said. I said nothing. Both of us thought of Ron Barricade. That was exactly the level of his social contacts. Victoria Principal, etc.

Carlton turned, fuming like some kind of cornered beast. 'And you know if I've heard it, everybody's heard it. They try to keep everything from me.' He was shaking inside, I'm sure, waiting for a phone call from the president, Mr Nixtor. He was a real terror, as all the ex-Mrs Nixtors could testify. 'Who did the casting on this?' Carlton screamed, throwing himself in a chair. 'I'll kill her. Him. Whatever.' 'We all did it,' Edwina said. 'We were sent a tape from the West Coast and we all agreed this guy had the most charisma. You, too, Carlton. You saw him.'

'How would I have known. I don't watch porn videos,' Carlton grumbled, going into his sulky phase.

'It's not as though we do,' Edwina said. 'Life hasn't come to that, yet, Carlton, that we have to screen our models to

make sure they haven't done porn films. Though some of the
best are going to eventually, or close to it.'

She got up. 'I'm going to check this out, Carlton. Don't
overreact. It's probably a hullabaloo over nothing. He probably isn't. Cindy what's-her-name is probably just hurling
these things out without checking them. I'll bet you anything
she said, "It's rumored . . . " or something like that. I'm
sure she didn't name names. How could she?'

Edwina swept out with her entourage, including me, leaving
Carlton sweating and swearing in the conference room. We'd
come over to present some layouts for our new makeup,
Playtime, but we weren't about to risk losing a week of work
by presenting them to the living volcano of hate. He would
scream whatever we showed him.

What a peach, Edwina! What instincts! 'I'm sorry I got you
into all this, Edwina,' I said. 'Well, wasn't it worth it?' she
said. 'And anyway, you didn't get us into this, I got you into
this. And I don't regret it in the least. I mean what are we
talking about? A television commercial. Thirty seconds. That
no one will remember two months from now. It's only advertising.' She turned to me. The elevator was coming. 'One
must live!' she said as the doors opened. Everybody inside
was wearing a navy blue suit and looked at me very carefully.
You could tell they found the idea of living a very iffy propo-
sition. Edwina stared at them all as she does. As though to
check if there was anyone worth knowing in the elevator with
her. And turned away. She was wearing a black and white
check suit and a huge ruby pin. She saw me looking at it. She
said, 'It's nice isn't it. I tore it from a rajah's turban. That's
how I like jewelry to look; as though you had torn it from
your father's crown before you fled the country. You know
that's how Nabokov's family lived for years. His mother had
worn her rubies to the opera the night before they fled Russia
and they were on her dressing table. Otherwise they probably
would never have escaped and he would never have written

Lolita.' The elevator stopped. Everyone fled, not waiting for
ladies first. They knew *Lolita* was not nice and that we were
not nice right along with the book. I love Edwina. 'They
probably thought we were hookers,' I said. 'Oh no, darling.
Hookers wear those little navy blue suits. They probably
thought we were the wives that men flee from *to* the hookers.'

And so it turned out that Cindy did have the names.
Someone had done some squealing somewhere along the line.
I called Graham and told him. He said, 'Does this mean I
won't get my residuals?' and laughed and laughed. He said,
'I hope they fire you and you have to come out here and
live.' Which is exactly what happened. Sort of. Not exactly.
Obviously I had to leave. Nixtrix was never going to pay
attention to me anymore anyway. They'd never let me supervise a shooting. They probably wouldn't even buy a script,
since I was the untrustworthy one. Yes, word had gotten out
that I was seeing Graham. That I had left my husband.

It would have been wonderful to run into someone's office
screaming, 'Lies, lies, lies. It's all lies.' Unfortunately it wasn't.
Curious, huh? You step outside. Do something that isn't
strictly professional, not even really knowing why you're doing
it. And kaboom. You're in a whole new world.

chapter 12

....

to california

'We must talk about your going to California,' Edwina said. We were in her office. She was wearing red and black, one of her best looks. A black suit and a large red cashmere shawl. The shawl probably cost more than the suit. And no jewelry. Sort of a Spanish look, at its best. Or Habsburgian, if you prefer, since Edwina is blonde.

'The jig is up here, Ninotchka. You can stay here as long as you like, but you can't go back on Nixtrix. Carlton Carlson would have a fit. He's calmed down since Jamaica Wind was such a success. And all the hoo-haw about the porn-star leading man just made sales go higher. He thinks so, too. But he's embarrassed, and hell hath no fury like an advertising manager embarrassed. And he'll never believe we weren't trying to put something over on him. Which we were. *N'est-ce pas?*' Edwina speaks French with an English accent. What a piece of work she is.

Edwina had outdone herself when Carlton Carlson called the president of Campanella, demanding that I be fired. The president came to Edwina's office and I heard her. She never acts angry when she is angry. And she never shuts the door to her office. So no one ever needed to get paranoid. You could always hear everything.

In her 'sweetly reasonable' voice she said, 'Oh, no, I think it's better that I go. Because you know I couldn't accept someone telling me whom I should fire or hire. Nina wrote a wonderful commercial. It's making tons of dough for Nixtrix. There are only ten people in the world who know our leading man has done porn movies. Unfortunately those ten people are in the Nixtrix management. I don't think it matters. Sylvester Stallone did porn movies.'

'Soft porn,' Mr Campanella said. 'A lot of people must have seen our man in those movies and it doesn't reflect well on Nixtrix. Or us.' He was using his strangled I-can-hardly-bear-to-talk-about-this voice.

Edwina said, 'Even if it matters, which I don't think it does, I'm the head of the department and the blame must rest with me. Not my staff. And that Stallone film wasn't so soft. The Italian Stallion?'

'How would you know about that?' the President said. He left it there.

'Look, George. They're pouring into the stores to buy Jamaica Wind. You know how you're always exhorting us. Telling us that there must be something in every commercial that captures their attention. Makes them think "This is my product. This is for me." Something's working. Maybe a lot of people recognize him and want what he's got. But no, I'll go. That will settle the problem completely.'

'Obviously you can't go, Edwina,' Mr Campanella grumbled. Then without a pause, 'So, how we doing on that Lavish Lashes commercial? Did you sell that new idea?' And the crisis was over. But it didn't go away.

I said, 'You're not at all intimidated by bosses, are you?' She said, 'They're all rubber icebergs for the most part.'

'Which means what?' I said.

'Which means that we think, as with icebergs, that what we see is only the tip of something massive and dangerous and powerful that is going to rip us apart. But these guys for the most part are just what you see, floating on the surface.

There's nothing important below the water line you don't see, much as they'd like you to think there is.

'No, Ninette, I think you must decamp to Los Angeles. You'll never land that guy living here. And you deserve a new life.'

'What about Fred the Second?' I asked her.

'He's going to boarding school you told me. You'd always planned that, so he would have a better chance of getting into Princeton. You're not going to be seeing him much anyway. Does it matter if you're two hundred or two thousand miles away? You're away. Ask for more money out there and put it into airfare. And Freddy will love it, actually. All that teen angst. The glamour of a mother in Los Angeles, slightly tarnished. Those kids love getting together in some filthy old dormitory and angsting away together. Now he's really got something to angst about.'

'You talk such heresy, Edwina. He's still only fifteen.'

'Honey, your life can be ruined at fifteen months, not at fifteen years.' Sometimes Edwina slips into a kind of showgirl mode. I never get the real facts about her past. All of her past.

She went on, 'No, the coast is waiting for you, my dear. They're dying for good writers out there. Neutrogena. Giorgio. Cleanola. They'll be thrilled you want to change coasts. And even more thrilled that it's for romantic reasons. Turning your life upside down because you want to screw someone makes perfect sense to them. Cleanola is the obvious beauty client you should go after; they're the biggest on the coast.'

'I'm not going out there without a job,' I told her.

'You could go out just for some interviews, my darling. You don't have to move out there lock, stock and barrel first. Now just sit down and we'll think about who we know out there.'
I was already sitting down.

'But more important, where do you want to live? I've always

fancied one of those dreary 1930s bungalows in West Holly-wood. Like a Raymond Chandler novel. All sort of down-at-heel. If you live somewhere like that I'll be out there all the time, hanging around in a back bedroom in a torn bathrobe. You'll just have to explain me to your friends as best you can.' Obviously Edwina and I were attacking the problem on the same trajectory. The decor first. Paying for it second.

chapter 13

....

nina in hollywood

So, there I was. On Orlando. In Hollywood. West Hollywood just off Sunset. And the place *was* Raymond Chandleresque. A kind of English cottage with a gigantic tree of some kind in the front yard that had completely killed any hope of a lawn. I rented it furnished. The bed must have been Emperor Size. It could sleep eight in a row. There were closets everywhere. People must have had an enormous amount of clothes in the 1920s when this house was built. Furs to wear to openings at Grauman's Chinese Theater I suppose. Everything was vast in small rooms here. The Chanel theory. Fill those rooms up. A gigantic armoire and two vast couches in the living room, and a large stone angel as you came in the door, and wood, wood, wood everywhere. Wooden walls. Wooden ceilings. Wooden floors. A castle jammed into a cottage.

A step up into the dining room which had a stone table. A great big slab of granite. Thank God there was no basement so I didn't have to worry about everything slumping into it during the night.

And a very large television screen in the bedroom. So I could watch my Chase Manhattan videos in almost life-size. Except I didn't have to; we weren't living together but he spent every night with me. What will the neighbors think, seeing his car in the driveway every morning? The nice thing about Hollywood is that the neighbors don't think.

And the job. Of course, the job. I felt as though I was Edwina's puppet. I knew exactly what she'd do in the circumstances and I did it. And it worked. I wrote a letter to Mr John Steer, the president of Steer, Stone, and Dorita, who have the Cleanola account. Followed it up with a phone call. Yes, Mr Steer would like to see me. I flew out and the docile Mr Steer, very nice, very calm, very Anglo-Saxon, said they were trying to get more of the Cleanola business and thought a classy New York writer from a hot New York agency would probably get the job done. And he hired me right in the interview. I think when I told him I'd just done the Jamaica Wind commercial he made up his mind. Everyone in the business knew by now that Jamaica Wind did twice the Christmas business of any other fragrance. And it was a re-launch, not an introduction. He was impressed. So now I had been made a Group Head and I was getting twenty thousand more a year.

Edwina says when people ask how much money you want you shouldn't be embarrassed. Just pretend they are asking how old you are and say a number. She says when she started you asked for the same number as your age, but now you doubled it. So I just looked Mr Steer in the eye and said 'Seventy-five to eighty.' He said, 'Will you take seventy-seven with a raise to eighty in six months if everything works out?' I said, 'That will be fine.' Knowing that if everything didn't work out I'd be at zero and out on the street. As Edwina said when I told her, 'Seventy-seven thousand is only a lot of money at the end of the year when you've earned it. It isn't so much if they dump you in six months. So you better work, my angel.' Tough love, Edwina style. She probably thought if I was in Hollywood to get my brains fucked out I wouldn't have any left for the job.

But that's where my puritanical side kicked in. I wouldn't

have said I was getting my brains fucked out, but I certainly was getting mine. Sometimes when Graham showed up I just opened the door and dragged him right down on the floor. Pulling his clothes off.

Did you see that scene in *Apollo 13* when they're re-entering space and they have to hand-maneuver the space ship and they do it by keeping the earth in the porthole? And they're guiding it with this weird handle, like one of those shower handles that goes all ways, back and forth and up and down? Difficult to do. But Tom Hanks does do it and keeps the earth centered in the porthole and they re-enter space at the right place on the right angle.

That's what I was trying to do with this sexual space adventure with Graham. I was trying to keep my real life in the porthole so I didn't spin off into destruction with my obsession. I had to steer this vehicle for the two of us, because he was completely caught up in this thing with me. It wasn't that he was obsessed with me, but he was experiencing something and it was exciting. It wasn't so much sex, sex, sex which he knew all about, but him, him, him. Which I suppose was very flattering. I guess if I had been a waitress at Hamburger Hamlet it would have been less so. I'm not so sure of that. It was more that I had some kind of Space Sex Odyssey going on and he was the passenger. He was fascinated to see if we were boldly going where no man or woman had gone before. Me, too.

chapter 14

nina thinks

Graham has a very strong back. I think my favorite part of intimacy with him, whether he is in me or not, is running my hands down his back, which is something like a smooth armor. His spine is set down in a valley between the curves of muscle on each side and his skin is very smooth.

I move my hands together up and down on his back and he lies on me with his full weight, breathing moistly and warmly into my ear. I call him my sweet baby, which he doesn't object to. I have the impression that it isn't so much he enjoys it, but that he enjoys that I enjoy it.

Last night he mumbled groggily, 'I must be heavy.' And I said, 'It is the weight of your problems that holds you in place.' What did I mean? He didn't seem to resent being considered a problem. Maybe he didn't draw that conclusion. And I have to admit that his weight *is* almost crushing. Making it impossible for me to move. And if I could move, where would I move to?

chapter 15

....

you'd better work

So many new things at once. I could walk down to Steer,
Stone. They're on Beverly. But I'd bought this stupid car. I
hated to drive but it was nothing to zip down Orlando and
across on Beverly into the parking garage in the basement. It
was so close it made me feel guilty so I often pretended I was
in New York and walked from one place to another. Or took
a taxi. But I came to like my beaten-up little Honda. People
would see me pull up in it and think 'Poor thing. An out-of-
work character actress who never made it and never will now.
Must have been pretty once but there are a zillion women
like her around this town.' Looking defeated is a kind of
disguise around Hollywood. No one could imagine you might
have more money than you were displaying. Since everyone
was running around flaunting the reverse. Hollywood is not
a culture that understands throwaway chic, even with all their
blue jeans and T-shirts and baseball caps. It's like Marie
Antoinette playing at being a milkmaid. Except in Hollywood
the tumbrils roll every day, every time a movie flops.

And the movie culture filters into everything. The agency
looked like a set for a movie about advertising. The people
all looked like extras who had been dressed to play the roles.
A Brooks Brothers suit? The account supervisor. A little Ann
Taylor number? Head of Research. They were like that in

meetings. They didn't seem to know anything about their work. The idea seemed to be to find someone you could pay who would do the work for you. Maybe that was where I came in.

My senior writer was quite all right, though. Fiona Fizdale. How do you like that name? Everyone must have come to Los Angeles originally planning to be in the movies. And skidded sideways into other industries when that didn't work out.

I took Fiona to lunch the first day and she filled me in on the Cleanola account. Mr Duress, Claude Duress, was the president of Cleanola and the agency was having trouble with him because the present Mrs Duress was my predecessor. That's right. I was replacing Connie Duress. She wasn't Connie Duress then, but had captured Mr Duress's fancy with her copy or with her something and immediately quit the agency. To become a talent agent. The story Fiona told me was that Connie Duress saved the company's life when she created the famous Cleanola line, 'You're only as clean as you feel. *Feel* clean with Cleanola.' Evidently this tapped into some great American yearning to not only be clean but feel clean.

Now after two years of marriage Connie wanted a divorce. I know you're thinking 'They went two years at this agency without a copy supervisor on the account?' but that's advertising. I'm sure no one wanted the job, figuring they could never match Mrs Duress, now married to the client. Except stupid me, of course. Who paid so little attention to the business I didn't even know about her.

Now that Mrs Duress was asking for a divorce the agency probably felt they must have a new supervisor on the business. Because all hell was breaking loose at Cleanola. Mrs Duress was asking for half the value of the Cleanola company on the grounds that it was her know-how that pulled it back from the brink. Naturally Mr Duress wasn't too crazy about this idea.

Our first big project was to be new slogans for Cleanola. They hadn't had a Group Head for two years but for some reason they had to make this presentation a week after I reported in. Mr Steer was very pleasant about it and explained that no one would hold me accountable on such short notice but they'd been working on this for about six months and hadn't come up with anything that pleased Mr Duress. No wonder Fiona was pleased to see me.

And of course there was only an assistant Art Director to help us. The Senior Art Director Azimuth Bendor was on vacation. A long vacation. Mr Steer said, 'He was so relieved to hear you were coming and it had been so long since he'd had a vacation he left immediately. Four weeks in Yosemite with the kids.'

I said, 'It's January.'

He said, 'Yeah, I know. Evidently they're crazy about hiking in the snow.'

I thought, 'He's crazy about being anywhere but here.'

At first I felt a little desperate. Five days. I knew nothing about the account. And despite Mr Steer's optimism, this had to be a crucial meeting. I was going to win or lose on this meeting. If Mr Duress likes me, fine. If not, my departure is written in the stars. And where would that leave Graham and me?

This was being a big girl. I remembered Edwina frequently quoting Coco Chanel, one of her idols. According to her Coco said, 'I never designed a good dress until I didn't care anymore.' So I just sat down and whacked away. I told Fiona we would knock out lines for two days then sit together and see where we were. I decided we wouldn't march in with hundreds of slogans but take in about twenty. And have them printed out and put on big cards with pictures. To put up about the room. An Edwina trick. It looked like so much more than just a handful of pages with lists on them.

By the end of the day I had a bundle. Three or four I really liked but I hid them in amidst all the rest to see what kind of reaction they'd get from Fiona and Ashley Brock, our little assistant Art Director. My favorites were:

'YOU JUST THINK YOU'RE CLEAN'
'COULD YOUR SKIN BE CLEANER THAN IT IS?'
'THE CLEAN MACHINE'
'CLEAN IS A WISH YOUR SKIN MAKES'
'CLEAN AT LAST'

The trouble with slogans is that they always sound dumb until you read them in a magazine or hear them on the air. The process kind of somehow legitimizes them.

Mr Steer had been hovering around my door all afternoon but I told him that the Creative Staff had to review the work first. The business people always want to make creative decisions and I started holding him at bay right from the start.

Fiona was gun-shy about saying what she liked and didn't like about my work but Ashley spoke right up. She was small and dark and not really pretty but I saw the hint of something stylish there. She and I overlapped on a couple of lines. She liked 'The Clean Machine'. Seemed a little surprised that an older woman from New York would think of something like that. I told her I had a teenaged son so he probably had infiltrated my vocabulary.

I liked a number of Fiona's lines so we finally boiled it down to about twenty we all liked. Then I explained we would print them out on the computer and stick them on boards with pictures. They both looked nonplussed and said 'What pictures?' I started flipping through magazines and soon, like kindergartners, we were pulling stuff out and spreading it around on the floor and deciding what lines would go with what pictures.

Mr Steer peered around the corner again. 'Can I peek?' he said. 'Tomorrow, tomorrow, tomorrow,' I cried out.

When I got home Graham was already there and I told him about what we were doing. 'You seem pretty excited,' he said, lounging across one of the big, ugly leather couches in the murky cave of my living room. 'I am, I am,' I said, walking around the room wondering if I had time to dust before we went out to dinner. 'It's fun, you see. It's not important but it's fun. They all think it's important but to me it's just fun. And you're fun. My whole life is fun.'

I climbed on top of him and hugged him.

He put his arms around me and held me tight. He was always so warm. 'Naughty Nina. You're going to wrinkle your suit.'

'I can iron it. Or press it. Or whatever. So what's cooking in your life?' I asked him, sitting up and sorting out my hair.

'Mimi Fandango over at Eagle is planning a new picture. He wants to call it *Chase Away Your Blues*. It will have a lot of sailors in it.'

'He?' I said. 'Mimi?'

'Mimi Fandango is a guy. I've never seen him out of makeup, but he's a guy. He's the director over at Eagle. I don't suppose they'll be real sailors. I don't think they have to look for real sailors when there are so many guys who want to be in these movies.'

'Really?'

'You should see the casting calls. There are hundreds of guys. Maybe not hundreds. But many. The women are harder to find.'

'And you're the best,' I said.

'And I'm the best,' he answered.

chapter 16

....

at cleanola

Claude Duress said, 'Do you know Edwina Grey?'

'I've worked for her for the last four years,' I said. 'She's the best.'

He said, 'The last time I saw Edwina I told her that she often did really nice work and she said, "Oh, you mustn't spoil me. It wouldn't be good for me to be spoiled." How do you know when she's being funny?'

'Never, really,' I said. 'Until it's too late.'

Mr Duress regarded me a little suspiciously under his eyebrows. He looked a little bit like a sulky gray-haired bison. He was the only one in the room wearing a sweater. A cashmere v-neck. I guess in his circles they don't know that the v-neck is completely out. Or was it coming back in? I was wearing my new pale blue linen suit. A Carolina Herrera look. I've decided that will be my style for this job. No menswear. Carolina Herrera all the way. Spoiled South American heiress. Definitely does not need the job. Pale blue and yellow and sometimes black. I was smelling of Vol de Nuit by Guerlain. Rather chic.

'She is the leader of our industry. She *is* Nixtrix,' he said definitively. 'And I am right behind her,' I said. Everyone from Steers, Stone froze and looked straight ahead at nothing. That 'Who is this person? Does she work for us?' look.

Without moving they all seemed to be sitting further away from me than moments before.

'That remains to be seen,' Mr Duress said rather jovially and sat down. Everyone seemed suddenly to be sitting nearer me again. 'Let's see what you have.'

So I did the whole dog and pony show the way I'd learned in New York. The little speech about how important Cleanola was and how they occupied a special place in the beauty industry and how their image must be reflected down to the last little word in the least important piece of collateral material. To establish how much the agency cared. Then I took our stack of slogans and one by one read the line slowly. Put the card with its shiny picture and slogan on the narrow shelf running around the room. Read the line again. Went back and got the next one. I'd shuffled the favorites down in the pack, knowing that clients always think you've either got your favorites up front or at the end. And they're certainly not going to like anything the agency likes. When all the cards were up, which took about thirty minutes, it seemed like quite an important little project. I had all the lines we'd done on handout pages, which I handed out to Mr Duress and his little band of lackeys. You are never sure what those lackeys do and it's not really very important to know since the boss was obviously going to make all the decisions.

Mr Duress then went around the table in the classic manner. Asking the least important of his staff what they liked first and working up in pecking order. Guys like Duress are tricky. In principle, they let everyone express themselves and then make a different choice. There was no disgrace in liking something he didn't like. But should he be in a whimsical mood and like a slogan or layout that an underling had chosen, that underling would then be given many points by his cohorts. Talk about the court of the Louis's.

Everyone liked the most eulogistic directions. Many liked Fiona's 'It isn't Clean if it isn't Cleanola'. Before making his own choices Mr Duress asked for the agency's recommendation. Mr Steer graciously nodded in my direction. Certainly he wasn't going to involve himself, if this was going to be an exercise in the agency being cut down to size by withering criticisms. Let them chew up the new supervisor.

I told Mr Duress I liked 'The Clean Machine' the best because it seemed to express the idea of super-cleanness without using clichés, and since there were many Cleanola products, from soap to facial cleansers to shampoo, this was a slogan that could be used with everything. 'It just assumes that dirt can put up no resistance. And we have to assume that our market is people who want to be clean above everything else,' I told him.

'I think you're right,' Mr Duress said. The agency people nearly fainted. Mr Steer had to steady himself with one hand on the table. I miss nothing. You could feel the warmth of the Cleanola group's gaze upon me. They were going to approve of me, even like me. Mr Duress had given the seal of approval.

But pretty cagey was Mr Duress. He had divined who had written what and said he wanted 'The Clean Machine' to go into test along with two other slogans, one of mine and one of Fiona's. I appreciated that. Keeping my senior writer on my side was important and he was doing that for me. It made me like him better.

Everyone from the agency was in a jolly mood as we got into our cars to return to the office. Fiona and Ashley and I went with Mr Steer in his Mercedes. To his credit he didn't go crazy, but he was obviously relieved that a first hurdle was over and that I might quite possibly be a worthy replacement for Connie Duress. He said that Mr Duress and his ex were going to court next week so maybe Mr Duress was feeling a bit relieved, too. That he could shed his wife and that his company wasn't headed to hell in a handbasket. I was careful not to think too well of myself too soon.

Mr Steer came to my office after lunch and said Mr Duress had called him and said that he was pleasantly surprised and impressed. He said, 'We may have a new Edwina Grey on our hands here. Let's hope.' That was certainly music to my ears. I rushed home feeling very peppy to share the good news with my paramour.

He came in soon after I got home and was happy for me. He hugged me. He had parental feelings for his little bird flying off into the wild blue yonder for the first time. His aged little bird. He *was* parental with me. But I never felt maternal towards him. Graham was someone who wanted to learn, but I don't think he needed nurturing. He only said to me the one night, 'When we met you needed affection and I needed attention. And as Simone Weil said, "Attention is a kind of prayer".' My eyes bugged. 'Simone Weil?' I said. 'Where did you hear about Simone Weil?' He smirked. 'I just read that in a magazine yesterday,' he said. 'Who in the hell was Simone Weil anyway?'

Graham had good news for me, too. I wasn't so sure his good news was my good news, but they were going into production next week with his new porn flick. They were thinking of calling it *Chasing The Fleet* now and were going to shoot it in a rooming house in Laguna Beach. He thought it sounded like it was going to be a lot of fun. He was going to be the proprietor of a hotel called The Palace Hotel (for Sailors Only). There were going to be some women in it but also guys on guys.

So here we were. The reality of my new life was upon me. I had to think how I was going to handle this and I had to think fast. Since demanding that he give up his profession was out of the question I assumed the role of business manager.

'What are they paying you for this?' I asked.

I could tell he was expecting a different reaction. 'I told Mimi Fandango I wanted double. Since the Jamaica Wind commercial I'm more of a celebrity. So I'm getting five thousand a day for three days. And if we go into overtime I get the same day rate.'

'Three days is a lot of fucking,' I said. 'I won't be seeing much of you while you're shooting.'

'You'd be surprised,' he said, pushing himself up against me from behind. I was at the sink washing lettuce for our dinner. It was one of those rare evenings when we were eating in. I remembered Edwina's advice. Was I putting a hoodoo on this romance by letting him see me cook? At least we hadn't taken to using the bathroom at the same time yet.

'Yes?' I turned around, pressing the front of me against the front of him. He pushed me harder against the sink.

'I *want* to fuck you. I don't particularly want to fuck any of them. In fact, I'll probably be thinking about you even more than usual during the shoot.'

'Maybe I'll visit the set,' I said.

'Hmmm. I wonder how that would be. I've never had somebody I was sleeping with on the set unless they were in the picture.'

I hadn't thought about that.

'Chase?'

'Graham.'

'Graham, who was your girlfriend before me? Did you break up with someone when we started seeing each other?'

'No. I didn't have anyone particular in my life. I was dating around. Usually with people in my pictures. You kind of don't know anyone else when you're in this business. Some women. Some guys, too, you should know. Some of them are really nice and really beautiful.'

'Will there be some of them in this picture?'

'I don't know yet,' he said. 'Mimi hasn't discussed that yet with me. There won't be anyone I don't like, that's for sure.'

We broke apart and I went back to washing the lettuce. He sat down. He had an erection and I was flattered. Or maybe he was just looking forward to doing the picture.

'There will be a lot of men in this one?' I didn't really want to look at him.

'It's safer.' So the subject had finally come up. 'With guys you always use condoms. In the strictly heterosexual films they usually don't and I'm not nuts about that idea. I told Mimi I was going to wear protection in all my scenes, male and female. He's pretty cool with that because he thinks they ought to be doing that in all the porn pictures anyway. To teach the public.

'Look,' he said and he pulled me on to his lap and his erection, the lettuce going everywhere, 'I think we've got a future. I don't know where this is all going, but we're certainly not going to fool around. I just had a test, I know I'm in the clear. Have you had a test lately?' I looked at him in amazement.

'I've never had an HIV test. Why would I? I've always been a married woman.' And then I realized how silly that was to say with Bertrand dipping his silly French wick who knows where. 'I'll make an appointment to get one tomorrow. And we'll use condoms tonight.'

'How about right now?' he said.

chapter 17

nina thinks some more

Have you ever suddenly found yourself saying things and doing things that are entirely unplanned? Your lips open and you speak and you think 'Where did that come from?' And then you have the scary feeling that the real you is someone you scarcely know. And if you left her alone to go her unguided way, what would she do?

I thought of myself as a stray passenger on a strange train. Where is the engineer? Where are we going? And what's to say that we aren't going to run completely off the tracks.

My mood exactly when I said to Graham, lying underneath him, 'I don't want you to wear a condom.'

He looked down at me with disdain, one of his better expressions. 'You're crazy,' he said.

'No. I'm on the pill so that part's all right. It's just that if you got AIDS and died I wouldn't want to live on after you. I'm ready to die for love.'

'Women, women, women,' grumbled Graham as he started to screw the daylights out of me, as he likes to put it.

chapter 18

chasing the fleet

Now I talk about the hard part. Where two cultures meet, and all the rest of it. My boyfriend made porn movies. He fucked complete strangers with abandon. Which was actually better to my mind than someone like my soon-to-be-ex who pretended he didn't and did pretty much the same thing.

Was this an open relationship? How much more open could you get? Since we'd met he'd been completely loyal to me, in his own way. In a funny way I suspected Graham's idea of betrayal would be to say negative things about me to someone else. I was sure in his mind screwing somebody was like saying 'How d'ya do.' But revealing something personal about your partner to somebody else, that would be a definite no-no.

I certainly didn't want to casually sleep with other people myself. Assuming there was somebody around town who might want to. But I was such a dit. Someone actually putting their sexual organ into your sexual organ is so personal, don't you think? Where for Graham I imagined it was the initial getting to know someone. That was definitely not going to work for me. Besides, I was so obsessed with Monsieur Graham I would never have the slightest urge.

Which left me accepting that it was okay for him to do this. It was his living. Uncle Fred would understand this frame of mind, but nobody else I knew. Edwina would understand but she wouldn't accept it.

I suggested we go to the Getty Museum on Saturday. 'You have to reserve,' Graham said. 'It's the garage not the museum. When the garage is full they stop taking visitors.' 'Maybe we could walk,' I suggested. 'They'd be very surprised to hear that since they're on the edge of a cliff overhanging the Pacific,' Graham said. 'I'll call them. There usually isn't any problem.'

So we went to visit the Getty. The old one, before they built the new monster one – the reincarnation of a Pompeian villa. On a similar coast, in similar blazing sun. Hard to imagine that even in Pompeii there were days when you could smell the fresh plaster, all the angles of the walls were sharp and clean and all the statues were glossy and looked brand-new.

Sort of freaky, the Getty, so totally lacking in any sense of history. Maybe that's good. We don't get a chance to romanticize it with veils of the past. This is it, kiddoo. Just like it was. And probably a very appropriate place to discuss sex. Those old villas probably saw plenty of it. Curious, isn't it, to think of a culture where it wasn't filed under the heading of sin? Just excess in certain cases, I suppose.

We walked along the pool, looking at the red tiles and the tile-red trim on the villa. And the bronze statues that lined the pool that didn't seem very beautiful or very beautifully made. Perhaps they thought of them as people do now about plaster dwarves and reflecting balls and wooden flamingos. It surely must have been a level above that. Graham brought up the subject first.

'You're thinking about my doing this movie,' he said.

'Exactly,' I said.

'So cool. So collected.'

'You know I'm not inside,' I told him.

'I know but I don't know what to say to you about it.'

'The other day I was running down that little mirrored staircase at the office we have between floors, and I saw myself, hair flying, and it didn't seem to bear any resemblance to the me I know. It seemed to be somebody else altogether.'

'Maybe it was someone I know.'

'Maybe *only* you know her, Graham.'

'Anyway, it's no joke losing track of yourself.' He looked at me carefully. 'Everyone must fall in love with you,' he said. I loved it when he said that.

He pulled a bougainvillea blossom off a bush and put it behind my ear. I am the least flower-behind-the-ear person you can imagine.

'You just open your mouth and say things other people can't bring themselves to. For such a nicely brought up person, Nina, you're not awfully repressed.'

I sat down on a marble bench. He came and stood in front of me.

'I have to figure this thing out. I love you. More than that, I'm obsessed with you. But I still have to let you be free to do what it is you want to do. If you hadn't I would never have even seen you. Heard of you. Nothing.'

He sat down on the bench and we both looked straight ahead. 'When I was in college I had a roommate with a pet monkey named Clyde,' he said. 'Clyde had an erection all the time. It didn't look like a human erection, more like the stamen of some kind of flower. Long and slender with a little flat thing like a miniature flower on the end. Unless he was sleeping it was erect. It was like an arm or a leg. And it changed the way I thought about sex. It was kind of equipment, ready to go. And I realized I was like that myself. I had this equipment and I was ready to go. I had an affair of sorts with my roommate and I felt I was just like Clyde.'

'Your roommate was a girl?'

'No.'

'You didn't worry about being a homosexual?'

'It wasn't like that. I think he was sort of like me. He wasn't in love with me. I wasn't in love with him. We didn't even care about each other. It was just flesh. Attractive flesh. It only matters when you care about the person.'

'But after you've had sex with lots of people, doesn't it make you different. Kind of careless?' I asked. 'Kind of jaded?'

'Maybe for some people. But sex doesn't leave any marks. When you love someone it's like you have a different body and when you make love it leaves marks on your soul. And you can see it on people's faces and bodies afterwards. I can see it on yours.'

I said, 'It's strange, isn't it? Love isn't really very romantic. Aldous Huxley said that making love was like two maniacs struggling in the dark. Trying to fight their way through to some kind of answer.'

'That's when it's good.'

I said, 'Otherwise you're thinking about whether you remembered to do the laundry. Men don't think about the laundry when they're making love I guess. They have to concentrate.'

'They can think about themselves doing it. I knew a dancer once who told me that when he took class and saw himself in the mirror he was so beautiful he got a hard-on.'

'But you didn't start doing this to show off your beauty, did you? I know you didn't. You're not at all like that. You don't even use face masks.'

'Any man who uses a face mask will eventually suck cock,' Graham said.

I got up and shook out my skirt. 'Let's go look at the French furniture.'

Actually I was feeling a little shaky. In front of a particularly horrible Louis Quatorze bureau. I asked, 'You've never done that?'

'Done what?' he said, standing behind me and putting his arms around my waist, nuzzling my ear. I would never have allowed that at the Metropolitan Museum but this was California. Nobody notices such things. 'Sucked cock,' I said in a low voice.

He pulled back and looked at me with a very surprised expression. 'Whoa! People don't usually say those kinds of things looking at Louis Quatorze furniture.'

'I'm sure they used to say things like that a lot *on* Louis Quatorze furniture,' I said. He took my hand and pulled me along to look at a hideous room-setting of chairs and a table with a large overly restored painting of nymphs and Gods. The Getty evidently thinks that bright red velvet and a lot of gilding was the seventeenth century. There were many low squat chairs evidently made for people with short legs and enormous rear ends. Or lots of skirts and tail coats more likely. I like French furniture but the Getty has collected the ugliest of everything.

'I have. But I don't particularly like it. I would only do something like that to please my partner. And never in a porn movie. Bad for my image.' The couple next to us from Arizona perked up when they heard 'porn movie' but we moved along out of earshot.

'How about anal intercourse?' I asked staring straight ahead at an awful Fragonard of a girl in a swing who seemed to have one leg longer than the other. This was definitely not my day for art.

'To quote Evelyn Waugh, for sheer pleasure give me a trip to the dentist,' he said.

'You are well read. Evelyn Waugh.'

'Well, I was crazy about him at one time. I dreamed of living with people who talk wittily. You talk wittily,' he said.

'Not compared to Edwina. I spoke to her yesterday and told her I had violated her rule and fixed dinner at home and she said, "I hope you didn't go to sleep on a full stomach. I hate going to sleep on a full stomach, no matter whose it is."'

He laughed. 'She's wild that dame. You don't meet anyone like her out here unless they're English.'

'She's a very English French woman. I love her. Almost as much as you. But in a completely different way, of course.'

'How about you?' he said. Dragging me along to a Greuze painting of some girl in a gauze turban. We weren't really concentrating. 'Speaking of anal intercourse.'

'Women don't do that kind of thing,' I said in a shocked voice.

'You know they do. You've seen the movies I'm in. They do it all the time.'

'The answer is no. And those women are professionals. They're actresses playing a role. I'm sure they don't like it.'

He looked at me, amazed. 'You really are a proper lady aren't you? We'll have to try it some time.'

'I can't imagine it. I can hardly handle it from the front.' Thank God the couple from Arizona had flagged at the Limoges china section and had gone back out into the sunshine.

'Is that true? You seem to be handling it fine. You said "deeper" the other night.'

I punched him in the arm. 'That would be so unlike me.'

As we walked back through the paintings Graham said, 'No one has pubic hair.' I said, 'Well, what is it about pubic hair that seems so out of place?' He said, 'Especially in a chicken salad sandwich.' It was my turn to laugh.

Back outside we walked back along the pool towards the garage. Graham said, 'You have to be careful about doing sexual things just because you're bored. I know Eagle Productions wants me to do weirder stuff all the time to sell videos. But I told them I definitely wasn't going to do any S and M stuff. That is not my bag at all. Hurting someone in the name of lovemaking shows a certain disrespect for love, don't you think?'

'Well, I certainly have never understood it. Unless it's some kind of religious thing. Where you go through the suffering to prove how much you love someone. Like St Sebastian and the arrows and all that kind of stuff.'

'Were you brought up as a Catholic?' he said.

'Not at all. Episcopalian.'

'Same thing, I suppose.'

'Hardly. I think Episcopalians think any display of emotion is in very bad taste. You can love God like you love your husband. But don't go overboard.'

'Anyway, I don't do S and M. And I don't suck cock and I don't take it up the ass. Eagle wants to push me into strictly homosexual movies and then I'll suck cock and they'll promote it and sell millions and then I'll take it up the bum and they'll sell trillions. And then what? I'm not getting into all that kind of stuff. I might learn to like it. I'll get into any kind of stuff with you, but not for money.'

I didn't know what to say. We got back into the car and headed back down the coast highway. I said, 'Why is it that sex is so important? Suddenly I feel like Eurydice. As though you're leading me out of the land of the dead, and I'd be lost without you. You're the only one that can do it.' I looked out the window. You couldn't see the ocean, the houses in Malibu along the water are too close together.

'I think sex exploration is like spelunking in underwater caves. It's dangerous and you can get stuck down there. It isn't enough to just explore things. You should only explore things that have some meaning for you. I think just lying down on top of each other is going to have a lot of meaning for us for a long time to come.'

'And the other thing?' I said. He didn't ask what other thing. He said, 'I like living with the pariahs. It isn't a world of the spoken and the unspoken. Nothing is hidden. People buy the videos I make to let themselves loose from that tight little world they live in. To make their sex more fun, to play out their fantasies. And then they go back and pretend they're someone else. In my world we don't pretend we're someone else.'

'But you pretend you're an actor and you go on go-sees and would do a movie or a play if somebody offered you a part,' I said.

'I think that's pretty unlikely, don't you?' he said, running a yellow. 'If I did get a part they'd have to deal with the fact I've done porn movies. I wouldn't be into hiding it. Traci Lords seems to be making it work. At least a little bit. I can't really imagine her becoming another Marilyn Monroe though.'

'So there's this and then what?' I asked.

'There's this and then there's you, I guess. Eurydice can lead Orpheus out for a change. Do you think you can do it?'

'We'll do something,' I said.

'Here's how I see it. Life is brief. We're here. We're gone. We have to live. We have to be ourselves, and not live lies. All those other people out there seem to think they'll live a million years and it doesn't matter how much time they waste. But we're just like the plants and pets. We flourish and we go.'

I said, 'But sometimes we don't go in a hurry. Being old and ugly and poor can last a very long time I think. That's what worries all these people with secret lives.'

'True,' he said. 'Want to go to Hamburger Hamlet?'

'I'd love to. With all that red plush it's pretty Louis Quatorze. It suits the day.'

I went on to plan our lives. 'We'll keep our bodies in great shape. We'll make love as long and as hard and as amazingly as we can for as long as we can and then get fat, knowing it couldn't have been any better.'

Graham said, 'Can you get fat at ninety?'

And then we didn't talk the rest of the way to Hamburger Hamlet. I sat beside Graham and wondered to myself why strong arms mean so much.

We didn't talk about sex again on Sunday but on Monday

morning I apologized. 'I wasn't much fun Saturday. I'm sorry,' I said. He said, 'Don't worry about it. Even when you're not fun you're more fun than most people.'

That surprised me. I said, picking up my purse and heading for the door, 'If I was Joan Greenwood I'd say something like "What a pretty speech," but since I'm not I'll just say that's certainly the nicest thing anyone is going to say to me today.'

'Want to go to a pre-production meeting with me tonight?' he said, very casually. 'At the Eagle offices. You could meet Mimi Fandango. You'll like him. Her. Whatever. And who's Joan Greenwood?'

'Why don't you pick me up at the office? I'll walk over this morning. I can leave at six. Joan Greenwood was an English actress who was my role model. She said things like "What a pretty speech," and "What effrontery!" Very pretty and blonde and invulnerable. I loved her. I wanted to be just like her. Very blonde and invulnerable,' I said.

'Well, you got the blonde part right.'

'I'm nuts about you,' I said.

'I know, I know, I know,' he said in his pleased voice.

That evening I was walking towards reception and I met Mr Steer's secretary in the hall. She's English. Muriel, wouldn't you know. Very cool. She said, 'The handsomest man in the world is in reception asking for you. I asked him if he'd like to follow me and he said, "To the ends of the earth." Is he a writer? That's too witty for an actor.'

I smiled enigmatically. As she left she said, 'I can see you have very good taste in *everything*, Mrs De Rochemont.'

'You caused quite a stir at reception,' I told him.

'I thought it would be good for your image,' he said.

Eagle Studios' office was on Melrose. I think it was decorated largely from the Mexican gift shop downstairs. You don't get those miniature serapes just anywhere. The reception was full of staggeringly handsome young men and some almost pretty women. The women for the most part were not too young. We waited in Mimi Fandango's office. Mimi had a large collection of miniature silver sombreros on her/his desk. I was going to have to decide on that personal pronoun very soon. The door opened. Curious to call yourself Fandango when you are so blond and large, and not at all Spanish. Maybe Mimi wasn't always, but now this big-bodied creature in a turban with blond bangs definitely was. I wondered if the bangs were sewn into the turban. Mimi looked very much like a football dressed as Ginger Rogers.

'Hey, howareya? Greattoseeya.' Ginger Rogers had the voice of Humphrey Bogart. Mimi, underneath all that Max Factor pancake makeup, had the same breezy but gruff manner. 'Who's this, who's this, who's this?' She advanced upon me with a large hand extended, nails nicely done with the new dark maroon Chanel nail enamel with black hair near the knuckles. This was kind of Mimi's thing I guessed. Female but not feminine.

'This is Nina De Rochemont, a friend of mine,' Graham said.

'You're not here looking for work, are you? Of course not. Too bad. Nice name, too. You're not related to the movie De Rochemonts are you?' Behind all that mascara Mimi's eyes were pretty shrewd.

'I'm afraid not. It's not even my real name. It's my married name. My maiden name was Morton. I'll probably go back to it soon.' We left it at that, Mimi was obviously not going to pry. 'So,' she said, sitting down at her desk, which looked like it had been torn out of a bomb shelter somewhere. After a heavy raid. 'So, so, so. Angela and you are going to be the stars of this little effort, Graham. She'll be here any minute. Rico Flick is going to make a guest appearance. And so is Brian Divine.'

'Brian's always hell to work with,' Graham said. 'Maybe if he needs work he'll have a little less attitude. Rico's fine, but

God knows what you're planning to do with that giant thing of his.'

'I'll throw it over my shoulder and burp it like a baby,' said a blonde woman at the door. Tall, very nice black dress, nice shoes, very nice black Kelly bag. Somebody's private secretary or somebody's very low-key wife. 'Come in, Angela, come in,' Mimi cried out. Angela came in, kissed Graham on the cheek, looked at me. 'Nina De Rochemont,' I said, standing up and holding out my hand. 'Hi, Nina,' she said and shook my hand nicely and firmly. 'Angela Lock.' Angela turned to Mimi and said, 'There you are, you fat bitch,' and leaned across the desk to kiss Mimi on both cheeks, leaving lipstick marks. 'You look wonderful, Angela,' said Mimi.

'I won't say you look wonderful, Mimi, but I will say you look wondrous. Great earrings,' Angela said. Mimi's earrings were large lion's heads with rings drooping from their noses. 'Versace,' said Mimi. 'Oh, I can see that,' Angela said. I got the impression that earrings for Mimi were like neckties are for some men. A must. But you just throw them on and go do your job.

I was beginning to wonder if Mimi was wanted in ten states or something like that. She didn't seem to care much about those little womanly touches. She was wearing those awful wooden German sandals and had black knee highs on the legs I could see under the desk. Comfort was obviously high priority. Yet no trousers. I decided she didn't want to be taken for a lesbian.

'We shoot next Wednesday, Thursday and Friday. At Guy's house in Laguna which has always reminded me of a hotel. We do some exteriors Saturday morning in the streets and on the beach. Neither of you have to be there. In addition to Rico and Brian I'm going to have Ann and Esther there for some of the group scenes. And four first-timers. Wanna see them? Let me run these kids past you. Their private parts are all fine. I've already checked that.' Angela said, 'I'm sure you have,' as Mimi stormed to the door, giving Angela a cuff on the shoulder as she went by. Girl friends.

The boys came in, one at a time. Bill and Bob and Kurt and Don and so on. They all seemed very nice and utterly interchangeable. 'Interchangeable Parts' could be the name of one of these little films. 'Did you like any of them better than the others?' Mimi asked afterwards. 'Your call, Mimi,' Graham said. 'But I think I'd lean toward the brunettes. We're getting a lot of blonds in this film. Brian's dark, but Rico's blond, too.'

'You're right, you're right. Of course I like blonds myself but we do need color contrast. That's absolutely true. Skin tone, too. It makes a difference.'

Angela got up to go. She didn't kiss anybody. 'You're not in this, are you?' she said turning towards me. 'No,' Graham said quickly.

'Not this one,' I said, answering for myself.

'Maybe the next time. You never know,' Mimi said.

I did kiss Mimi good-bye as well as shaking his hand. It's not easy for a woman alone in the world, even if she's a man. My feeling was that Mimi was a very okay person. And I was just assuming he was alone.

'Does Mimi have a boyfriend?' I asked Graham in the car. He looked at me surprised. 'Your little mind just never stops, does it? Actually she has a girlfriend. I've met her. A very nice schoolteacher. Was a schoolteacher. She was fired when the school board found out she was living with another woman. They were already living together at the time Mimi started doing drag full time.'

'Mimi sleeps with *women*?' I said.

'Mimi sleeps with a lot of people. Or would like to. I don't know how lucky she gets. I don't think she leans on anybody in casting calls, but certainly a lot of those guys are going to throw it right in his face. Her face. And some of it is pretty hard to turn down.'

'Only in Hollywood. Only in Hollywood,' I groaned. 'Now I'm beginning to sound like Mimi. It's very catchy, that style. What was or is her real name?'

'I think it's Max. Started as a light man. Someone made him up in the dressing room one day and the rest is history. This is only hearsay. It was long before my time out here,' Graham said. 'Let's go to my place, shall we?'

'Let's, and we'll have some light instead of crawling around in my cave where the sunlight never falls,' I said.

'I like crawling around in your cave, but I like to go home once in awhile to get clean underwear.'

I loved where Graham lived. A little rabbit warren of apartments sunken into foliage up above Sunset. Very 1930s with the carved Southwestern railings and tiles around a tiny pool and blue painted wooden ceilings in the verandas leading to the apartments. So temporary, so charming. Maybe that was why it was so much fun to live in Southern California. Nothing was for keeps. If it rained hard enough the adobe washed away and you could start all over again when the sun shone again. The perfect place for an industry based only on images and make-believe. For people like me, so afraid of making a mistake, a world where nothing was for keeps was a big relief.

Graham's apartment was a big relief, too. Everything white with beige carpet everywhere. No pictures, no mirrors, some cushions and a low table in the living room. A mattress with white sheets and duvet in the bedroom. And square French pillows. Only one photograph on the walls. By someone named John Dugdale. It was a smallish, dark photograph in a dark brown frame. Looking as though it had been taken long ago. You could see a countryside in the rain, a narrow frame house to one side with trees massed behind. And all alone in an open space beside the house was a small figure under a large black umbrella.

So evocative. Of those days in May when the leaves are

bursting from the trees and the sky is lavender gray, the wind blows the long grass and the air smell is wet. When you're very young those were the days when you knew something was going to happen. When I asked Graham who he thought that was under the umbrella he said, 'That's me, waiting for something to happen.'

We ordered a pizza. Does that count as eating in? I put on his white terry-cloth bathrobe and we sat on the floor in the living room to eat. At least I wasn't graceless in the kitchen.

'So how do you feel about my doing this film?' Graham asked.

I said, 'First of all, what was that meeting all about? There was no discussion of the scenario, there was no script, you didn't discuss money, you didn't even get an address.'

'It was to look at us,' he said, lifting a large triangle of cheese, tomato, anchovy and sausage towards his mouth. 'To make sure the cast wasn't fat, or doing so many drugs we looked like hell. Or didn't seem to be about to go over the edge. We looked fine. The kids looked fine. Mimi had seen the others, who really don't need to know what's going on. His cast is willing, ready and able.'

'But what about lines?' I wanted to know.

'What does it take to learn "Nice place you've got here"? We make most of it up anyway. It's like commedia dell'arte. You know what the scene is about and you go in and improvise. But you're not answering my question.'

'If I had a choice I'd just as soon you didn't make the film. I'd just as soon you didn't sleep with other people for a living. But I'm not complaining. Those are just the facts. It's the human instinct. First, I want someone everyone wants. Then I want him all to myself. It's a failing.'

He pulled me over to him. 'I just can't keep my mitts off you. Why is that?' he said.

'I dance to your music, kiddo,' I told him. 'Kiddo' is an expression I've picked up from Edwina which she probably picked up from some sailor while she was fleeing the Nazis. 'I dance to your music and that's the way it is and I'm not going to say I'm not going to think about the rest of it. Of course I am. But I'm not going to discuss it with you.'

He pulled the bathrobe open and pressed me against his body. He was only wearing boxer shorts. He pulled them off with one hand. 'I have my clothes off so much I feel like I'm wearing clothes when I'm not.'

'Maybe it's an occupational hazard. You're going to have to be careful.'

'I mean with you.'

'Are you naked with me all that much?'

'I mean when I am I'm not at all aware of it, and I don't remember it being like that with anyone else.'

'With Angela, for example,' I said.

'Please, if you're going to be jealous of someone, don't make it Angela. Whenever I've been naked with Angela I've been very aware of it with all the lights, cameras and crew. Not to mention the sandwich-makers and God knows who all. She always draws the maximum on set. She's just a pal. It's like screwing a guy. Great body, proud of it and knows how to use it.'

'Well, I'm not at the point that I don't notice it when I'm naked. And as a fashion person I have to believe that dressing it up makes it more interesting.' I rolled away from him and pulled my bathrobe around me. Before I could get up he was on me. We wrestled like kids. I grabbed his crotch. 'No fair,' he grumbled in my ear and grabbed both my wrists and held me down with the weight of his body. And then I didn't mind being naked one bit.

chapter 19

....

at the gym

I was leaving the office on my way to the gym when Muriel, Mr Steer's secretary stopped me. At the end of our Cleanola meeting in the afternoon Mr Duress had asked me to dinner. This came out of the blue, sort of. I realized Mr Duress was favoring the agency's work because he was favoring me. I was just playing my Edwina card: the fascinating creative person. It certainly had never occurred to me that Carlton Carlson at Nixtrix hankered after Edwina. Perhaps he did. Perhaps Edwina slept with him. I had to find out if I was to handle this correctly.

Mr Duress had stopped me in the door as we were leaving and said, 'I wonder if we could have dinner some evening to discuss directions for your Clean Machine concept.' Thank God I kicked in immediately, 'I'd love to Mr Duress. Could I bring my boyfriend along? He's so handsome I'm afraid to leave him alone even for one evening.'

The Duress face fell. Did he think a swell-looking dame like myself didn't have a boyfriend? Had he heard I was in the process of getting a divorce? Who knows. 'You'll like him,' I went on. 'He knows I love my job and we talk about work all the time. He'd love to meet you, he's heard all about how great you are.' Was I laying it on a bit too thick? Usually that's impossible. 'Let me think about it,' he said and walked quickly

off towards his office. Oh-oh. Well, if I blew it I blew it and
I certainly was not going to go out with Mr Duress. Kismet.
It is written in the stars.

Muriel said, 'Mr Duress just called and wondered if Wednesday night next week would be all right with you. For
dinner. Alone.' Her face was perfectly clear. Signaling
nothing. Duress had obviously called Steer's office to make
the request official, and Steer just passed it on to see if the
fatted lamb was willing to be offered up to keep the account
and keep her job. Tacky. Those nice bland men so often are.
'Of course, darling,' I said with my biggest Hollywood
smile. 'Of course. Anything for Mr Duress and Cleanola,' this
in a voice loud enough for Mr Steer to hear it in his office.
But I was boiling when I hit the gym.

As soon as I got to the stationary bicycles I saw Petitfour
St Albans, the miniature monster of hairdressing. So cute. I
hadn't seen him since we were all in the Caribbean together:
I blew a kiss towards his sweaty face as I jumped on the bike
next to his. 'What are you doing here, Pete?' I wanted to
know.

'Pert Plus,' he said. 'They love me. The same commercial,
over and over again. It's so easy. Long, flowing, beautiful hair.
Even though nobody is wearing long, flowing hair.'

'Who's the girl?' I asked, pedaling madly away.

In his little black lycra shorts and pink and black striped
top he was pedaling away equally furiously, as though we were
on some kind of fashion marathon. All we needed was Gloria
Vanderbilt on the next bike.

'Anna Apples. Remember her?' I did. We had used Anna
Apples for a mascara shoot before she had made off with that
real estate tycoon. 'She's still working with all those bucks
she landed?' I said. 'Oh, you know how those girls are. They
want to show the world they're just hard-working little things
that really didn't hitch up with anyone just for the money.

And that hubby of hers. He needs a hairdresser just for those eyebrows.'

'And you? You're here because of that guy, aren't you?' he asked me. I admitted I was and then added, 'I have a terrific job, too, of course. It was kind of a career decision on a lot of levels.'

'I have to hand it to you, Nina. You've got guts. But then, who wouldn't have run off with that guy? He is gorgeous.'

We trailed each other through the gym, the arm machines, the leg machines, the ass machines. We had the same drill since he's not planning to make himself look like Arnold Schwarzenegger. He told me he was staying with his friend Anita, whose troubles outdid anyone else's.

Anita had just found out that the young Russian male au pair she had recently hired at her boyfriend's suggestion was actually the boyfriend of *her* boyfriend, Anatole.

'Did she drop him and get rid of the au pair?' I asked from the chair where you press two big springs together for your inner thighs. Pete was on the next one where you press two springs apart for your outer thighs. 'No, she didn't really want to break up with Anatole. He's Russian, too, and a painter and she loves the arts so she's kept the au pair. When I came in last night her son was in the upstairs hall shouting, "Will someone get this faggot out of my room?" '

'How old's the son?' I said. 'Thirteen, I'd say,' he said, moving on to the leg curl machine where you lie on your stomach and roll the weights up towards your thighs with your ankles. Supposedly great for the buttocks. I thought of Freddy. At least I wasn't putting him through anything like Anita's son was undergoing.

'And this is a very good friend of yours, Pete?' I said, climbing back on the machine. 'Yes, she's fun. She's rich. Her father was in parking lots I think.' I wanted to be like Petitfour. Breezy and accepting and just whirling through life, having fun. Instead I had to go home and call Edwina and ask her what the hell to do about Mr Duress.

'How long are you here for?' I asked our Mr Pete on our way out together. 'I'm shooting tomorrow for two days, if we don't run into overtime. And I might stay the rest of the week if I'm not booked back in New York.' He gave me Anita's phone number in Beverly Hills and I gave him my new card. 'Tiffany's,' he said, holding it up to the light. 'Nina De Rochemont. So simple. So chic. No one would ever guess you were such a little sexpot, would they?'

'Am I, Pete? I don't feel like such a sexpot. I feel like I might be a little crazy.'

'That's what it feels like to be a sexpot, Nina, my dear. Call me.' And he ran off towards the parking lot. A very masculine little guy, whatever you might want to say about faggots.

I walked home, slung my gym bag into the corner and called Edwina at home without even taking off my coat. It was ten o'clock in New York and I had never called Edwina at home before, but I thought this situation deserved some immediate action.

She was home. I imagined her in some white linen monk's robe. Hair pulled back. No makeup. Looking like some French sixteenth-century philosopher. Descartes, maybe. 'What are you wearing?' I said. 'It's Nina.'

'Actually an old tartan bathrobe an ex-lover left here. That needs to be washed desperately. What's cooking?'

'I think Claude Duress is coming on to me.'

'I rather suspected he would. Not to be morale-lowering, my dear, but he's desperate. Wife leaving him. Financial problems. No girlfriend. Doesn't look good for a monomaniac, does it? You're perfect. Ad lady with a bit of a reputation,' she said.

'So what's my plan?'

'I'll come to Los Angeles next week. You're having too much fun out there without me and I have a thousand things

I could do out there. See Ninthe Eliot. Do some castings. The weather is shitty here anyway. Can I stay with you? And I'll call that old fart Claude Duress and tell him I'm coming and I'm going to barge in on his intimate dinner because I long to see him. I've got a million things on him. And I actually like him. There is something sexy about him, you have to admit, Nina.'

'I know,' I told her. 'That's the terrible part.'

'And there's something sexy about you, too. And sexier all the time I'm sure, with that fabulous Graham hanging about,' she said.

At that point the fabulous Graham came barging in.

'I keep calling him Chase,' I told her.

He made signs asking who I was talking to. 'I'm talking to Edwina,' I said. 'I'm getting an Edwina fix at the end of my strenuous day.'

Edwina said into my ear, 'You know when they asked Tallulah Bankhead why she wanted to go to Hollywood she said, "I'm going to Hollywood to fuck that divine Gary Cooper," and she did I understand. I think that's what people go to Hollywood for, so don't blame yourself for weakening. It could happen to any of us.'

I said, 'Adieu, Edwina. Adieu, adieu.'

She said, 'I think I'll fly in Wednesday and be there in the afternoon, so we can plan our attack on that poor Duress fellow.'

I said, 'Try to set it up so that Chase . . . Graham can come too. He's working in Laguna Beach this week, but he's okay next week.'

'Tell him he *must* be there,' she said and hung up.

I fell on top of my lover, who was lying sprawled out on a couch. 'Your day?' I said, feeling much cheerier now that I'd talked to Edwina.

'Exactly. My day. I had a long talk with Mimi and she has a question for you,' he said.

'Shoot,' I said, getting more comfortable on top of him.

'You smell good,' he said. 'Did you just come from the gym? The only woman in the world who smells better after the gym.'

'It's all that St Laurent *Paris* welling up from deep in my pores. What does Mimi want? It had better not be my underwear.'

'Even worse. She wants your brains. She asked if you would do the creative direction on the shoot. She knows you come from Nixtrix and you're working on Cleanola. She thinks you can class up her act. She wants Angela to look fabulous so she's willing to hire a great hair and makeup guy. And wants your advice on clothes and the sets and so on.'

'I'm hardly an expert on how to look slutty,' I said.

'Oh, come on. You and Pete St Albans made that Russian dog look fantastic in the Jamaica Wind commercial,' Graham said.

'He's here working on Pert Plus. You know? Long flowing hair. I wonder. He'd probably love it just for the guys at no extra charge. Enlarge his circle of acquaintances. I'll call him and ask him. Of course I'll give Mimi my advice. Free, of course,' I said, getting up off my adorable lug.

I dug the number out of my bag and called Petitfour at his friend Anita's. A teenage boy answered. I felt a pang. I asked for Petitfour St Albans and he shouted 'Pete' loudly and laid the phone down.

I explained to Petitfour what was going on. He asked if I would be on the set and I told him I wouldn't. He was free as a bird to do as he pleased with the ladies. And the gentlemen. He then asked me if Graham was going to be there. I said, 'He's the star.' 'I suspected as much,' he said. 'Well I'm certainly not going to miss the chance to see what stole you away from New York and your not so happy home in the living flesh. But I can only work Thursday and Friday. They'll have to do the all-boy stuff the first day.'

'There's a lot of all-boy stuff as I understand it,' I said.

'Oh, goody. Tell this director I know they have tight budgets and I'll work half-fee if I can stay on the set for the boy-boy stuff.'

'I'm sure that's no problem,' I assured him.

Graham then called Mimi and I could hear her squealing in bass pleasure from my end of the room.

'She says this is going to be her most elegant film yet,' he said after he hung up.

'Maybe she can try her version of *Philadelphia Story* next. There's a threesome in there somewhere,' I said.

'And a foursome as I recall,' Graham said. 'Can you imagine? Cary Grant, Hepburn, Stewart and somebody else. The reporter. Ruth Hussey?'

'Cary Grant would have loved it. The rest of them would have been horrified. Great clothes, though.' So we tore ours off and took a shower together.

chapter 20

....

shooting in laguna

Graham asked me if I would drive down to Laguna with him on Tuesday evening. Petitfour St Albans would be there and Mimi wanted a last pre-production to discuss clothes (what there would be of them) and hair and makeup. I was the 'look' consultant.

Mimi had picked a great location. It was really seedy. The whole house was done up in a kind of nautical theme. A sign had been made up that read The Palace Hotel (for Sailors Only) and was leaning against the wall in the front hall. To be put up outside when they did the exteriors.

Mimi had called in the cast the night before just for me, because I couldn't be there in the morning. Angela was there looking a little sullen, probably resenting having to spend the extra night in Laguna. There were two other young women who weren't all that bad. Petitfour was going to be able to make them look pretty good. And our young stud muffins who didn't look alike but did in some way. They were all relatively short and had the same kinds of gym-enhanced bodies.

Petitfour was in his element and loving it. And he soon had everyone else worked up by the professionalism of it all. This was, after all, the makeup and hair guy who did Cindy Crawford. And had been in Linda Evangelista's last commercial.

'I saw a picture of him at a party with Johnny Depp and Kate Moss in *Vogue*,' one of the actresses was telling one of the young guys. This was movie-making!

We sat in the little 'salon'. There was an enormous sword-fish on the wall and two oval mirrors with frames made of rope. Large rope. Should I say cable? The coffee table was one of those round cable spools that you see washed up on the beach. I know I'm going to see this in the film, I thought. The room was all blue and white with a few glass fishing floats on the mantel. I probably don't need to add that the chandelier was a circular ship's helm.

Mimi was in one corner unpacking a large canvas carryall full of sailor uniforms. She turned to me. She was wearing a blue and white striped matelot sweater and a blue-jean skirt. A large matelot sweater and a large skirt and they were tight. Her hair was tucked up into a captain's hat with gold braid on the visor. She saw me eyeing it. 'I bought it just for this shoot,' she said, cocking it over one eye even more saucily. The big gold Versace earrings were what made it work.

'The earrings pull it all together,' I told her.

'That's what I was thinking,' chipped in Angela. And to me she added in a lower tone of voice, 'That and the Five O'clock Shadow.'

'Now my idea is that the three girls . . . sorry, women . . . will be in red, white and blue. Let's see what you brought for clothes,' Mimi said.

'I can do white,' Angela said. 'I have a nice white Azzedine Alaia. Tight. Very tight.' She pulled it out of a garment bag. It looked like nothing off. I could imagine what it looked like on. I wanted to strangle her with it. The other women didn't have red or blue clothes.

Petitfour said, 'Pants. White pants and T-shirts. And little strappy shoes.' I agreed and said, 'If you can wait to shoot the exteriors with clothes I'll come back down Saturday morning and bring the T-shirts. I know exactly where they are. I saw them at Neiman-Marcus.'

'I'll pay you back,' Mimi said.

'You're darn right you will,' I said.

'Can I cut your hair a little?' Petitfour asked Angela and they were off on how he was going to make her look wonderful.

Then it was time to go back to West Hollywood. I was taking Grahams's car and would come back and get him on Saturday. When he was all fucked out.

Petitfour came out on the porch to say good-bye.

'This is going to be fun,' he said.

'Not too much eye shadow,' I said. 'The idea is to *not* look whorey.'

'Gotcha,' he said. 'The Nina De Rochemont look. A lady who's kind of gone all to hell with herself.'

'That about sums it up,' I said, not too sure that I cared a lot for the definition.

'Did Mimi ask you if you wanted to be the fluffer?' Graham asked Petitfour.

'Fluffer?'

'That's the person who stays behind the camera and fluffs the boys up when they begin to droop. And I don't mean with your hairbrush.'

'Do I get to fluff you up?' he asked Graham.

'I never need fluffing,' Graham said.

'I suppose I could, but it'll cost extra,' Petitfour said.

'Mimi's not going to pay you to do it. There are tons of guys around town that want to pay her for the job.'

'What a business,' I said. 'I'm getting out of here.'

Inside I could hear Mimi saying loudly, 'And no fucking around tonight, do you hear me? Save all that for the camera. You can fuck around all you want when the shooting's over.'

'You don't really like this, do you?' Graham said as he opened the car door for me.

'I don't like it at all. But I'm just not going to think about it. This is what you do. That's it.' I turned to him faking a great big smile. 'I love you and that's the story.' He held me very close. 'My little pal,' he said.

In the car I let myself feel very shitty and then pulled myself together again. What alternatives do I have? I could walk out on him. I could make a big scene and walk out on him. I could make a big scene and he could walk out on me. Maybe someday I'd wake up and say to myself 'What am I doing?' and not have any feelings for Graham at all. But I had to remember that he was not cheating on me. And maybe our intimacy was going to make him feel differently about what he was doing in these films. Really. Hello! What a fool you are, Nina. And I rolled down the window and let the night air blow through my hair and pretended I was my mother when she was a teenager. Rolling through the night air, looking forward to love.

So Wednesday I kept busy and didn't think very much about what they were doing down in Laguna. We were doing extensions on The Clean Machine concept and thinking of headlines like:

YOU AREN'T CLEAN WITHOUT THE MACHINE

How about 'Do you know what it means to clean New Orleans?' Sometimes I hate myself.

Graham called me in the evening. 'How did it go?' I asked him and then laughed and laughed. 'No, don't tell me. About the penetrations.'

'I know, it's stupid, isn't it. If it was just Angela and me we'd get on with it and get it done. But the little young guys are kind of erratic. Either they come right away or they can't come at all. We're running behind schedule a little bit. Mimi keeps a can of Evian spray mist on the set. When someone gets close to coming she hits his winkie with that and it usually calms him right down. She says she learned that trick quite by chance sleeping with a French millionaire in a hotel in Paris. Got him over his little failing in a jiffy. Do you know what premature ejaculation is in French?'

I admitted I didn't. He said, 'Ooh la la so soon.' And laughed.

'How's Pete doing?' I asked.

'Angela looks fantastic. It's another woman altogether. She's really keeping the whole thing moving. And I think Petitfour has found love with one of those sailor kids. He's not doing any fluffing. He told Mimi he didn't want her to think he was sex-crazed. We're using *Penthouse* and *Hustler* to keep the so-called heterosexuals in action.'

'We're going to have to do something about this situation. I don't know whether I hate you or I'm jealous of you but either way you've got to stop doing this or I have to start doing it,' I said.

'Then all your friends *would* say I'd ruined you. I think you can get a grasp on this without doing it.'

'I don't want to pretend in my mind that it doesn't exist. That it isn't happening. That way lies insanity,' I said.

'I think you should come down early Saturday morning. We're running behind and we'll have plenty of sex shots yet to do. And you can visit the set and see how it all works. I can handle that if you can.'

We said goodnight and I felt a pang. There was something really good about Graham.

So another day was spent at my desk. Mr Steer had asked my group to work on some fragrance ideas for one of his other big clients, Federico. 'Power,' I said to him. 'It's all about power. Get out of here and let my brain turn. I've got thousands of ideas.' I waved a piece of typing paper over my head and turned to hit those keys.

I was definitely getting more flamboyant in these California climes. Maybe I wouldn't let myself go around Edwina for fear of being too much like her. But 'Let 'er Rip' was my new policy.

And I did some great stuff for Federico. Very Hollywood. Very Za-Za Gabor revisited. This great blonde spraying clouds of Federico around her as she strides down Rodeo Drive. Finally saying, 'I wish I had a whole swimming pool of Federico!' Finding herself beside a pool she hurls the bottle in the air and does so. Somehow I imagined Angela Lock doing this part. Would I have the nerve to cast her considering my history? I think I would.

That evening Graham and I didn't have a lot to say to each other when he called. He did say that he was looking forward to coming home with me on Saturday.

'You won't be all out of the mood?' I said.

'I'll be very much in the mood for some love,' he said. Tears suddenly jolted out of my eyes. What was going on here? In the midst of all this fucking we were falling even more in love with each other.

When I pulled up in front of the house in Laguna a couple of the crew were putting The Palace Hotel (for Sailors Only) sign up over the entrance. Mimi came running out to meet me. She was wearing a kind of short kimono in black over black stretch biker's shorts and her German health sandals. The turban was black. So was the nail enamel. Where did she find time to do all this stuff to herself in the midst of the shooting?

'Honey, am I glad to see you. These so-called heterosexuals need the sight of a good-looking woman to perk them up. They're so bored with the three pussies we've got here, one look and they get a soft-on. Even with your clothes on they'll be glad to see you. I don't shock you, do I?' She shot me a sideways glance out of those crafty little eyes. Only when you looked into her eyes did you see quite clearly that Mimi was not a girl. Some kind of Napoleon was in there looking out. Women just don't have that look.

'Why should I mind? I love being flattered. I haven't had this kind of attention for years.' We bourgeois. The more out of our depth we get the more we act as though everything is perfectly normal. I was never going to be able to get on Mimi's wavelength so I decided I might as well do the garden party number.

'You've got the T-shirts?' Mimi said, looking at the Neiman-Marcus shopping bag I was carrying. 'Yes, and I'll just keep them after the shoot so you don't have to pay me anything. They're in my size and actually I could use them,' I told her. 'Yeah, and every time you wear one you can think of us and the movie we made together.' She took the bag out of my hand and sailed into the house. I walked in behind her. Everyone was in the reception room. Naked. Except for Petit-four, the crew and a ton of lights. 'We've been having a hell of a time with the lights,' Mimi shouted at me from across the room. 'This place must have been wired before World War I. I guess we're lucky we haven't burned the fucking place down. Pardon me. I forget there are ladies present.'

'Places, please.' They were doing the big *partouze* scene with the entire cast. Graham and Angela and a large, dark man were standing on the cable spool table, Angela sandwiched between them. The two other women were lying head to head on the couch, a man standing between their legs at each end. Another large blond man was standing between the camera and the table with two young men kneeling on each side of him. One prepared to attack his almost wildly out of proportion front, the other, the crevice of his buttocks.

'Does everybody feel comfortable?' Mimi shouted from behind the camera. 'This is the master so you must be inserted and you must be erect for this, all of you guys. I'm going to cover all of you separately with handheld later, and you can relax then.' The men all had erections and the man that was getting the blowjob was wearing a condom, as was Graham. The others weren't. Petitfour shouted, 'Just a minute for hair,' and ran on to the set, combing out the two girls on the couch. He looked up at Angela who had a new kind of helmet cut and did look spectacular. She had great breasts. If they'd had some assistance here and there, they certainly didn't look like it.

'Action,' Mimi shouted and everyone started inserting and moving. Graham hadn't looked at me when I came in. He probably couldn't see me very well with the lights glaring, and what are you supposed to do when you see someone you know during a porn shoot? Wave and smile over your sex partner's shoulder? Anyway they fucked with what looked like real abandon to me. I cowered back in a corner by the door. Petitfour was on the other side of the camera ignoring me. Very professionally his eyes kept shifting from one head of hair to another. He wasn't watching crotches. He probably had seen enough of everyone's crotch in the last two days.

Mimi kept shouting, 'Zoom on the group on the table.' 'Zoom on the cock-sucking.' 'Zoom and pan on the couch. Keep it lively. More faces, girls. Act like you're liking it. I could use some little shrieks and groans.'

Finally she yelled, 'Cut.' The lights were turned off. Petitfour went on the set immediately to check for makeup repairs. 'Okay, I'm going to groups now. I'll do Angela, Graham and Brian next.' The lighting men were shifting the lights around them. Graham looked straight into my face over Angela's shoulder. And Brian's shoulder, too. He was planted firmly against her pelvis and Brian was pushed up against her buttocks. Angela saw me and gave me a 'Whaddya gonna do?' kind of look.

There are certain things that happen to you, and once they do you can never go back; you are never the same again. You can never pretend they didn't happen to you. There was my wonderful lover with his body pressed into someone else's

body, pushing slowly in and out of her, as the other man did
the same thing. Their arms were all around each other. They
were sweating in the heat of the lights. The camera was
running. What can I tell you? Your brain just goes somewhere
else. You are somewhere you never imagined being doing
something you never imagined doing and it's happening.
That's all. It's happening and your whole frame of reference
has exploded. Now you're on another planet. It looks like the
same planet, but it is definitely another world. And I had
become another person.

Mimi called 'Cut.' And then said, 'How close are you guys
to coming? Want a break? Okay, we'll do Rico and his boys.
Over here. Ready Rico. You came, didn't you Gary?' she said
to one of the studs sitting on the couch. He hung his head.
'That's okay, we'll do you last.' I took a breather.

As I was sitting on the porch a young woman came up the
steps carrying a cooler and a picnic basket. 'Hi, I'm Debbie,'
she said. 'Are you in the movie?' I told her I wasn't, I was
Graham's girlfriend. Might as well go for it. 'My husband's
Gary,' she said. He was the one who had come ahead of
schedule. 'I told Mimi I'd bring some lunch today. I always
do that. Always. This is only Gary's third movie, but I like
doing it. We're from Dallas and since I'm here I might as well
do something, right?' She sat down beside me in the other
rocking chair.

Well, here's a new breed of person, I thought. I guess I've
got something to learn from little Debbie. 'You don't do this
kind of . . . work yourself?' I asked her. 'Oh, no, I couldn't.
My body really isn't good enough, and I don't think I'd like
it. I'm too shy. But Gary seems to have a knack for it. He
started just doing heterosexual stuff, but everybody does that.
So now he's doing some of the homoerotic things, too. He's
doing anal penetration in one of the scenes. It doesn't bother
him and the money's much better. You don't have to keep it

up so much that way. Poor men. Women really have it a lot easier, don't they?'

I agreed with her. Chatty Debbie got into a confidential mode. 'We rehearsed before we came out here. We went into one of those sex aid shops and got a strap-on dildo and I did it to him. It was kind of fun.' I guess I looked surprised because she added, 'You should try it. It gives you some idea what it's like to be a man. Gary says he likes the way it looks on me. I have kind of a boyish figure. I don't have much in the line of boobs. And I'm certainly not going to have those implants. I don't like the idea of having that artificial stuff in my body.' Debbie certainly had her principles. I said nothing, just rocked and tried to look interested.

She said, 'You're worried about AIDS aren't you? I am, too. But you know they're really careful. They always use condoms and nobody ever comes inside anybody. They have to save it for the money shots. You know, when they come for the camera.' This girl was a mine of information. 'I tell people in Dallas we're working in industrial films and we are in a way, aren't we?' She giggled.

'What's for lunch?' I asked her, peeking into the basket. 'I didn't make everything. Just some sandwiches. But there's a little kitchen at our motel so I made cookies. Chocolate chip. Want one?'

Mimi opened the door. 'We got that one,' she said over her shoulder. 'Oh, hi Debbie. You're a lifesaver. We're starving.' Debbie and I went back inside. The men had pulled on shorts and the women had on bathrobes. Petitfour was setting hair for the afternoon shoot. What a little professional. We all sat around and ate Debbie's sandwiches. The cookies were a big hit. 'If we were shooting in Dallas I would have made some pie,' Debbie said. 'I make great apple pie.'

'If we had you around we'd all be fat by the end of the shoot,' Angela told her. 'Take these cookies away from me.

They're too good, Debbie. But I guess I must have lost some weight this morning.'

'Okay, girls. Eat everything you're going to eat, because I'm going to do lipstick,' Petitfour said.

In the afternoon we did the exterior shots; Angela and the other women pulling up in front of the hotel in Graham's convertible. I had to admit they really looked cute. The T-shirts looked fine with a little clothes-pinning in the back. Angela getting out of the car in her Azzedine Alaia was pretty stunning. She has great legs. Fred the cameraman did a low shot and had the reflectors in exactly the right place to throw the light into her face. I suggested they put a white card on the dashboard to push light up into her face for the shot at the steering wheel. They aren't really beauty people so they didn't know about that trick. 'Umm, she really looks good,' Fred muttered.

'I learned that trick from Renée Russo,' I told him.

'She's still using it,' Fred said. 'She looked great in *Get Shorty*.'

Then we did the shot of the four sailors coming down the street. They looked cute, too. Short but cute. And since they were all about the same size I'm sure it didn't look too much like the Seven Dwarfs going to meet Snow White.

The shots of Graham greeting them at the door were basically the same set-up. Fred and Mimi got the lights set and first Graham opened the door for the three women. Angela and he improvised some pretty good dialogue, with Angela explaining they just couldn't find a hotel and could they please make an exception and take them in for the night? Graham did a kind of country bumpkin thing, scratching his head and reluctantly letting them in.

'We've only got one double bed left,' he said. Angela quickly replied that one bed would do just fine. The fact that nobody had any luggage didn't seem to bother anyone and I didn't bring it up. This wasn't an Ingmar Bergman movie after all.

They did the same shot with the sailors and Graham used the same line about only having one double bed. It was actually rather well done since with good editing the impression would be that it was the same double bed he just gave to the three women. I'm sure he improvised this since I didn't see any evidence of a writer on the set.

Then I had an idea. Mimi was re-setting the lights for a final shot in the little living room lobby. 'You've still got Brian and Rico here,' I said to Mimi. The two guest artists. 'Why don't you have Brian be the handyman and walk up the stairs carrying luggage for the girls. And Rico can lean out of that door at the end of the hall in a white apron and a big spoon in his hand and be the cook. Then you've kind of established what they're doing here. Instead of their just magically appearing from out of nowhere.'

Mimi cocked her head at me. 'You're not bad, are you?' she said. 'Fred, can we do that?' She explained what she wanted and Fred said he could do it handheld with one light on it. And Mimi had the bright idea of having the sailors shout 'What's for dinner?' at Rico when he appeared and had him call back, 'Me!' Which was kind of funny in fact.

'Now just everybody mill around here in the living room for the last shot,' Mimi called out. 'Sit down, stand up, take each other's chairs.'

'The girls' hair is a mess,' Petitfour said. 'I should reset it.'

'Forget it. Just move around fast, ladies,' Mimi shouted. 'Don't let us see what your hair really looks like. This isn't L'Oreal,' she added for Petitfour who looked kind of pissed-off.

And they were done. 'We really need one more undershot of anal penetration,' Fred told Mimi. 'We really never got a good one.'

'Okay, we'll use Graham and Gary. Gary's good at it.' The rest of the cast was milling about, saying good-bye. They all wanted to head out for Los Angeles ahead of the traffic.

Gary got naked and bent over the cable spool coffee table. Debbie sat on the couch like she was waiting for a doctor's appointment. Fred lay on the floor holding the camera, pointing out where he wanted the light beside him. 'Reflector?' his assistant asked. 'Yeah, over here. On the left,' Fred told him.

'This is a scene I definitely do not have to watch,' Angela said. 'I must have had a yard of cock in me in the last three days. I need a break. Good-bye,' she said, taking me by both arms and looking me straight in the face. 'I think you've got something, Angela,' I said.

She said, 'Could we have lunch one of these days?' and kissed me on both cheeks. I noticed she didn't say 'Do lunch.' I liked Angela. I said, 'Sure, I'd love to. We can talk about Graham.' He turned and looked at us from over by the camera where he was taking off his jeans. He wasn't wearing any underwear. I guess they'd run out of Calvin Klein undies. He didn't look pleased.

Angela and the other women and the guest artists and the other sailors all left, after shaking hands all around. It was pretty funny, Gary bent over the table, rear end in the air, reaching up to shake hands. Graham naked except for sweat socks bidding everyone adieu in a very gentlemanly way.

'I don't really have enough space in here,' Fred said. 'Somebody's got to sit on the table and brace Gary's shoulders so he can get far enough away from the lights.' One of the assistants held Gary's shoulders. Gary looked pretty bored. Graham fiddled himself erect and put on a condom, ripping the package open neatly with his teeth. An assistant came up with a tube of lubricant and a towel and fingered the lubricant up Gary's rectum. 'How does that feel?' he said. Gary grumbled, 'Get outa here.' Debbie laughed. The assistant handed the lubricant to Graham who put it on his condomed member. It *is* big.

And then he inserted it. From where I was standing I could

only see his back. Those broad shoulders tapering down to his narrow waist and hard buttocks. They squeezed and released, squeezed and released. With the camera whirring and Fred gesturing for the reflector to come closer and Mimi crouching down to make sure the camera angle was good, it was like doing a package shot for the end of a commercial. Almost everyone gone, no glamour, just getting the job done. I noticed again that Graham was tanned all over and wondered when he did it?

'Graham, can you do a money shot on Gary's back?' Mimi asked. 'Sure, why not?' he said. 'That's my guy,' she said. He pulled out and pulled off the condom. The crew automatically moved lights and Fred stood up with the camera. Graham began pulling at himself and I decided to go back out to one of those rocking chairs.

They were done very soon. I heard them packing up and Graham came out with Debbie and Gary. My honey leaned over and kissed me in my rocking chair and I hugged him very hard. I got the feeling Debbie and Gary didn't think I was very professional. I got up and went in and shook hands all around. Mimi had the red and blue T-shirts neatly folded and back in their Neiman-Marcus bag, which she handed me. I kissed her good-bye on both cheeks. 'You were swell,' she said. Somehow I think she knew this had been pretty traumatic for me and felt the best way to handle it was to breeze right through it. I guess drag queens have to breeze through a lot of stuff. Petitfour was all packed up and looked all bright-eyed and bushy-tailed. 'That was fun, wasn't it?' he said. 'Sure beats a L'Oreal shooting, doesn't it?' I said to him. He laughed and ran off towards his car. He seems to be always laughing and running off towards his car.

Heading back to West Hollywood I talked a lot. Too much. I didn't want portentous silence between us.

'I could have kept you out of there but I wanted you to see what it was like,' Graham said.

'I figured that,' I said.

'There's no point in pretending I'm going off to the office.'

'I know, I know. It's okay. Really it is. I learned a lot. About a lot of things.'

'Like what?'

'Oh, like penetration isn't all that important except when it's with the person you love. Do you think having intercourse casually like that makes having intercourse with someone you love less important somehow?'

'It's like sticking your finger in your ear,' Graham said. 'It's just my flesh. It's not me. It sees some other flesh and an orifice and it responds. But you, Nina, you are not just an orifice.'

'Do you think you can love what a person is so much that you are sexually aroused by them, no matter what their body looks like?' I asked him.

'In your case, yes. I always knew you were lovely, but from the first I always had a sense of you. The person Nina. Not just a good-looking blonde from New York.'

'Do you think we've been waiting for each other all our lives? It's like that awful Gore Vidal book, looking for the other half of your persona. It's such a cliché. It's dreadful. I'm almost ashamed of loving you so much when it's so much like movies and books.'

'Yeah, wasn't that book something? He thinks he's very special and different just because he never took it up the ass. And that poor guy who spent his life with him and never got fucked. Some lifestyle.'

'Not to digress,' I said.

'Not to digress. It isn't dreadful that you love me so much. It's an honor for me that someone like you could. It makes me nervous. I keep thinking I'm going to wake up some morning and you're going to be gone back to your life in New York and your obsession with my body will be over because that's really why you love me. Or started loving me. You saw

me in a video, Nina. You saw me fucking people and
wanted me to fuck you. Isn't that true? How should I feel
about *that*?'

Now I really did feel dreadful. 'It's true. It was what you
looked like that obsessed me. And it still does. Except what
you look like is now you. In all your fun and niceness and
kindness and sweetness to me. I don't know if I would love
you in another body but I think I would if I could have gotten
to know you as well as I do now.'

'It's funny isn't it? Men are supposed to love beautiful
bodies and women love the person within and we've just
turned the whole thing around, Graham.'

'Maybe you're really a gay guy and I'm a lesbian,' he said.
'And my name isn't really Graham, either.'

'I've got to learn a new one?' I said.

'My name is really Ralph Smutney. And I didn't graduate
from St John's University. I've never been to college. I'm
originally from Waco, Texas, and I think we ought to sort
some of this stuff out.'

I reached over and took his hand and shook it. 'Nina
Morton from Briarcliff, New York. I don't give a damn what
your real name is. We're way past that, my darling.' And I put
my arms around his muscular waist and my head on his
shoulder. He put one arm around me and drove with one
hand. Like high school sweethearts. A couple of crazy high
school sweethearts driving on the San Diego Freeway towards
West Hollywood.

'Why did you wait until now to tell me your real name, Mr
Smutney?' I said in his ear.

'I was afraid you wouldn't like me,' he said.

chapter 21

the dinner

As the Bible says, 'And so it came to pass.' Edwina called me on Monday and said she had spoken to old Duress and he was game for us all to have dinner together Wednesday evening. He wanted to go to Le Dome up on Sunset; still chic, not insanely noisy like Spago, and not too 'see and be seen'.

I went home early on Wednesday to be there when Edwina arrived. Travel heavy is Edwina's motto. Her taxi pulled up in front of the house and two vast suitcases emerged, followed by herself. She looked very chic in black and white check with royal blue. The cab driver, a young hippy-dippy type, had fallen in love with her. As he heaved the suitcases to the door he said to me 'She's so droll,' which I guess pretty well summed it up.

I somehow carried her luggage to the guest room. She loved the house in all its gloom and outsize furniture. 'Isn't it funny they didn't seem to be at all interested in sunlight and fresh air in the 1930s,' she said. 'Women were supposed to be pale and unathletic and England was the divine prototype. Imagine the swath Lady Sylvia Ashley cut when she came out here and picked off Douglas Fairbanks! Senior, that is.

'I love my room! Do *not* think I've come permanently just because of all this luggage but you know once you have the shoes and the purses and the tissue paper and plastic to keep things from wrinkling it takes up quite a lot of space. I hate all that "roll your little Gucci like a wet towel and take off" that the fashion magazines keep hustling. You always wind up looking like your clothes came from the Gap.'

Her bags were open and everything was emerging already on hangers and being hung up. 'Great closets,' she said. 'They knew how to live better than we do. All these new buildings have low ceilings so the architects can put in more floors. Ivana Trump's apartment. It looks like a meat-packing plant; vast and the ceilings just clear my head. How can one look tall and proud and swell in a place like that?'

Talking steadily she emerged from the bathroom in a cotton robe, blue and white striped, and bare-footed.

I made tea and we threw ourselves down on the chester-fields in the living room. 'Nice, really nice,' Edwina said. 'Like a California version of Coco Chanel's apartment in Paris. Everything too big for the room. That gigantic armoire, that huge statue, these enormous couches. Now about tonight. I'm wearing gray.'

'I'm wearing blue. Dark blue. With my new topaz earrings,' I said.

'Perfect. I'll wear pearls so as not to outshine you. And lots of mascara. Do you remember that wonderful line from *The Prince and the Showgirl?* "When you are young you must wear a lot of mascara. And when you are older you must wear *much* more." My philosophy exactly. Men never notice mascara. They think it's just you. I shall wear mascara on my deathbed.'

She was on a roll. 'I love it here and I'm going to stay until Sunday if you don't mind. You don't have to do a thing to entertain me. I plan to stay in that fabulous bed and scream and tear at the sheets and eat cookies and read and really get a good rest. Complete bed-rest. That's what I need. Which you never get in your own home because you're always remembering you have to defrost the refrigerator. Now about

Claude Duress. First, you have to let me talk about all the
real reasons I'm out here so he doesn't think we're ganging
up on him. If he thinks I'm job hunting so much the better.
It's great to have people think your job is shaky when it isn't.
Keeps them completely offguard.'

'And I'll tell you how much I love working for him,' I said.

'And I'll tell him he's a king of the industry. A czar,' Edwina
said.

'As for his new-found passion for you?' she added. 'How
are we to combat that? It won't be enough that you're out of
the running. You *are* out of the running aren't you? He could
be a fabulous second marriage you know. Everyone in New
York would call you the second Georgette Mosbacher.'

'Please. I don't think I can get that much lipstick to stick
to my face. I am *definitely* out of the running; there's a serious
magnificent obsession going here,' I said.

At that point the magnificent obsession walked in. All blond
and messy hair and rippling muscles under his T-shirt. Edwina
said what I was thinking. 'What a guy,' she said as he bent
over the back of the couch to kiss her. 'Poor Mr Duress.'
Graham (or should I call him Ralph now? I decided to forget
Ralph) sat down beside me facing Edwina and put his arm
around me. I think we looked all right as a couple, I really
do. I was obviously older but not *that* much older. I could
only hope and pray.

'We're figuring out how to discourage Claude Duress from
being interested in Nina personally while keeping him fascinated with her professionally,' Edwina told him.

'How do *you* do it?' I asked. 'How do you keep Carlton
Carlson from crawling all over you?'

'Firstly, Carlton Carlson knows that I am completely out
of his league, professionally, intellectually and sexually. He'd
be terrified of coming on to me. Secondly there is Mrs
Carlson, who is a real bruiser in Bill Blass. She'd kill him.'

'We could tell him we're getting married,' Graham said. Forget the Ralph forever I decided.

'Are we?' I said, looking at him.

'Are you?' Edwina said.

'Are we?' he said, looking back at me.

'Can you?' Edwina said.

'Yes, I think that's a very good idea,' I said after staring into the air over Edwina's head for a minute. I turned and kissed him gently on the cheek. 'And no, I can't. I haven't even started divorce proceedings yet.'

'*That* is totally unimportant. We've solved it.' Edwina got up from the couch. 'You two are getting married. I'm going to be the Matron of Honor. It's going to be in my apartment in New York when your divorce comes through. You plan to continue to live in Los Angeles so Graham can continue to pursue his career in the cinema. Now we must dress and look our most elegant.'

And we did. My lover went home and came back in a navy blue suit I'd never seen before and a very discreet tie. Edwina wore a gray linen jacket with a darker gray linen pleated skirt. The jacket had beautiful embroidery across the front and down one arm. I suddenly realized it was a woman's profile with her hair flowing down over the sleeve. In pale beads with pearls in the hair. 'What an incredible jacket,' I said when she appeared in the living room. 'It's a copy of the Schiaparelli jacket designed by Jean Cocteau. Done in 1937 I think. Suits your house perfectly.'

I wore my navy blue with the chiffon sleeves from Jil Sander. Right up to the neck. No necklace. Just my Bulgari topaz earrings. No other jewelry. Not even rings.

'Nina, you look like a very elegant and sexy nun,' Edwina told me, looking me up and down. The Fashion Patrol, we used to call that look at the office. You could hear the sirens wail if you had on the wrong kind of shoes. 'When an American is elegant she outdoes them all. You look as though you could run hard and fast somewhere. That hidden something. That independence. I love it. Let's get the hell out of here,' she said.

Claude Duress was waiting at the bar. Graham was introduced. Both men were polite but distant.

It could have been awkward without Edwina. Very. She launched immediately into tales of a round of castings and pre-production meetings that even convinced me. She cleverly added the slant that she had so much to do because of my absence, and how much I was missed by Nixtrix and how wonderfully well the Jamaica Wind commercial was doing, which she believed was entirely due to Graham's presence in it and so on and so on. I'm not sure to what degree Claude Duress was taken in by this flow of amiable charm. He basked in Edwina's presence but he was far from stupid.

People were looking at our table. It's not often that Hollywood has someone of Edwina's presence who isn't recognizable as a celebrity. They probably thought she was a foreign princess. Which she is.

'And Claude. How are the children? How's the divorce going?' she asked him. So forthright, Edwina.

He didn't blink an eye. 'Edwina, how could I have been such a fool?' he said, not sounding at all as though he thought he had been such a fool.

'Sex, I suppose,' she replied, taking a drink of her wine. She had coquilles St Jacques and was drinking red wine with them. She never drinks water with her meal. She believes it forces liquid into your cells, causing cellulite.

I looked down at my sole. Grilled. No butter.

'It can get to you,' Mr Duress said.

'It's the most important thing,' Edwina told him. 'It's worth whatever you have to pay Claude. It may be expensive per fuck, but it's worth it.'

'I figure mine at about fifty thousand apiece,' he said. 'If she gets what she wants.'

'Well, that is *cher* but on the other hand would you have wanted to go through life without? You can afford it, Claude. What none of us can afford is to miss the thrills.'

He chewed his steak thoughtfully. I could see he wasn't going to agree with her. Not with all those millions at stake.

Graham hadn't said much during the meal. He had devoted himself manfully to his salad and his cote d'agneau. Now he said, 'What can you do when your body takes over? It doesn't know anything about taxes and alimony. It just decides what it wants to do, and we follow along. Don't you think that's how it works?'

'For some people. For lucky people,' Edwina told him not looking at Claude Duress. She wiped her mouth, not giving a damn about how much lipstick she might leave on the napkin. She was done eating. She took her compact and lipstick from her purse and made up her mouth again. She always wears Revlon's Fire and Ice, in the evening, year in and year out. That's her look. Of course Nixtrix would like her to wear one of their lipsticks, but you can't have everything.

My Graham spoke. 'I guess I'm among the lucky people then. Nina and I are getting married, Mr Duress. We told Edwina this afternoon.'

'I think it's fabulous,' said Edwina, taking one last look at her mouth in her compact mirror and closing it with a decisive click. Dropping it into her purse, she added, 'Let's have some champagne, Claude. I feel like having some champagne and this gives us the perfect reason.'

Mr Duress did not look nonplussed. He was a savvy little critter. 'My congratulations,' he said. 'You *are* lucky. She's going to be a wonderful help to you in your work.' I realized he knew who Graham was and what he did. Edwina realized it, too. There was just a flicker in her eyes. She straightened her back and gestured for a waiter, who came right over and took the champagne order.

The waiter said, 'No desserts?'

'Not necessarily. I might like some ice cream. I like ice cream and champagne together,' Edwina told him.

'Has *your* divorce gone through?' Claude Duress inquired politely of me. This guy knows plenty, I thought. 'It will soon,' I lied. 'We'll probably be married in the autumn at Edwina's apartment in New York. But we'll live here. I love him very much.' I reached over and put my hand over Graham's on the table and we both looked at my client. I hoped I was behaving with dignity and not like some superannuated love-besotted fool.

Suddenly an awful little man was standing at our table. A crew cut. Black horn-rimmed glasses. A white wool jacket and an awful tie with roses on it. 'Edwina! Claude! Together again! It's been five years at least!' he said very loudly. Edwina looked at him as though someone had dropped a load of manure beside the table. I had never seen her eyes look so hard. Duress' face was completely blank. Edwina said very flatly, 'Hello, Fred. I thought I told you to wait in the car.' Claude Duress had the same look.

Fred was undeterred. 'Who are these beautiful people?' He squealed when he talked. 'Hi, I'm Fred Farmer. You probably read me in the *Post*. What's going on here, Edwina? Are you about to jump ship at Campanella and join up with Cleanola?'

'Caught in the act. Fred I'd like you to meet Nina De Rochemont and Graham Grant. They're getting married.'

'Is that right?' He shook our hands. His was little and wet. 'Mind if I join you?' he said as the champagne was arriving. He pulled a chair over from the adjoining table. I was actually rather enjoying myself. He had Edwina and Duress on the spot and I was longing to know what that spot was.

'Nina is a dear friend who worked with me at Campanella and now works at S.S. and D. on Cleanola. Graham's an actor. Claude and I are having a little engagement celebration with them. That's it. Over and out.'

Fred had a little notebook in his hand. 'How do you spell

De Rochemont, Nina? Are you connected to the movie De Rochemonts?' I spelled De Rochemont for him and said I had no connection to the movie De Rochemonts. I didn't bother to explain that my soon-to-be-ex-husband wasn't either. I noticed he looked at my hands and saw I wasn't wearing any ring.

'And how do you spell Grant, Graham?' he asked. 'Like Hugh,' Graham said. 'And what was your last movie?' Fred asked.

Graham laughed. 'There is no last movie. But I'm supposed to go to Hawaii next month to do a pilot for a TV series. Wish me luck.'

Turning to Edwina and Claude Duress little Fred said, 'And what's going on in your lives these days?' Edwina said, 'Practically nothing, and if anything was you would be the last to know, Fred. Now drink your champagne and leave us in peace.' Claude Duress was puffing on a cigarette and looking like a pre-Columbian idol.

'You could cost me money Fred, if you talk about me carelessly in the press. You know how I'd hate that,' he said.

Fred babbled, 'I'd never say anything about you, Claude. You're a king of the beauty industry.'

'I've already told him,' Edwina said.

'And Edwina is the Empress. You're the best. The two of you. So smart, so intelligent, so chic. What's to say that's bad?'

Edwina said, 'I'm sure you could find something.'

Fred Farmer didn't take no for an answer. He shmoozed. He smiled. He wheedled. He charmed. He was awful. Edwina looked as though she was at a circus that was not particularly amusing. Duress answered direct questions with a low grumble. Graham looked bored. I tried to look amused. But nobody was spilling anything. I wasn't even sure what there was to spill. At one point Edwina said, 'Why do people talk when they have nothing to say?'

Graham excused himself and headed for the men's room. While he was gone Fred Farmer finally threw in the towel. 'It was wonderful to see you again,' he told Edwina. 'Nothing like the pleasure of seeing you,' she replied.

Mr Duress said nothing. He didn't even grumble as he shook Fred Farmer's hand. To me, Mr Farmer said, 'I'm sure I'll be seeing more of you.' I smiled. Sardonic replies were Edwina's specialty. I could never compete.

Edwina and Claude Duress seemed unwilling to even mention that Fred Farmer had been at the table. Edwina said, 'I never got my ice cream.'

'Did we ever order it?' Claude Duress signaled a waiter. Edwina ordered ice cream. I ordered two cappuccinos for Graham and myself. Duress had American coffee.

Graham reappeared from the men's room. He seemed pleased with himself, and Fred Farmer swarmed past the table right after him, his face flushed, clothes seeming tighter on his swollen little body. He didn't look at us. I was sure Graham had said something to him.

As we waited for the car to come around he told me. 'That Farmer guy followed me into the men's room and wanted me to meet him later. He said he would pay.' Graham didn't seem to be particularly miffed at this. 'What did you say?' I said.

'I told him I thought he had kissed enough ass for one evening,' Graham said and turned to help Edwina into the car.

chapter 22

....

at home

'This guy doesn't seem to have any downside.' Edwina gestured at Graham with her cigarette. We were sitting around my Ludwig the Mad living room, having bid adieu to Claude Duress at the restaurant.

Graham and I were sitting on one large leather couch and Edwina was stretched out on the other one, her shoes on the floor.

'True,' I said. 'He's loyal, courteous, honest. And handsome.'

'And great in bed,' Graham added.

'That's your profession,' Edwina said. 'That doesn't count. No, but really. You don't drink to excess. You don't take drugs that I've noticed. You don't even smoke. You might be fooling around but if you are you're doing it professionally.' Graham and I exchanged a look.

I knew what Edwina was doing. Asking the questions I wasn't going to. And trying to shed a little light of reality on our goo-goo love nest.

Graham said, 'My biggest fault is that I'm very passive. I play the ball as it lays. Going after Nina is probably the most aggressive thing I've ever done. I just felt like I had to have her.'

'Nina was fairly aggressive about finding you once she'd

seen your cassette,' Edwina said. 'I don't think you'd have escaped at least meeting each other.'

'But Edwina,' I said, 'you're the one that kick-started this whole thing. I would never have figured out how to track down Graham. I would have just sat around with my video cassettes obsessing.'

'Anyway, it seems unreal to me,' Edwina said. 'Girl obsesses, girl meets boy, boy is perfect.'

'I'm not perfect, Edwina,' Graham said. 'What am I? I'm on out-of-work actor who has never worked very much. I'm a porn actor, and most people think there's nothing lower. Everything I've done has been because it was the easiest thing to do. I'm not stupid but I'm not really a catch.' I felt bad. I took his hand. His fingers clenched around mine. He's breezy in that Hollywood way but underneath he has that little edge of not feeling so great about himself.

'So where is this all going? What's the plan?' Edwina said. She sat up and looked at us, her hand reaching for her shoes. Edwina doesn't like to talk idly.

'I don't know, Edwina. I'm a good bit older than Graham. I just have to play it by ear. I'd like to spend the rest of my life with the man of my dreams, but *quien sabe?* I'm not going to goof up what's going on right now by worrying about where it's going.'

'But you ought to make a plan for where it *could* go. Things left to themselves always work out somehow, but they never work out for the best. And I mean never.'

'I know I want us to stay together. When I'm seventy and Nina's eighty, I want to be there to take care of her and love her and let her know that she made my whole life mean something. That's all I know,' Graham said.

'Bravo,' Edwina said. 'Nobody has ever said anything like that to me or about me. That was an admirable speech, and you are to be admired. Unless that was all bullshit.' I said nothing. I just pondered.

chapter 23

....

making a movie

I'd only been in Los Angeles three months but I was beginning to fall in love with it. Such a curious town. Actually more foreign to me than any city in Europe.

The greenery. The houses all in some period: French Provincial, Elizabethan, Federal, Georgian, Modern. An occasional Munchkin cottage. With all the authenticity of a stage set, which of course they were designed to look like.

The people seemed to be largely electronic. I got the feeling that people were like television sets. They got up. The set goes on and things play on the screen all day long, but none of it is considered, none of it is retained. There is no slow accumulation of character or knowledge. Life is to be lived. You live it. At night you go to bed and switch the set off.

What saved me is that advertising is actually a real business. We were connected to other agencies in other parts of the country and the world. The staff behaves in an orderly, legal way. Who would think advertising would be a solid little island in the midst of a raging sea?

Which brings us to the possibility of my doing a porn movie. Was I going mad? Well may you ask. I criticized the scenario of the movie Graham just made and he said, not in any angry way, that I should write one myself. And I thought about it. Porn movies are so formulaic. I'm sure they never do any research to find out what their audience really wants to see. I always tell my clients they should go window-shopping in Paris where you are forever seeing something you didn't know you wanted.

For a drag queen, I don't think Mimi had much feminine sensibility. I wonder how much of a sex life Mimi has actually had. Giving someone an occasional blowjob wasn't exactly having a woman's sex life.

So I started thinking about it. What real-life situation could possibly result in all these high-jinks and permutations that these films seemed to require?

I decided the sexiest thing would be to do something like a feature where you actually saw the real sex parts. Like *The Year of Living Dangerously.* You saw a lot of Mel Gibson nude, but it would be really sexually arousing to see him getting it on with whats'er name. They probably couldn't do too much because she's two feet taller than he is. But how about Michelle Pfeiffer and Kurt Russell in *Tequila Sunrise?* Or Michelle Pfeiffer and Jeff Bridges making bamboola in the Baker Boys? Unless I'm very wrong he would be great. Very nice body. And if my sweetie was a porn star, he at least could be making a porn movie of stature.

Graham gave me a short story collection he had of erotic stories, one of them telling the sexually explicit side of an imagined affair between Ingrid Bergman and Humphrey Bogart while shooting *Casablanca.* Quite hot, actually.

So I began imagining what kind of story I could weave for just Graham and Angela. Something like *Bridges of Madison County* where you actually saw the sex parts. You know, the doomed lovers. I knew women fantasized about this, and men did too, I was sure. You were sinning and you were being unfaithful but it's justified because of your great love. I suppose it was exactly my own story.

This was the story I concocted. Angela plays a writer living alone somewhere like Maine. A beautiful New England house.

Gardens. The movie started with her calling for someone to help with the garden. Graham appears. Was this too much like *Lady Chatterley's Lover?* I asked myself. Probably couldn't be *too* much like it; the more like it the better. I saw Angela in a flannel skirt, gray cashmere sweater, brogues. A gray Persian cat in there somewhere.

They look at the garden together. Close-ups of stamens and pistils. She is a bit older than he. Angela is. At least I would like to think.

He leaves; dust whirling down the road as his truck disappears. Poor sad Angela, mourning at the door. And then at dusk, he re-appears, to water plants, as they shouldn't be watered in the broad daylight. Was this getting to be too much for a porn film? She asks him in for a drink, a cup of coffee, something. And you know the rest. Except this is where I had to really kick in.

I saw a four-poster. A chaise longue.

I thought we should have time lapses and make things happen over a period of several weeks. I wanted to see them making love in the garden itself, two beautiful bodies in the flowering borders.

And down by the river. They must have rivers in Maine. Probably too cold to go into. I was thinking of *The Go-Between*. Julie Christie and Alan Bates. Caught in the greenhouse by her mother. But some standing up in the reeds along a slow-flowing river, that could be beautiful.

I decided to call it *Chase My Love*. Too gloppy? It was certainly a far cry from the sailor's epic they'd just finished.

I read it to Graham and he had a few criticisms. He asked if he couldn't be a landscape architect, married with two children. That added to the hopelessness aspect, and made it more interesting for the married men who would watch.

I called and asked Mimi to have lunch. She was rather thrilled when I told her I wanted to discuss a scenario. We decided on a Saturday, so I wouldn't have to rush, and there would be less likelihood of business acquaintances sitting at the next table. Lunching with a drag queen might be pushing it a little.

If any restaurant could handle Mimi and me at the same table it would be The Tattooed Rose. And it's in Venice, which meant less chance of my bumping into co-workers.

Lunch with Mimi Fandango at The Tattooed Rose was fun. All the waiters were in black leather, so Mimi enjoyed that. She kept growling to our waiter, 'We have to do a movie.'

I explained the story line and that I had imagined it would be for Graham and Angela. 'Very classy, very classy,' Mimi said, actually paying attention to what I was saying. Mimi was jealous of her reputation and wanted to upgrade her image. It was never going to lead to Meryl Streep, but, she liked the idea of her films being more like features.

I had added a scene where the couple make love in a rainstorm and get covered with mud (straight out of *Lady Chatterley* of course) and Mimi loved that. 'Hottest, hottest,' she chanted. 'Do you think we could work another guy into the story somewhere?' she asked. 'I'd love to get a three-way going at some point.'

'Do you think a three-way is very romantic, Mimi?' I asked her.

'Oh, it can be, it can be,' she said. 'But maybe you're right. It gets too carnal, that way, I suppose.

'I have to talk to my backers,' she said as we dabbled with our desserts. Mimi had ordered the toasted angel food cake *and* the brandy caramel ice cream and had put them together on the same plate. That kind of excess was probably what made her a good director. Did I say 'good'? Maybe excessive director is closer.

I couldn't help but wonder who the backers were. Porn is a very big money-making industry. But who were those 'someones' making all that money? The Mafia came to mind immediately. This was going to be interesting. Maybe I could do an exposé on the porn industry?

I like Los Angeles best in the late afternoon. Driving in from Venice on Sunset. The light long across the highway. Smelling the eucalyptus. Something fresh and moist in the air as the sun began to relent. When I got home I said, 'I wish our life could just go on like this forever.' Graham said, laying on the couch, 'It will, just as long as we keep on planning to do something more with it. The moment we let up, it will begin to fall apart.'

'Are we going to do something more with it?' I asked him.

'Time will tell, time will tell,' he said.

I put my hand on his hair and looked out the window and knew I was the one who was going to have to do something more with it.

chapter 24

....

making a movie, take two

Mimi called on Monday. 'We've got a deal,' she said.

'That was quick,' I said.

'Yeah, I called them yesterday and talked about it. They liked it because I liked it. And because you wrote it.'

I was surprised. 'They don't know me from a hole in the wall, do they?' I was wondering who in the hell 'they' were. 'Mimi, nobody in Los Angeles knows me. I just got here, and I don't even work in the movie industry. How would anyone know about me?'

'Beats me,' she said. 'The minute they heard De Rochemont they were really interested. They wanted to know if you'd be involved with the shooting. I told them that Graham was your boyfriend.'

'Is this good?' I asked myself. To Mimi I said, 'It isn't the Mafia is it?' He laughed. 'Worse. They're business people. It isn't drug money, I promise you that. They're just business people who like the porn business. Maybe it's to meet the performers. Beats me. I'm not asking them why they want to give me money. I just take it and smile.'

'This is a crazy thing for me to be doing, you know that don't you, Mimi? I wouldn't lose my job or anything, at least I don't think so, but it might make me slightly less hireable in the future.'

'Yeah. But on the other hand it might lead to you writing features. Which is even bigger money than you're making now. You ever think of that?'

I hadn't. Nor did I really wish to.

'So what are our next steps, Mimi my dear?' I asked him.

'I'm scheduling the shooting right now. I've got to check Graham's availability and Angela's, and then line up the crew. We should shoot up in the Napa Valley. Maybe around Glen Ellen. M. F. K. Fisher country. That looks something like New England in places. More intellectual anyway. Not like around here.'

'How do you know M. F. K. Fisher, Mimi?' I said.

'*Map of Another Town*. Great book. She was brought up around here, you know. Then went to France. Lived in Aix-en-Provence. The most beautiful city. The hottest.'

I was flabbergasted. 'I'm just so surprised you know about her, Mimi,' I said. 'She's my favorite writer. So ladylike and so emotional at the same time. And I think she was probably very sexy. We're bound to be good friends, with her in common.'

Mimi said, 'I thought we already were.'

'We don't really know each other all that well, Mimi,' I told her. 'But this advances the cause. We'll pretend we're doing a movie of one of her books. I think she'd be pleased.'

'With all those penises?' she said.

'I doubt she was a stranger to penises,' I said.

'You're right. She was probably one hot babe in her time. I read a lot, you know, Nina. I don't go out very much and I don't watch television, so I am pretty up on literature. Right now I'm into May Sarton's journals.'

'You're a hoot, Mimi. You and I are the only two people in LA that even know May Sarton existed.'

'No, no. Not true. Very hot lesbian, May Sarton. Very beautiful when she was young. She's sort of my role model.'

'Are you thinking of becoming a lesbian, Mimi?' I asked.

'I *am* a lesbian, Nina. So watch your step.'

'Mimi, you spoil me.' I thought of how Edwina would handle this. It was definitely a man speaking when Mimi said, 'You're *worth* spoiling.'

'Back to our movie, enough about me, Mimi. If we're shooting in a month I could probably take off a week to be there. I'm of two minds whether I should or not. I might freak out.'

'Do you think your hairdresser friend could be lured into coming along too? He did a great job on Angela. You should see the rushes. She looks like Michelle Pfeiffer,' Mimi said.

'I'm sure Michelle would be glad to hear that. Yes, I'll try to get little Mr Petitfour to tag along. There won't be a great variety of males, but maybe Graham will be enough.'

'Oh, I think Graham will be more than enough,' Mimi said. Hmmm. Was Mimi trying to tell me something or just making trouble? I hung up.

Of course it wasn't half an hour before Angela called me. She didn't really sound like Angela. She sounded a little excited, which wasn't Angela at all. I had left a message for her that morning about the possibility of some work in Europe.

The story? The director, Roger Flint, had called from Zurich during the morning. He was doing a hosiery commercial and the principal girl had just fallen through. They had to have a blonde with great legs who could dance and they had to have her immediately. They had been through every agency in Europe and New York and there was nobody. Everyone who could possibly do it was booked. Besides, what blonde with great legs would be in Europe or New York in the winter time anyway? He'd called Edwina in New York and she'd put him on to me. I immediately thought of Angela. Roger had said the girl didn't have to be very young, she just had to be glamorous. Angela was completely unknown in

Europe. This could be a breakaway step for her. I'd called and left a pretty complete message before lunch.

'They need you Wednesday in Zurich,' I told her.

'They haven't even seen me,' she said.

'They're taking my word for it,' I told her. 'I've spent my adult life working with beautiful women in television commercials. They trust me and you're it. Can you dance?'

'Like a fury,' she said. 'This sounds so great.'

'This is how it goes, Angela. You tell them you are an actress. You have never modeled. You have done commercials here and quite a bit of lesser-known film work. You're waiting for your breakthrough. And you're twenty-seven. Got it?'

'You're sure they're not going to say "Who sent us this old hooker"?' she said.

'Not at all. Every woman needs a great makeup artist and hairdresser. You had one in the last film and you looked wonderful. You'll certainly have the best in Zurich. Roger would never work with anything less. And you'll love him. Not literally, of course. He's a real gent. He'll make you look fabulous. He has no choice. His back is up against the wall. You're perfect for this.'

'I'll just pretend I'm you,' she said. 'A lady who knows how to let it all hang out. Am I right?'

'Angela, I like you. I've met some of the most interesting and nice people in the past few weeks. You. And I'm beginning to like Mimi, too.'

'Did she come on to you?' she asked.

'In a very gentlemanly way,' I told her.

When I got home Graham was there, lying on one of the leather couches in what was becoming our routine. I sat down beside him and hugged his waist. He put down the *New Yorker* and clutched my knee.

I told him Angela was on her way to Zurich. 'My little do-gooder,' he said. 'Don't be disappointed if she doesn't become a European film star. She's made a lot of money and she's hung on to it, she isn't going to wind up in the gutter.'

'I was thinking more of an emotional gutter,' I said.

'We are all in the gutter but some of us are looking at the stars. Oscar Wilde,' Graham said.

'I'm just old-fashioned enough to think she might be happier if she was earning a living with her body not so directly,' I said.

'You have a much more private feeling about your body than a lot of people. You think much more highly of yourself than some of us.'

'But you don't have a poor opinion of yourself, do you? Tell me you don't.' I put my head down on his shoulder. He pulled me more on to the couch. To hell with wrinkling my skirt.

'It took me awhile. I've made certain adjustments, like stepping out of the middle class altogether. I don't see anything from their point of view anymore. But I remember that point of view.'

'Graham, have you slept with anyone else since we started seeing each other?' I don't think I had an accusatory tone in my voice. I was just remembering what Mimi had said about Petitfour St Albans. He laughed. 'You were there,' he said. 'You saw me having sex with any number of people when we were making the movie. That's something else. And I don't know how much longer I want to keep doing this. I kind of didn't mind your being there and I kind of did. I mean, really, what's the difference between what I do for the camera and what we do together? To me, they're worlds apart, but when you think of it our making love is a kind of pornography, and I don't like to think of it that way. So maybe I'm going to have to give up pornography.'

'I didn't mean that. I meant *really* having sex with someone else. For the pleasure of it.'

He didn't tense up and we still felt comfortable lying there together. But he didn't answer.

'Well?' I asked.

'I'm thinking. I'm thinking. Jack Benny used to say that when a mugger said, "Your money or your life"? I'm thinking. And I think I'll tell you this. I slept with that Russian model when we were on location in St Thomas. She was begging for it. It took about ten minutes and I don't think either of us thought about it again. And I let your uncle's boyfriend suck my cock when we took that hike down to the beach. He was such a nice guy and I think he was sort of desperate for a little change of pace. I don't think you should tell your uncle.'

I sat up. I wasn't shocked. I was pissed-off. 'And while you're falling more and more in love with me you're having it off with anybody who comes along. It's kind of sleazy, Graham. Let me make one thing very clear. No matter what I find out, I'm not leaving you. No matter *what*. You are the one I love and I'm here until you kick me out and even then I don't think you'd have a lot of luck. This is obsession, my darling. Maybe some morning I'll wake up and be de-obsessed.'

He held his hands up, one finger across the other in the sign of the cross, warding me off. Weirdly this was definitely a discussion, not a fight.

'I know that. And we do have to do some re-thinking. I wouldn't be at all happy if you were sleeping with that old guy we had dinner with, your client. The one who knows Edwina. I wouldn't like it at all. But if you did because you wanted to, I'd handle it. And I know all that shit about men wanting to spread as much sperm around as possible so as to maximize their fleeting presence on earth, and that they don't want women to do the same thing because they want to make sure that those babies are theirs. But it goes beyond that for me. When somebody wants me very much, it seems selfish not to. I am, after all, not really this body and face, which seems to appeal to a lot of people. So if I'm the pilot in this little separate sort of space vehicle, I just don't like to say no to someone because they're not beautiful enough or special enough. I don't want them to go away feeling worse about themselves. Rejected. For what reason?' I'd never heard him say so much.

'You're sort of the Florence Nightingale of sex, aren't you?' I said.

He pulled me back down on top of him. 'I'll give you Florence Nightingale,' he said. 'And it's time for your medicine.'

'No.' I pushed myself up a little so I could see him. 'We should finish this. I'm not going to sleep with someone else just because the urge takes me. Or because I feel somebody is deprived and should have the pleasure and privilege of my body. I don't think my body is such a pleasure or a privilege, frankly.'

'It is, it is,' he said, pressing himself up against me. I could feel he was getting hard.

'It's just that I'm afraid you'll lose the ability to see the difference between me and your charity cases. I think it's possible to fuck too much. You lose your edge.'

'Fuck Freak. That's what they call that. Fuck Freak. No, I certainly don't want to wind up like that. Certainly it's a far greater pleasure to have my way with you than anyone else, because you are really here for me. The rest are paper dolls. And I know that my fucking you makes a lot of difference to you. It means a lot to you. And I'm not so sure it means a lot to those others. I have to think about this.' He began to pull my clothes off. One thing about a great love affair is that it's tough on your underwear.

chapter 25

....

the warsaw

Angela called from Zurich. They loved her. Not only had she saved the day but the client, Fabulegs, thought she was the greatest hosiery model they'd ever worked with. She sounded breathless and much younger than she had in Los Angeles. Mr Fabulegs wanted her to go on to London immediately to do some package and catalog pictures. What did I think?

I told her that although the money was less than she would make doing her 'regular work' there was more potential for big bucks in London.

'Make every decision based upon money,' I told her, parroting Edwina. 'It all boils down to the same grim people making stupid decisions, so at least you can go home at night knowing you got top dollar.'

Angela was a very good egg and underneath it all I'm sure she was thrilled, but it would be too much like an old Joan Crawford movie for her to admit she'd have loved to stop doing porn and putting out for a living. Tough LA girls just don't do that.

Then Graham called. 'I'm booked to work in Miami next weekend. Miami Beach to be exact. Some place called The Warsaw Ballroom. Want to go?'

'Of course, darling. Do you think I'd miss a chance to see you strip?' I said. 'You've had plenty of chances to see me strip,' he said. 'But never in public,' I said. 'But never in public.'

For the next two weeks the long distance calls poured in. Mimi checked in from New York. She was there peddling her sailor's hotel film I guessed. She was pretty well set to go ahead with the romantic movie I'd written. She wanted to go into production after Graham came back from Miami.

Angela called from London. Someone in Paris had heard about her Zurich shooting and wanted her to come over to audition for the Dim people. The Fabulegs company wasn't very happy about this and were muttering about putting her under contract. 'A contract girl,' I chortled into the phone. 'Ooh, Angela, you and Cindy Crawford and Claudia Schiffer. Way to go.'

'It's all happening so quickly,' she said.

'I know, I know, everything in life is a cliché. The movies aren't wrong, you know, Angela. You're out or you're in. Go with it. Does your agency have a good lawyer?'

'I changed agencies. I needed an international one so I've gone to Elite. John Casablancas gave me a really good deal. He thinks I'm going to be hot. He even came on to me.'

'I thought he was married and I thought he liked his models young,' I said.

'He is. He does. Do you think this is all part of the baby boomer trend? Middle-aged women are going to become chic?'

Angela was beginning to sound with it in the New York way. She'll probably wind up running a hosiery company. They say Madame Rubinstein made it all the way from hooking in Sydney, why not Angela?

Edwina checked in, too. She felt she might have to do a little fire control work with Claude Duress. I told her the Cleanola account seemed to be in open waters. The Clean Machine campaign was testing very well. We were putting

together new commercials for the fall. I'd had no calls from
Duress of an up close and personal nature.

I told her about Angela and how well she was doing in
Europe. 'Sainthood is yours, Nina,' she said. 'Now you're
saving girls from a fate worse than death.'

'It wasn't the morals thing, Edwina. Who am I to talk? I
just thought Angela was too smart for this business and she
could do better elsewhere.'

'One could say the same thing about Graham.'

'You took the words right out of my mouth,' I said.

'Is that your crafty plan, little Nina? To sneak him into la
vie bourgeois,' she said.

'Maybe he's sneaking me permanently out of it. Oh,
Edwina, isn't there a third choice?'

'You could both join me in Upper Bohemia, my darling.
You and I weren't in exactly the same worlds, even in New
York. I think you're whirling through space right now, but
hang in there. You'll wind up in a world that's to your liking.
If it's one of a kind and only Graham and you are in it, that's
not such a terrible thing. One can get along without belonging
to a country club you know.'

'It's just kind of scary. What happens to old porn stars?'

'Much less than you think. There are probably people all
over Hollywood running restaurants and laundries and taxi
services and even married to important people who used to
do their stuff for the camera. And in private for money. It's
only when *all* you can do is fuck you probably don't have
much of a future.' She sounded as though she'd known a
number of people who were limited in this way. She bid me
adieu and wished me luck. She is such a good parent. She
worries about you, she does all she can for you, but finally
she pushes you into making all your decisions yourself.

My own mother never wanted you to think she was thinking
about you or worrying about you. But even she called. She
wanted to know when I was next coming to New York.

She didn't say she missed me, but just the fact she called indicated that if we were getting a little closer she wanted to keep the contact up.

'How's the job going?' she asked. My mother knows nothing about advertising. She once thought that as a copywriter I wrote copyrights. I explained that the words in an ad in a magazine were written by somebody. Me. And also the words you heard on television advertising. I was that person. 'But where do the ideas come from?' she wanted to know. There must have been mothers like her in Ancient Rome whose daughters were virgins at the shrine of Vesta or something like that. 'God knows what she does in that inner sanctuary and I *certainly* wouldn't want to do it myself, but it's a job. Of course there are all those laundry bills on those white chitons and headdresses don't come cheap, but hey!'

My mother isn't stupid. I'm sure she feels a little creaky and unsure of herself being a woman whose world used to be so neatly defined. And now life is all over the block. I told her I had no plans to come to New York and suggested she come visit me. My mother never likes to do anything she hasn't done before. She murmured something about she'd 'see'.

And then Freddy the Second called. Funny wasn't it? I worried about him the most and thought about him the least. My own child. I guess I worried about him so much or at least about my failing him that I didn't let myself think about him. 'I love you, Mom. I always knew you were special but I didn't know there was only one of you. Claire has absolutely no sense of humor.'

'Do you see a lot of her?' I asked him in what I hoped was a truly neutral voice.

'Not much. She stays over once in a while but I think Dad is bored with her. She tries to be French and she isn't. And she thinks she's a great cook and she isn't. Hours of work and it's all very neat and intricate and it doesn't have any taste.'

My opinion of haute cuisine exactly and I'd never coached him. Freddy was beginning to show signs of being a bit of a wit. Which if he was before, he was only allowing his friends to know about.

'I want to come out and visit you, Mom. All my friends envy me very much. Nobody else has a Mom who ran off with a porn star.'

'He's an actor, Freddy,' I said.

'Yeah, but he's also Chase Manhattan. Very cool, Mom. *Very* cool. I really want to come meet him. That's about as prestige as you can get.'

'Oh, Freddy, should you be knowing about these things?' I said.

'Mom, I already know about these things. Relax. I don't suppose there's any chance of me watching them make one of those movies?' he added.

'Totally out of the question. No one is allowed on the set. I mean, how would you feel?' This seemed like a terribly adult conversation for me to be having with my fifteen-year-old. And furthermore I was lying.

'Yeah, I guess you're right.' I might have been refusing him roller blades. 'I can hardly even imagine doing it, let alone doing it in front of people.' So he's still a virgin. At least I've learned that much. My little boy. I sort of lost him when he was about seven and now he seemed to be coming back. He had been a very dear little boy.

I told him that he could come out on his spring break, which would be just about the time Graham would be winding up the new movie. I'd been sending money to Bertrand regularly which I guessed he'd been using for Freddy's school, but I told him I'd send him the plane ticket and we'd buy some clothes while he was out here.

That night Graham told me he had wangled a ticket to

Miami out of his manager for me to go along as his 'dresser'.
They wanted him there on Friday evening so he could see
the club and they didn't have to sit around all day on Saturday
wondering if he was going to show up. You never can tell with
porn stars. They had done a lot of advertising for the event
and sent a handbill with his picture, bulging out of a pair of
half-buttoned torn-off jeans. Very vulgar and really quite
great. I kept it and put it in my memory book.

We stayed at the Delano, the new Ian Schrager/Phillipe
Starck hotel. It's white. White. But it has something. I've
always been a sucker for curtains blowing in the wind. And the
Delano has curtains blowing everywhere. The front terrace is
completely curtained with two-story curtains blowing. It must
be *fabulous* in the rain. Everyone is in white and the staff are
all in white and as handsome as porn stars themselves. Some
ambience.

Our room was not very large but was very white. What is
it about all those white linens that makes you want to soil
them immediately with your bodily fluids? Flying seems to
put one in the mood for bamboola, too. And of course,
Graham was always in the mood.

But I hated doing the obvious, so I suggested we go to the
pool. If I ever had my dreams come true I want a château
with a descent of steps like those at The Delano's to the pool;
the width of the building with grass planted between the
stones and set with rows of pots of little star-like blue flowers.
You don't just go down stairs like those. You descend. They
are grand. And you are grand.

The pool was amazing. The water came precisely to the
edge surrounding it. So it was flat, flat, flat. And it was so
shallow at one end that a table and chairs stood in it. I hated
to give anyone credit for imagination, but it was strangely
beautiful. As were all the near naked people lying around the
pool. The women were topless, which I didn't think I was
quite up for yet. On the Côte d'Azur you'd probably look like

a figure of fun in a top but here there was a certain uneasiness. You could tell the European women; experts at not wearing a top yet showing nothing, all arms and towels and turned away positions. I could only do that with some coaching. Graham was enjoying himself. As much with the guys as the women I supposed. Los Angeles has never gotten out of floppy shorts surfer mode. Here the brief swimsuit was in, in, in. The sugar daddies were in just as good shape as their toyboys. Quite a feast for the eyes there at the pool. Lots of enclosed couches with curtains to draw, but even these advanced folk weren't about to clamber back there and get it on. I don't suppose. Am I wrong?

Going back from the pool I noticed a large marble table with an inlaid checker board and a bridge lamp, sitting on a stretch of lawn. Otherworldly. You could imagine yourself doing things here you wouldn't in more familiar surroundings.

Actually we went upstairs and did things we usually did. I was perfectly happy to have this handsome man whom I loved climb on top of me and make really great love. I felt no need to put on black leather and take a little whip to him, or to hang from the chandelier or do handstands in the corner. The more I learned about sex, and I'd been learning a lot lately, the more I sensed it was as great as the feelings you have for the other person. I asked Graham if he would love me forever and he said, 'I wish someone would threaten you so I could kill them.'

We were all screwed up, time-wise. Having made love we hadn't had dinner yet. And it was only six o'clock in Los Angeles. We had dinner on the terrace at the top of that big sweep of stairs. Through the trees the pool glimmered, lights went on and off in the cabanas around the pool, there was a huge, haunting moon, the famous 'Moon Over Miami' was hanging over us and planes were sailing through on their way to Rome or Zanzibar or Bahia. Was this romantic or what? What did we have to eat? Who knows and who cares? We were both all in white, both blonde. A fantasy, and so nice because I wasn't in it for the fantasy and I was living it anyway, as a bonus.

We took a cab down to Ocean Drive to check out the action and there was mucho. Block after block of little restaurants and cafés, all packed with beautiful people. The sidewalks, too. Bronzed gods on skates, lithe blondes on skateboards, motorized skateboards, gorgeous couples arm-in-arm. Pretty fantastic. It was the only place I'd ever seen with 'intimate' street lights. The night seemed to be full of flickering shadows, candles on tables, lights hidden in greenery, everything lit to look its most tantalizing and temporary. Set in a phantasmagoria of Art Deco hotels. Curves and zigs and zags and pastels and whites and curling metal balustrades and porthole windows. Somehow more modern than modern. The human body seemed so ridiculously attractive against all these shapes that have nothing to do with the body at all.

Graham wanted to see the Warsaw Ballroom where he was going to perform so we ambled up to Collins and 15th Street, just one block off the ocean. Curving around a corner with windows in black plate glass, the Warsaw must have been a nightclub in the 1930s. Graham spoke to the man at the ticket window who seemed suitably impressed and we were ushered into a black laser hell with a large bar at one side. The music was a hurricane of sound against which you could hardly stand. There was no one there. Graham shouted into my ear, 'No one starts coming until midnight. They're all home having their disco naps.' It was very strange. Something was happening but it didn't involve people. It didn't even seem to need people. There were posters and flyers at the door and on the bar with pictures of Chase Manhattan. 'See Manhattan By Night' it said on the flyers, with evidently his most popular look, abdominal muscles forever and hardly-there torn-off blue jean shorts. And it's mine, all mine, I thought. You can't help but feel a little possessive when a large share of the world fancies your man. Graham seemed completely unfazed by it. He walked around the bar, checking out the small space at the center where the two oval bars hooked up. The bars were like a figure eight, with the dance space at the center. 'The go-go boys work the bars, I just work on the center platform. I'm not there for people to put money in my jockstrap,' he told me. I was beginning to understand that this wasn't exactly the New York City Ballet.

People were drifting in now as midnight approached. Mostly men but some young and pretty girls among them. They danced in a physically exhausting manner that did not seem to exhaust them. Older men went to the bar and a fabulous-looking Latin guy suddenly appeared on the platform in tiny white shorts, a tight T-shirt and work boots with heavy white sweat socks. All of his muscles seemed to be working simultaneously in every possible direction. In moments the T-shirt and the shorts had been peeled off and he was in a tiny white thong. He completely ignored the men watching from the bars on both sides and actually seemed to be enjoying dancing. The dancers on the floor paid not the slightest attention to him either. Red laser lights were zapping the darkness and smoke was being released from somewhere to make the atmosphere even more murky. The dancer in the white thong started picking his way around the bar as a man with a skin the color of very dark honey took his place, wearing knee-length blue jeans, which he had lowered to give the slightest glimpse of pubic hair. His predecessor moved along the bar smiling distantly at his admirers now and swooping down on one knee while they tucked money into his minuscule white crotch cover. It seemed to be the price you paid for touching his body, however briefly.

'Let's go find the manager,' Graham bellowed close to my ear and we climbed a kind of staircase terrace that wandered up one wall. Upstairs across the back, there was another smaller bar. A very nice looking young man with a beautiful

body had his jeans fly undone and was showing his penis to
two men at the bar. They were inspecting it rather politely I
thought. The bartender was a roly-poly person with a big
smile who looked like something out of a George Grosz
drawing. 'This is decadence,' I thought. 'True decadence.'

No one else seemed to think so. Young girls passed in pairs
looking for someone. Nearby couches had chatting people,
talking about their jobs, I suppose. The young man's penis
did look rather large, but I suppose the regulars had seen it
many an evening at the Warsaw. Like a line from *Sunday,
Bloody Sunday*. 'Here comes that tired old penis again.'

Graham asked where we could find the manager. The bartender gestured to a door behind the couches. He didn't need
to be told who was asking. As we walked away he pushed
some of the publicity flyers in front of the polite men and the
penis man and pointed to Graham.

Through the door was a kind of lounge with some shabby
armchairs and a little coffee machine and a fat man at a
battered desk. The desk looked like it had been at the Warsaw
since the 1930s. This was probably the chorus girls' dressing
room. I could just see Joan Blondell talking to Ruby Keeler
in the mirror. In a nasal voice, of course.

The fat man looked up and said, 'Chase Manhattan. You're
a day early! You don't work until tomorrow night.'

Graham laughed and told him we'd come by just to say
hello and to look over the club and to reassure him he was in
town.

He introduced me and the fat man said, 'Hi, I'm Fred
Faricanelli. You're lucky you caught me. I manage Thrust
too, and I'm usually over there on Friday nights. Gotta keep
an eye on the boys. Make sure they're in on time. Call in
replacements if somebody doesn't show up.' Some of the
other go-go boys were beginning to turn up. A tall Latin, very
pale with a long mane of dark hair. A short-haired kind of
Irish tough kid with a really beautiful body and much attitude.

A shorter black guy with a fantastic body and some major tattoos around his biceps, which were about the size of my waist. I didn't realize black men had tattoos. These were very elaborate floral wreath designs in navy blue, quite beautiful. I was beginning to feel dizzy. Graham was very cordial and went around and introduced himself to everyone, including the Latin guy in the white G-string who had just come in from his turn on the bar. He had a lot of money clutched in one hand, hopefully some of it was more than one-dollar bills. The dancers were obviously thrilled to meet Chase Manhattan. None of them made any attempt to be cool. I wondered if I looked enough like a floozy. I was wearing a miniskirt but no big hair. They probably thought I was his manager. Or his mother. Freddy the Second would have been so proud of his mother, hanging out with this lot.

We walked back to the Delano. Miami Beach was a nighttime town. At nearly one in the morning the action was building. The streets were full of young people, the traffic lights holding up lines of cars. Very Latin. Like the capital of a South American country. It's the sea air flowing over your body that makes the difference. It's as though you were being incessantly caressed. I probably needed to go to Maine for awhile to cool off.

We slept in each other's arms, tucked away in our tiny little white nest. I never slept in Bertrand's arms. He didn't like to be touched in his sleep. Graham loves to hold and be held. I don't know about other women, but I was willing to put up with a lot from a man who actually wants to put his arms around me whenever I'm within reach. It was all very well to be a team, but being a physical team is so reassuring.

We slept in and did the big trick again. Exactly the same way we had the evening before and it was just great. I said to Graham, 'Shouldn't you be saving yourself for tonight?'

'Oh, it's not going to be *that* exhausting,' he said. 'And we'll take a disco nap this evening. It will be like another day altogether. This will be our fuck for today, and tomorrow we can treat ourselves to another one before we go back to California. And there we can treat ourselves to even more, day after day.'

'Sounds good to me,' I said, and pulled him on top of me. He's so smooth. He does shave some of his body hair, but he doesn't have much. Like some kind of merman, surging up over me out of the waves.

Graham wanted to go to the gym at the Delano before we took our disco nap. The modern traveler, he carried practically no clothes but always his gym kit. I went with him and did my little circuit training I always do, while he went at it for the abs and pecs and biceps. They should call Miami Beach 'Pec City'. What an array. There were bronzed beauties in every direction. Getting ready to go out for the evening.

There were three young men lying on the floor near my bicycle machine, discussing some other absent gorgeous creature. They were doing their abs. Huge brawny backs strained upwards. Rippling rows of stomach muscles crunched. Tiny white shorts strained to contain what was jammed within. Thigh muscles bulged.

'I think he's the cutest. The very cutest,' one said.

'He's a really nice guy, too,' his friend responded.

'I could really get interested in him. I was always interested in him. As I say, he is the cutest.'

'And nice,' the third one grunted.

'What's he doing?' the first one inquired.

'He's working as a trolley dolly airline steward these days. So he doesn't get to work out as often as he used to,' the friend replied.

'I'm sure he's still the cutest,' said Mr Number One.

'Oh, he can get shredded,' the friend said. 'But sometimes he gets out of shape. Puts on weight.'

'Oh, I'm sure he's still the cutest.'

'And so nice,' the third friend threw in again.

'Let's go over and do thighs,' Mr Number Two said. 'At least I'm going to.'

The other two men got up with him. Young guys. Strong guys. Looking for the same. All the prom queens in the world should probably go kill themselves.

We got up from our disco nap at eleven o'clock. This was definitely not a lifestyle I could pursue for any length of time. Graham had an erection and looked at me inquiringly. I said, 'Just tuck that thing into your jockey shorts, young man. You have work to do and you must be fresh.'

'You say all the wrong things,' he said. 'Now I *really* feel like doing it.'

I said, 'I want it to be special. A quickie is so unappealing.'

He said, 'It will be special. I promise you. And it won't be so quick, either.'

I ran into the bathroom and shouted 'Sex fiend!' through the closed door. When I came out he was in a T-shirt and jeans and had a little gym bag all packed. I saw the famous torn-off jean shorts in it. And work boots. He saw me look at them and said, 'I hate wearing those work boots that everyone seems to find so sexual. What could be dumber than to be naked and wearing sweat socks and work boots. As though only blue-collar men could be a good fuck.'

'It's weird, isn't it?' I said. 'Women have the same idea. Do you think homosexuals are more intelligent than the average man?'

Graham was brushing his hair in the mirror. 'I've known some very stupid homosexuals. No, I think the breakdown is about the same, it's just the more intelligent ones are the ones that create literature and theater. And they do seem to yearn to be overrun by working-class males. Stanley Kowalski. Without Tennessee Williams there would never have been a Marlon Brando.'

'But heterosexual men seem to go both ways in their dream images. There's Marilyn Monroe and then there's Meryl

Streep. The Slut and the Angel. There doesn't seem to be any Angel equivalent in the homosexual dream category,' I said.

Graham joined me at the door. 'I'm not so sure that Meryl Streep is any man's idea of a dream woman. More of a woman's idea of a dream woman. Maybe her career is being held in place by a great lesbian following.'

We had a sandwich at the snack bar, if you could call it that, in the lobby then set out on foot for the Warsaw. By the time we got there it was jumping. There were six go-go boys working the bar. The full set.

Again, two worlds seem to be functioning in the same place at the same time. On the dance floor female–male couples and male–male couples were surging and sinking in the waves of sound that seemed to be reaching right into your corpuscles. And at the bar, four feet away, a sea of tentacle-like dollar-waving arms were reaching, reaching, reaching towards the buttocks and groins revolving above them. Perspiration was the rule of the day in both domains. Sensation was everything, consideration was nothing.

Graham threaded our way through the flickering lasers and hazy smoke up the stairs, through the crowds hanging over the railings watching the dancers and the strippers. Many pretty young girls laced the crowd. There were even some at the bar pressing bills into whatever catchments the dancers could offer.

When we got to the lounge Mr Faricanelli was there. Graham said, 'My arrangement is that I'm paid before I go on. I hope you're ready for that.'

Fred looked dismayed. 'I thought we were going to send a check to your manager.'

'No, I think we made it very clear,' Graham said pleasantly. 'I was in the office when my manager was talking to you. I'm supposed to have the five grand in cash before I go. I have someone with me to take care of it.'

'Didn't we agree on four grand?' Mr Faricanelli said. I tried to look ladylike. My purse wasn't big enough for me to have a gun in it. Freddy the Second would have *loved* this.

'Mr Faricanelli, we've got all this in a fax in the office. You know I'd never go so far as to threaten you that I won't go on, but I think you know I won't if I haven't been paid. And everybody in the business would know that I came here at my own expense and you welshed on it. You'd never get a real porn star in this place again. It's a different business from the days when you ran the Torpedo Club, Fred. Porn's big business now.'

Mr Faricanelli went to his beaten-up desk and took an envelope out of a drawer. 'It's all in hundreds,' he said, handing it to Graham.

'Real ones, I hope,' Graham said. They both laughed. Fred said, 'Oh, yeah. We're real careful with that these days. These came from the bank. They've gotten real good with the crap ones. They're coming out of Syria I understand. We don't accept 'em downstairs at all. It's too dark and they're too good. Some of the kids get them pushed into their jockstraps. But hell, you don't know what you're getting until they get back up here, so it doesn't do those big spenders any good.'

'Count this, will you darling?' Graham said, handing the envelope to me. I did. I'm from a world where you just stuff money into your bag and never count it. It would be too insulting. But in this world it would be too crazy not to. It was something like chess. No exchange of money until every move had been made. Graham and Mr Faricanelli had been perfectly good-tempered through their exchange. I think Mr Faricanelli would have been disappointed if Graham had been a wuss and let him get away with something.

I took the envelope, sat down and neatly counted it out in my lap, slipped it back into the envelope and folded it over into my purse. It was all there. Graham had gone into the bathroom off the lounge and came back out wearing the boots and sweat socks, his cutoff jeans and a tight T-shirt and a cap. He got down and did some pushups. I think he must have rubbed baby oil or something on his arms and legs. They looked pretty shiny. And pretty sexy. I never get over how beautiful he is.

'Put me in, coach, I'm hot,' he said to Mr Faricanelli. They went out the door together. 'I'll be right back,' he said to me over his shoulder. From somewhere he had a towel slung around his neck. I guess it gets hot down there.

The music stopped and I could hear Fred Faricanelli's voice over a loudspeaker. I decided to go out on the balcony in front of the upper bar. It was like the announcements they make on subway platforms. So much reverb you only catch words here and there, but I heard 'Chase Manhattan' and 'Hollywood' and the music erupted and he came bounding up the little steps on to the center platform and the crowd screamed and screamed. It was like someone coming into a boxing ring. All those young men and older men and pretty girls and they were thrilled to see him. Or thrilled to be up in the middle of the night carrying on, eating up their lives in a frenzy of sound and light and other people's bodies. I suppose it all dates back to the Roman arenas. We want to have a good time and we want to have a good time all together.

The music was a tape he'd given to the disc jockey before we came upstairs, and it was very fast disco. The song 'I can be this, I can be that, what do you want me to be?' And my boy can move. We'd never danced together and you can imagine how a lady in her late thirties dances. I could always move, but flinging my pelvis around was never my thing. Graham had great moves. Moving rapidly. Stopping suddenly. He was really dancing, not just moving his body provocatively for his audience. He pulled off his T-shirt, slowly, dancing really wildly while his head was caught in it, his arms pulling it upwards. And then he threw it into the audience. He put his cap back on once the T-shirt was gone and I could just see his eyes glinting back under the brim. He never looked up in my direction. Perhaps he thought I really would stay in the lounge and not watch his act.

His shorts came off next. He seemed to be quite expert at getting them off over his boots. Naturally he had on white underpants, but not Calvin Klein. I think they were the same ones he always wore. But then he took the towel, which was lying at the edge of the little platform, tucked it around his waist and pulled his underpants off under it. These he stepped out of, one foot at a time, dancing through the whole thing. Female strippers must not go through all this I thought. They're not taking off real clothes. Once the underpants had been thrown to the audience Graham undid the towel and danced on holding it in front of his groin. There he was, completely naked except for his cap and his shoes. I have to say, it was pretty sexy and he was pretty expert in keeping that towel between him and his audience.

He has a beautiful butt and from the back his dancing was quite wonderful, seeing that fantastic back flowing down into his buttocks and down into those strong legs. It had the crowd going and people were trying to reach him to put money in the tops of his boots and throwing bills on the little stage, but he ignored it. From time to time he swept down and scooped up the bills and threw them to the bartenders on either side.

As the music built up even louder and faster he suddenly stepped off the platform on to one of the bars and started moving around it. The crowd didn't expect this and they were leaping up like trout pushing money his way. Holding the towel in front of him with both hands he flapped it over their heads so they could get quick glimpses up under it. I guess that was what they were truly there for. A glimpse of that legendary cock. Not so huge but *so* perfect.

I felt like I was at some sort of temple ritual. I didn't wish he wasn't doing it. He was like a symbol of beauty and fertility. It was only right that people should adore him. I did.

He circled one bar and then circled the other. By this time men and women were pushing from one side of the bar to the other to get one last glimpse under the flying towel. Once back on the central platform all the other go-go boys came on and formed a circle around him, all dancing their heads off. And when the music stopped suddenly, they all raised their arms above their heads, the lights went off, and when they came on, the boys were there by themselves and Chase Manhattan was gone. The crowd screamed. The music began again, and the boys ran out on to the bars to get the money from the crowd that hadn't been forced upon Graham.

There must have been a back stair because he was suddenly in the lounge, the towel around his waist, the shorts in his hand, his body soaking wet with sweat. I threw myself at him, soaking wet or not. 'You were wonderful, wonderful, wonderful,' I mumbled into his ear.

'I thought you would either like it or hate it,' he said. 'I was really worried. I wanted you to see it but I thought this might be the end of it all.'

I pulled his towel off him and started wiping him down. 'This is only the beginning,' I told him. He turned around and let me wipe his back. Mr Faricanelli came in. He looked pleased. He said, 'Let's go to dinner. I'm paying.'

An amazing town. Mr Faricanelli took us to dinner at The Versailles in the Spanish section across the bay. It was four-thirty when we got there and the evening was young. All the tables were full. The salsa band was playing up a storm. There were children at some of the tables. One of the twelve-year-olds had a cigarette.

We had sangria. We had paella. We had the works: plaintain, black beans, bread that evaporated when you put it in your mouth. You could see dawn outside the front door when we were finished. Mr Faricanelli was kind of fun. He told us all about the early days of running a club in Miami Beach, when all the gay men on the beach could only keep one nightclub afloat. Now there were five or six going great guns. And there were all the special nights. The lesbian nights. The Hispanic nights. The drag queen nights.

From what I gathered the whole scene was breaking down into everybody going everywhere. As I'd seen at the Warsaw. Mr Faricanelli said, 'Everybody thinks gays have all the fun so they want in on it.'

I said, 'But what do all these people do that they can stay up all night? Don't they have to work the next day?'

'In the restaurant and night club business,' he said. 'We've got hundreds of them now. And all the people who work in them have their fun, too. So after their places close they want to go out and the fun just goes on and on. You'll see when we go back. Most dance places don't close until noon. Once you're inside you don't know that it's daylight outside. And you don't care.'

He was right. We went over to see what was going on at Amnesia. Very chic, with dancing in the courtyard. The fact it was broad daylight deterred no one. Everybody that could get bare was bare. The music was deafening. The bars were serving soft drinks, but nobody seemed to object.

'I'll drop you off at Liquid,' Fred said. 'I'm going home. I've gotta get some rest. There's just more of the same coming up. Next weekend's the Winter Party, and that starts Wednesday and runs through Monday, when we have the big After Party. These folks are relentless. They want their parties. I don't know where they all come from but there's just more of these partygoers from hell showing up in town all the time.'

'Great for business,' I told him. He said, 'Yeah, but where's it all going to end? D'ya think it's because the end of the century is coming?'

'I'd put some money aside to open a nice monastery if I were you,' Graham said.

'Not a bad idea. Down in the Keys. They can pray and swim at the same time.' Fred laughed and pulled away from the curb in his Lincoln Continental convertible. We were in front of Liquid. Lots of kids were sitting around smooching and holding hands and ending their evening. It was seven-thirty a.m. A blonde in an upswept hairdo and tight blue jeans came rushing out of the club and ran over to a dumpster to throw up. She wiped her mouth off with the back of her hand and went back in the club. The kids didn't notice her.

'Let's go back to the hotel, my darling,' I said to my boyfriend. 'I think I may have had enough nightlife for one evening.'

He took my hand and we strolled up Collins Avenue in the early sunshine. Nobody seemed very intent on going home. The drag queens looked a little the worse for wear, but whose hair and makeup wouldn't need a little attention after eight hours of thrashing about in nightclubs? As the clubs were closing the fruit stands and coffee shops were opening and the club kids were digging into bacon and eggs and lots of coffee.

Back at the Delano stragglers like ourselves were heading for their rooms. 'What time's our plane?' Graham asked. 'Four,' I said. 'Let's catch some shuteye, and then we'll have lunch and head out of here about 2.30.' The boy at the door, all spiffy in white shorts and jacket, said, 'I caught your show Mr Manhattan. It was great.' He looked at me speculatively, wondering where I fitted into the picture. I said, 'I was here yesterday, too. I'm not just coming in to say good-night.'

He stammered. 'No, no it wasn't that. I was just wondering if you were Mrs Manhattan.'

'No, no such luck,' I said.

'But she will be,' Graham said. And we left it at that. Since we had put off Mr Duress with our supposed engagement we had never really talked again about our future. I couldn't imagine it. So I just didn't think about it. And I didn't know if Graham did or not.

As we got ready to get into bed Graham said, 'What about sex?' I said, 'You're too romantic. Save it for the plane.'

He pulled me up against him, my back against his chest, and said, 'I'm going to hold you to that.' And he did.

I was only worried about the stewardesses seeing us coming out of the little bathroom. And actually it *was* kind of exciting. Me, a respectable (could I still say that?) advertising creative director, mother of a fifteen-year-old, with my skirt up, sitting on the edge of a tiny sink. Although it did pass through my mind that this wasn't perhaps the first time he had made love in an airplane. But you can't worry about everything. When we came out nobody saw us but we must have looked guilty because a stewardess looked at us sharply and nodding her head towards the bathrooms said, 'Were you smoking?'

Graham grinned, 'I don't know. I didn't look.'

chapter 26

. . . .

mother's visit

My mother was in Los Angeles when we got there. She was
staying at the Château Marmont. I called her as soon as I got
the message on my machine.

'Hi, Mom, what are you doing here and why are you staying
at the Château Marmont?' I don't call her Mom very often
and I had certainly never called her Alicia. That she would
not have approved of at all. As a little girl I had called her
Mama. Then Mother. She *was* a Florence Henderson type,
but in a Gina Rowlands kind of way. There had always been
something a little too reserved about her for Mom to stick.

And suddenly I felt like somebody who *needed* their Mom.

'I'm so glad you're here. Come over right away. With your
bags. I have a guest room and the Château Marmont is a
nightmare. Particularly for my very own mother.'

'What about your boyfriend?' she asked.

'He's certainly not sleeping in the guest room,' I told her.
'And he's not here every night. Some nights I stay at his
place.' I paused. Did this sound rejecting? 'But not while
you're here,' I added. I followed this up with, 'Did you just
come out to see me? Why didn't you call? Are you all right?
And what gives with that Château Marmont? Check out of
that dive.'

'It is strange here isn't it? I'm in the suite by the pool where

John Belushi died. They tell you that, as though it will make you like it better. I think if you hadn't shown up today I'd have killed myself, just to fit in with the mood. It's awfully rainy here.' My mother isn't usually this amusing. Los Angeles must be having an effect on her already.

'That's how the song goes, Mom. "Hate California, it's cold and it's damp".'

She sang back into the telephone, 'That's why the lady is a tramp.'

'Oh, God, is that what they're saying about me in New York. Always so proper and what a tramp. I can just hear it.'

'If they are, they aren't saying it to me. I'll be right over. I've got your address. And I'm staying at the Château Marmont because I read in *Vogue* that Lauren Hutton always stays here. She shouldn't tell people. That elevator that goes straight from the garage to your floor says it all, doesn't it?'

'It's for those dwarf-fucking parties,' I said.

'I'm not going to ask you what you said because I heard you perfectly. Actually I came out because I had a feeling you needed me and would never ask. I asked myself what my own mother would have done and I knew she would have gotten on the next plane and flown to where her child was if she felt she was needed. So I did. I called Friday and you weren't here but I came anyway.'

'How long have you been here?' I said.

'I came out Saturday. I tried calling Friday night but got no answer so that decided me. Am I getting erratic?'

'Nicely so,' I said. 'Now get over here.'

I thought about her mother, Blanche. Voted the most beautiful girl in White River Township when she was two. My grandmother was beautiful in that Madonna-esque World War I style. I remember when I was little she came to New York once a year. And one time when I told her she was pretty she said that the men in her family always married beautiful women, so every generation got better looking. It was true. I remember her sisters-in-law, Aunt May and Aunt Mary. Even when I saw them as a child they were tall and elegant and wore beautiful clothes and stood up very straight. My grandmother had beautiful legs all her life. Which is where my mother got hers. And I guess I got mine. Uncle Freddy has very nice legs, too. When I was a teenager he and I were walking down the street in New York behind a woman with monstrous thighs, ponderously forcing one past the other as she walked. 'That's one thing we don't have to worry about, Nina. We'll never know what it feels like to have one leg touch the other when we walk,' he said.

My mother had a solid upbringing with Blanche. And at her funeral – I must have been about fourteen – my mother said, 'Well, there goes the last person I *know* I can count on.'

My father said, 'Alicia, what are you saying? What about me?'

She turned and looked at us. She was wearing a dark green dotted Swiss dress. It was June, and her hair and skirt were blowing in the wind as we walked back to the car. She turned and said, 'She would have crawled across the Sahara Desert on her hands and knees for her children, Lawrence. I'm not sure you would do that for me.'

When she arrived from the Château Marmont I heard the cab stop and opened the door as she was reaching for the bell.

'I've been thinking about Bahma,' I said. That was my name for my Grandmother Blanche.

'She's certainly something to think about,' she said, dragging her suitcase in behind her. She waved good-bye to the cabdriver from the door. He saluted her back. Always Wisconsin-friendly, and yet something like royalty about her. Very accessible but not.

'I think you're getting more like her,' I said, taking the bag away from her and leading her towards the guest room. God, it was heavy. 'What have you got in here?' I asked.

'I suppose you think I don't need a raincoat? And an umbrella?'

'All of this furniture came with the house. I'm renting it furnished,' I said.

'I could tell, this isn't exactly your taste. But it's rather splendid isn't it? The perfect setting for a romance. Oh, you've got a piano.'

My mother plays and sings quite well. Nothing operatic and certainly not German art songs. Popular music. Nightclub music.

As a little girl she used to play and I'd sing along with her. That's why I know all the words to 'Stars Fell on Alabama' and 'I'll be Seeing You' and 'Ooh, Ooh, Ooh What A Little Moonlight Can Do For You'. She was a teenager during World War II and most of her repertory dates from that period. 'How Deep Is The Ocean' is a great favorite of mine. Ever heard Etta James sing that? Distinctly cool. Maybe that's why I cry so easily in the movies, though my mother doesn't. She's like Freddy the Second; deeply embarrassed when you cry.

She didn't unpack her bag right away but went over to the piano and played and sang, 'Laugh and the world will laugh with you, cry and you cry alone. No tears, no sighs, remember there's always tomorrow,' and it trickled off. 'I've been singing that in my head all day,' she said.

'It's really not at all that way here, Mom. Things are very good. Who knows for how long, but so far I don't have to put a brave front on anything.'

'I think it has more to do with me,' she said.

'Maybe you're tired of laughing and having the world laugh with you. Though in your case it's more smile and the world will smile with you. Smile pleasantly. And God knows what you're thinking.'

'Maybe.' She got up from the piano and went over to the huge angel near the door and touched it. 'Bavarian, I think.

Maybe I needed to see you as much as I thought you needed to see me.'

'I'm okay, I really am,' I told her. 'I'm cutting the job very well. I'm becoming another person with Graham.' Suddenly I felt sad and heartsick about saying good-bye to the old Nina. What would my mother think of the Warsaw Ballroom and men showing their penises at the bar? Maybe I was getting to be too big a person, maybe I was seeing more of the world than was absolutely necessary.

Graham walked in. My mother had never met him but he knew immediately who she was. They both smiled at each other. I said, 'Graham, this is my mother, Mrs Morton. You can call her Alicia, and Mom, this is Graham Grant.'

'What a pleasure to meet you, Mrs Morton,' he said.

Graham said he had heard Mother playing as he came up the walk and asked her to play some more. She demurred but he said he wanted to sing with her. Perhaps he'd hire her to be his accompanist when he went for a singing audition. We never sing together, in the car or anywhere. It just hadn't occurred to me. She played and he sang, 'Shine On, Harvest Moon' in a nice baritone voice. Not bad. Really. Something like Robert Goulet, whom I rather like.

Have you ever had the experience of looking at something and seeing it as though it was already in the distant past, and feeling nostalgic about it? As I watched Graham and my mother it was as though I was seeing them long ago. As though I was looking back on this, finding it charming and ideal and somehow unreal. Perhaps it was the song. Perhaps it was the fact that they were not at all uneasy with one another. And it made me think that Graham and I would be looking back at it together, from some far-off shore, wherever the rising seas had carried us. The bubble burst.

'Let's go eat,' I said. 'There's no food in the house, we must go out.' I went to get my raincoat. I heard Graham say, 'Nina believes that one rule for a romantic relationship is to never eat in.' 'What a good idea,' my mother said. 'I would have loved to have lived my life so wisely.' 'My other rule is never go to the bathroom together,' I said, coming into the room.

'That's very good, too. But I imagine you break both of those rules, don't you?' she asked Graham.

She was being a little flirtatious, behaving in a more sophisticated manner than she ever had with Bertrand. We don't really see our parents until we see them relating to other people in their adult roles. Or perhaps I'd been the daughter long enough. Maybe my mother was seeing me as another adult, now that I was behaving in ways so unlike herself.

We went to dinner at Hamburger Hamlet again. Just down Sunset in all that red. I loved it.

Mother said, 'It's just like the 1950s. It looks like Ernie's used to in San Francisco.'

'When were you in San Francisco?' I asked her.

'I worked there after college. Before I came to New York and met your father. I had the dumbest job. I was one of the girls on the main floor at the *San Francisco Chronicle* who took small space ads. You didn't call them in back then. You came by and stepped up to a little window, just like a bank, and paid cash. We went out a lot. I never slept.'

We all ordered hamburgers with red relish. I should have ordered a salad but I'd just flown in from Miami and I needed my strength.

'It must have been fun in those days,' Graham said. 'It was always the wildest American city, San Francisco.'

'There were so many places to go. The Fat Black Pussy Cat. The Purple Onion. The Hungry 1. Mort Sahl always played The Hungry 1. It was my first real city. I thought it was so thrilling. The Fairmont Hotel had all these bars running down the hill. The Merry-Go-Round Bar, that really turned. And what was it called? The Pago-Pago Room? It was filled with parrots, I remember. And below that the Tonga

Room. The Tonga Room must have been the gymnasium at one time. It had a huge pool in the middle and the band was floating on it on a platform. And every half-hour or so they had a make-believe jungle storm and it rained over the pool and lightning flashed and there was thunder. Sometimes they forgot to pull the band out of the way and they would get drenched.' She laughed, remembering. We laughed, too. It made me a little sad, seeing her so animated and having fun. She must have been like that often when I was a small child, but in later years she was so calm and controlled with me. Always.

'The most magical moment of all that time,' she went on, 'was coming out of the Tonga Room one evening, late. We were usually with naval officers. I had three roommates and everybody knew boys who were passing through San Francisco on their way to duty somewhere. Nice boys, the kind of boys we'd all gone to college with. Anyway, we came out of this nightclub on that steep hill that runs down from the Fairmont. Is that Sacramento? And a cab was going downhill, with a man playing the clarinet beside the driver. A black jazz musician. One of the boys yelled, "Hey!" and the cab made a U-turn right in the middle of the hill and came sweeping up in front of the nightclub door. And we all jumped in and drove all over San Francisco, uphill and down, in the middle of the night, with the clarinet playing. It was wonderful.'

'Did any of the girls ever sleep with any of those guys?' I asked her.

'Oh, you couldn't with three roommates. They would have been shocked. And I was never in love with any of those men. They were never around long enough. It was a different world. Tight girdles and tight shoes. The shoes had narrow pointy little toes at that time. Beautiful, but you longed to get home and take all that tight stuff off. Of course, girls didn't. And I don't remember a man really wanting to all that badly. I might very well have gone along with them if they'd really made an effort. I don't think a lot of men are all that interested actually. They make a pretense of it for other men's sakes.' She laughed again. All this on one glass of white wine.

Graham said he was enjoying her very much and she said she felt the same way. They clicked. He dropped us off and said he was going to go on home and leave us free to discuss him at length. Which was exactly right.

My mother stayed all week and Graham saw more of her than I did. He only had a few auditions to go to during the week and was able to take her to the Getty Museum and to Venice and the Museum of Modern Art and shopping on Rodeo Drive.

She didn't really come out of her manner of keeping a little distance between us, but that was her style. But she started calling me honey, which I remembered was an expression of her mother's. I didn't remember her using it before, so that was an advance.

One evening I told her that if my becoming obsessed with Graham and finding that Bertrand had cheated on me hadn't all happened at the same time I would very likely still be in New York and still be working for Edwina. But it seemed to be my fate to be dragged off in this new direction.

'I think it's very dangerous,' she said, 'but on the other hand I'm a little jealous of you. Your father never cheated on me and I never had any real reason to leave him, but it was smothering to have so little going on in my life. At least so little that interested me. My mother worked all her life as a teacher, so all the cooking and cleaning and shopping she did with the back of her hand. I often thought of that up in Westchester, driving you to your ballet lessons and picking you up at the dentist's. My mother did all of those things in her spare time. I think we were alike and you are like us, Nina. You're not all that interested in housekeeping and mothering. You need more. And somehow life has swept you off into more. Just promise me one thing.'

'What's that?' I said.

'You won't get a tattoo.'

'Oh, I don't think there's much chance of that,' I told her. 'Unless Graham suddenly decided he wanted me to have one. He doesn't have any, so I think we're safe.'

'It makes any woman look like a French taxi-dancer,' my mother said. 'You might as well have "slut" tattooed right on your forehead.'

'Except for the fact that being a slut isn't really looked down upon any more,' I told her. 'Luckily for me,' I added.

'Oh, Nina, I don't think anyone thinks you're a slut. They just think you've gone a little haywire and will have to pay for it later. Your job is to see to it that you don't pay for it later. And who wouldn't be jealous a bit? Graham is one of the most dashing and interesting men I've ever met and he loves you very much.'

'You like him, don't you?' I said.

'Actually I like him very much. And he isn't French. One gets a little tired of the French after a while. Talking with them is like picking up broken glass with your bare hands. You have to keep a close watch every second, they're so quick to take offense. So delighted to take offense. Bertrand was all right, but even so.'

'Bertrand stayed out of the way a lot, so one had downtime,' I said.

'Which reminds me,' she said. 'I think you should have Freddy here for his school vacation. Now that I've seen Graham I know they would get along fine, and I think it isn't his school but his home life that he needs a break from. I haven't met Claire but Freddy tells me she's pretentious.'

'The unpardonable,' I said.

'Well, you know, darling, the best people are never hoity-toity. It's only those jumped-up ones who feel they have to put on airs to be taken for the upper middle class. What is it? A gentleman is someone who is never rude to someone else unintentionally. And that's true of being a lady. It doesn't have to do with whose bed you sleep in. Being a lady has to do with being sensitive to the people around you and never letting someone leave you feeling worse about themselves than when they arrived. Claire isn't a lady, I'd guess, and Bertrand isn't even going to see the difference.'

'Oh, Mom, you do say nice things in the most roundabout way,' I told her.

She came over to me and hugged me.

'But, honey, you know I love you and will always be here for you.'

I hugged her back, hard. In our family this kind of emotion is tantamount to the immolation scene in *Götterdämerung*.

'I plan to bring Freddy out for his vacation,' I said, letting her go.

'I think he'd love it,' she told me. 'He's started playing the guitar so I'm sure he thinks he'll come out here and become a Rock 'n' Roll star overnight.'

'Since we seem to be going off in exotic directions in this family, why not?' I said.

Mother never brought up Graham's line of work and I didn't think it appropriate to talk about it. I don't think she clearly understood what it was in the first place. Maybe I underestimated her. And maybe it was not really clear in my own head.

The day before Mother left we got a call from Angela in London. She wasn't going to be able to make it back to do the new movie with Graham. I felt relieved, on a lot of levels. More than I realized I would. I guessed I really did want to rescue Angela from her life of sin, which was of course easier than rescuing myself. I thought if Angela can make it out we all can. And I didn't really fancy Graham making love to someone else, particularly someone that beautiful. Someone uglier, perhaps. Was this wild thinking or what?

Angela had inspired those hosiery manufacturers and they

wanted to do one of those 'I dreamed I wore my Fabulegs pantyhose in Shangri-la' campaigns and were going to take Angela all over the world to do them. David Bailey was going to shoot the pictures and they were leaving on Saturday for Bahia. I hoped this wasn't someone in management falling in love with her and wanting to go to the ends of the earth with her to pursue their romantic dreams. I don't think so. I think Angela would have said something.

Which left us without a leading lady. I had to leave this in Graham's capable hands. He'd think of something.

Mother went back on Sunday. Rather early, since she wanted to arrive in New York at a decent hour. Saturday evening she played the piano and we sang together. Graham didn't know a lot of the lyrics but was a good sport about learning or listening. 'Moonlight Becomes You', 'Dancing In The Dark', 'I Didn't Know What Time It Was', 'I Took A Trip On A Train', and my favorite, 'I Didn't Know About You'.

'I ran around in my own little crowd.
The usual laughs, not many but loud.
But then what else could I do?
I didn't know about you.'

It was bittersweet to me. Even when I was so young I didn't know what love was.

And so we took my mother to the airport. For me, it was like seeing off a good friend, an older woman, still attractive, who was very dear to me. Somehow my mother acting more like a mother made her less mother-like to me and more someone I knew and liked for themselves.

And then we came back and made rather violent love, before lunch. We came in the door and while Graham was in the bathroom I took off all my clothes except my pearl necklace and got into bed. When he came out he saw me there and began to take his clothes off. He got into bed with his jockey shorts still on. I said, 'Shouldn't you take those off.' He said, 'How silly of me.' And did. He climbed on top of me and I was ready, with no smooching, no writhing about. He just went in and it was as though it was something we had to do. Or that I had to do and he understood and was there with me to do.

chapter 27

....

new directions

'So what are we going to do with our lives, Nina?' Graham said the afternoon after my mother left. We were lying together on the couch, me reading May Sarton's journals, he, *The Oysters of Locmariaquer*.

I put my book down. I was getting pretty tired of May. Her long disquisitions on how much she loved solitude were mostly veiled complaining. Don't tell me that one can get along forever loving how the sun falls on the tea set.

'Well, we can't just put things off, can we?' I said. 'I love being with you and I'm not particularly haunted by the future at this point, but we should think about next steps I suppose. Tell me this, what do you imagine you'll do when you stop making porn films?'

He studied the angel's face in the corner of the room.

'I guess I think I'm going to become a movie star.'

'Do you want to become a movie star?' I said.

'Doesn't everybody?'

'I don't. I'd hate it,' I told him.

'That's an interesting approach. I've always thought that when you're good-looking you want the whole world to know about it.'

'I guess I'm not that good-looking. And I think I was brought up to think that good looks are a little suspect. Not entirely in good taste. That's my mother's background seeping through.'

'I don't think my parents had such clearly formed ideas. About anything,' he said. He never talked about his family, so this was interesting.

'How were they brought up?' I said.

'My mother had been an orphan. She was actually somebody's illegitimate child. And the people who adopted her didn't treat her well at all. She was glad to escape them. She was brought up in Maine and I guess in Maine people think the norm is having a hard life. If it isn't hard you make it hard. Anyway, she got herself to college in Ohio and the rest is history.'

'Do your looks come from her?' I asked.

'More from my Dad. But I'm better looking. One of his brothers is who I think I look like. He was blond and athletic. The grandfather was German and came over when he was a little child. That's where the blond came from. That and never discussing anything important with your children.'

'So how did you wind up here?' I said. 'I went to college for a little while. Everybody here is from a junior college in Waukegan, or worse. And they're all good-looking. And they're all willing to do whatever it takes to get ahead in the movie business. So I decided that instead of screwing people in the hopes of getting a chance at a part in a movie I'd screw people in front of the camera and get paid for it directly. It's my talent, Nina. I love to fuck and it doesn't bother me to be watched doing it. I wouldn't say that I *have* to have an audience.'

'No, I wouldn't say that either,' I said.

He laughed and came down to my end of the couch and pulled me over to him, putting one leg between mine, which felt good.

'Instead of losing myself in my sexual mania, I'd like to

finish this conversation,' I said. 'Then I'll lose myself in my sexual mania.'

'*Our* sexual mania,' he said, removing his leg but leaving his penis pressed firmly against my thigh. Which felt good, too.

'Should you *not* become a film star, what are the other possibilities?' I said, taking his face in my hands and looking into those eyes.

'Hairdressing?' he said.

'I'm sure you'd be excellent, but I was thinking of something that might be more demanding, mind expanding, something with a future, where you might make money.'

'I've become so dependent on my cock,' he said.

'You're a lot more than a cock with a man attached.'

In a more serious voice he said, 'It seems to me that we're both trying to draw each other into our worlds. You know about advertising so you think in terms of my doing something there. I know about porn films so I think about you doing something in my field.

'What do *you* think I should do?' he said.

'It's the only thing I really know something about, but I thought you might make a good copywriter. You're amusing, you talk well, you have a good vocabulary, you're alert, you see what's going on around you. I'd give you this little project that Edwina gives people and we could see how you do,' I told him.

He said, 'I'll make a deal with you. I'll make a try at doing some advertising copywriting if you'll consider doing a film with me. The new one. The one Angela can't do. Won't do. Will never do now if I'm right.'

That shut me up for a moment. Everybody's a critic, but I certainly never thought my body was good enough to do a sex movie. I was thirty-eight years old for God's sake. I wasn't drooping but I wasn't exactly busting at the seams either. And I certainly didn't plan to have silicone or salt-water bags or any of that stuff inserted in my body. As a matter of fact, if my breasts were even smaller I wouldn't be upset. I hated it when I ran downstairs and I felt them flopping. They're real appendages.

'Could we ease into this?' I said.

'I thought you'd kick me off the couch for even bringing it up.'

'My reservations are all aesthetic,' I said. 'Am I beautiful enough to do this? And do I want the camera to investigate my most private parts? That *does* seem a little humiliating. Like sharing your gynecological examination with the world.'

'Only one kind of porn film does that stuff,' he said. 'I was thinking of ours as being more beautiful than heavy duty detail.'

'What would we get paid?' I said.

'You would get paid more than I would. It's the ladies that get the major money for this kind of film. When I do an all-out full gay movie, then I can touch the bigger dough. But I like to play it across the board. You'll probably get twenty grand as a completely new face. I'd maybe get ten. It's probably a three-day shoot if I don't have any trouble getting wood. And with you in it, that's highly unlikely,' he said.

'Here's what I'd like to do. I don't want to get paid,' I said. 'I want you to get paid, and top dollar. But I don't want to do it for money. If I do it, and I haven't definitely decided I will, I would do it with you and for you. A kind of living proof that you and I actually are lovers and do love each other and did love each other, etcetera, etcetera.'

He held me very close to him and said, 'I realize that in some ways I'm trying to drag you down to my level. But actually, I think if someone like you does a movie like this you'll be dragging me and it up to yours. Which is pretty high in my opinion.'

'Shall we get up and start your little advertising project then?' I said.

'Or shall we fuck first?' he suggested.

'Fuck afterwards,' I said. 'I'd love to fuck right now but then we'd lose all this drive and objectivity and goal-orientating we've got going. And besides, then what would we do later?'

chapter 28

graham's lesson

'This is Edwina's advertising project. That she has young aspirants do to see if they have any talent. I didn't have to do it for her. I already had a book from working at Stirtz and Staller. And I was at Elegance, Inc. before that,' I told Graham. 'The poor project-doer has to choose three ads they hate and using the same product or subject, do one they like. Then they have to select three ads they like, and pretend they work on those accounts. And do the next ad in the campaign for each one.'

We dug out all the magazines in the house and I sat Graham down to look through them. 'You can select anything. And don't pick things just because they're guy things. You can certainly work on things like fragrance and lingerie if you've got a feeling for it. Many men do.'

'Are any of them straight?' he asked, leafing through an American edition of *Elle*.

'Come to think of it, no,' I said. 'But that doesn't make it impossible. You just might have a gift for writing about cupcakes. Don't fight it.' I went back to the couch and May Sarton while he busily flipped through magazines, ripping here and there. I was beginning to wonder what I would have thought of the noble May in person when he interrupted me, 'Can we talk?' I put May aside with relief. Always complaining

about the weather, decides to live in fucking Vermont and
then moves to fucking Maine! I ask you.

'So what do we have here?' I said, sitting down opposite
Graham at the big stone dining table. He had neat little piles
in front of him.

'Here are the ones I hate,' he said. 'This was the easy part.
Finding ones I liked was much more difficult. Here's Bijan of
course. I'm sure that everyone includes his ads among the
ones they hate the most. And on top of it he has to include
the number one non-star in the world, Bo Derek. Are there
really that many rich people without taste in the world?

'Then here's poor Tommy Hilfiger. His ads look exactly
like Ralph Lauren, except they're the ones Ralph Lauren
threw out.

'And I'm torn between two liquor ads. I don't know if
Bombay gin is worse than Johnnie Walker Black Label or not.
You couldn't want to buy any of this booze because of the
ads.'

I could tell he was interested. 'Edwina would approve of
these choices, I'm sure,' I said. 'And so do I. They're all
terrible. Let's see what you like.'

And he laid out an Absolut ad, an ad from the new Saab
campaign with the drawings, and an ad from a watch campaign I was vaguely aware of, Tag Hauer.

'Tell me why?' I said, feeling almost maternal. I wanted my
child to do well. I never think about advertising but it is
my vocation and I do think I'm pretty good at it.

'The Absolut ads are writer's ads, aren't they? I mean they
wouldn't be funny if there wasn't a good word there to go
with Absolut. Like this Absolut Rosebud with the sled in the
shape of a bottle.

'And the Saab campaign, the layouts aren't so great, but
there's something really nice about seeing a car ad that isn't
the same stupid car. There were a lot of stupid automobile
ads in these magazines, but they're selling you a new penis

every year. They're really too dopey to criticize. The Saab thing is pretty nice. And it seems modern with those goofy drawings. I love all the hair flying out of this convertible and it says "A Driver's Dream. A Hairdresser's Nightmare". It seems kind of swift.'

'And the watch ads, I'm not sure what they mean. Precision I guess. But that horse jumping the gap between two skyscrapers; I always get a funny quiver in my thighs every time I see that ad. And the one of the hurdlers going over the giant razor blades. I mean, I notice those things. So I think that's good. An ad that makes you quiver in the crotch has to be some good. Or is this a guy thing?'

'I don't disagree,' I said, 'And the Tag Hauer line, "Success, it's a mind game", I think is good although I can't say I really get it. But it's unusual. And you really don't expect this kind of stuff from the Swiss.'

'Are they Swiss? I didn't register that. Well, yeah, that makes even more sense of the precision, doesn't it?'

'So this is your project. I'll give you three days to take the terrible ads and do good ones and take the good ones and do more of the same. You can just sit down with a pencil and paper and describe them for me. If you want to do sketches, you can. Or if you see pictures in magazines you think can illustrate them, that's good too.'

I was getting a kick out of this. This was my area. And I did love to teach. Maybe I should have become a teacher. They must have loved Graham in school. He hadn't had a project in a long time that required him to do something with his mind, other than learn lines and things like that, so he was having fun.

'Maybe I'll go with you tomorrow when you go in and look through your magazines. And get an early start. Shall we go to bed now?'

'Did my mother just leave this morning?' I said. 'It seems like weeks ago.'

'We had a honey of a fuck this morning, maybe we should skip it tonight,' Graham said.

I pushed him down on the bed and climbed on top of him. 'You'd like that, wouldn't you? Well, nothing doing.' And we had a pillow fight and then we pulled each other's clothes off and then we really tangled. What would I ever do without this guy?

chapter 29

....

mimi calls

Graham was at my office going through material torn from magazines for his advertising project when Mimi called me.

'Can we talk?' she said.

'Of course, Mimi,' I said so Graham could hear me. He turned his head when he heard the name. 'What are you wearing?' I asked. I'm always curious about what drag queens wear at home. A torn kimono or jockey shorts and an old T-shirt?

'I have nothing on but the radio,' she said.

'I thought you were going to tell me you have nothing on but Arpege.'

'Jungle Gardenia,' she said. 'By Tuvache. I like a fragrance that rocks men right back on their heels.'

'I have the perfect girlfriend for you,' I said, thinking of Edwina and her penchant for making people cower in elevators.

'I'd love to meet her. Any friend of yours has to be fabulous. But I'm not just calling to chat. I've got the money for the shoot. It's a go. We just have to set a date. We'll do it on a weekend because I know you're working. I'm counting on you to come up with a good name.'

My heart sank. The day of decision was upon me. Graham

was looking at me with a blank face. I said, 'Have you heard from Angela, Mimi?'

'No.'

'Bad news,' I said. 'She has a big advertising job in South America.' I paused. 'So I'm going to do it. If you want me.'

There was dead silence. Then a voice that didn't sound like Mimi at all said, 'I can't believe this. *You* are going to do a porn film?'

'How about the weekend after next, Mimi?' I said. 'That should give you time to get things set up. Graham is here and I'll talk to him about it.'

'And we have to do stills right away.' The different voice said, 'This is incredible. Now there's *no* problem with money.' The real Mimi's voice returned. 'This is fabulous, darling. Fabulous. Fabulous! One night next week probably.'

'Stills?' I said, sounding stupid. 'Package cover stills. Have to have a really good photographer do those. Not like the stills we do on the set for the magazines.' Mimi was all gung-ho enthusiasm. She obviously just loved to get her teeth into a new project. I'm sure she didn't notice that I sounded a little less than thrilled when I said, 'Just let us know when you need us, Mimi,' and we said good-bye.

'You should see your face,' Graham said. I said nothing. Was I really losing my grip? Or was I just losing the grip on the old Nina that I didn't want to be again anyway. I decided I was *not* going to call Edwina and discuss this. Even she would thumbs-down this one. Edwina always said that no matter how much a slut anyone was, it was important to act like a lady. And I don't think ladies do porn movies. I was smart enough to figure out that one reason I was even considering doing this is that I would be throwing my lot in with Graham irrevocably. And making it harder for him to consider leaving me. Oh, I was quite aware of the little tricks I'm capable of.

'One can't help but have second thoughts about making

your first porn movie,' I said finally. He looked towards the door. I follow Edwina's lead. Leave the door open and say what you will. They only really pay attention when you're trying to keep them from finding out what's going on.

'Mimi said we have to do stills for the package cover next week,' I said. 'They always do that. That's nothing. Just nudity. Beautiful nudity. At least the most beautiful the photographer and the models can muster.' He headed for the door. 'I've got a lot of stuff from your files. I'm going to go home and work on my project. I'll probably have something to show you tonight.'

He disappeared around the corner. We didn't kiss goodbye. That's a bit gloppy for the office. They were already agog that a superannuated creative director could have such a gorgeous boyfriend. Of course they thought he was in it for the television commercials he could get or the contacts he could make, but they didn't see that as a negative. That is a given in Hollywood. You wouldn't be with someone if there was nothing in it for you. What they admired was when you made the best deal possible. A really good-looking boyfriend who in fact has the potential for making it, instead of some good-looking loser. This dates back at least as far as Clark Gable, who married his much-older acting teacher. She knew everybody in Hollywood. I'm sure she let him go without a complaint, knowing he had to have a young and beautiful wife like Carole Lombard to really make it.

I didn't have any time to ponder the looniness of doing this movie. I had a call from my mother. 'This is early for you,' I said. 'It's after lunch, dear. The time goes the other way. It's early for you,' she said.

'Oh, of course. It was swell having you here, Mom. I just loved it,' I told her.

'I had a good time, too. I think Graham is a darling, and I don't think there's a thing wrong with marrying him. You look wonderful and if it were a man marrying a younger woman no one would even give it a moment's notice. I think you should go ahead.'

'He hasn't really asked me. Well, he has but I'm not sure how serious he was.' I considered telling her about the porn movie but restrained myself. This was really my business and there was no reason to distress her.

'I really called to remind you that Freddy's holiday is upon us. It starts next Friday and I know he has been rather counting on coming out to see you. I know you've probably had it with guests, but Freddy is a bit more than a guest and I think you should do it. I'm getting preachy in my old age, aren't I? But I do think you should, honey.'

I told her I'd organize it immediately.

In addition to everything else, Cleanola was about to launch a fragrance. Claude Duress had told the agency that since they had a first-rate Creative Director finally and one that knew the fragrance business, he was considering doing a new fragrance for his own company. Which meant going to Cleanola every single day with all those names. This had been going on for a week and there was no end in sight. The other two writers and myself each dreamed up twenty names every day before heading over to Cleanola at the end of the day. Just as I had done in New York for Nixtrix. At least it was on the way home from the agency, but it made for long days.

I think Claude Duress just loved to have us around. He had some of his own people working on it too. So the six of us sat around and read our lists and told each other how much we liked each other's work and then the big cheese made his selections for the master list.

As with every manager I'd ever worked with, Duress didn't seem to have a clear picture as to what his company *was* exactly. I pointed out to him that a name like *Scarlett* for a fragrance was pure Revlon and that *Harlow* could work for Max Factor, but that we represented purity. He always agreed and then came right back liking a name like *Typhoon*. But as the little sign on Edwina's wall read, 'Someday this job will be done and when it is, we will have done it.' So be it.

The next day I called Freddy's school and left a message for him to call me, did my twenty names, had a sandwich at my desk, not all in that order, then went off to see the Cleanola people. Duress liked Aquarelle, Westwind, Angélique and Trevi. He did not like Norvege, Strata, Fidele ('Are you crazy? Everybody will think this is a Cuban fragrance!') or Majolica. I was actually with him on this. He *would* let you insist on a name going on the master list if you were forceful about it, only to discard it later. One lived in hope.

I had hardly walked in the door at home when Freddy called and we set up for him to fly out the next Sunday. He would come down from school on Saturday and stay overnight with his father. He chose a nine a.m. flight, which meant he was eager to see me or wanted to steer clear of his father and the dreaded Claire.

And Graham was beaming with delight, pleased as punch with what he'd done on the advertising project. Please. Could my plate get any fuller? A big advertising push and a porn movie to do all in the next two weeks. Not every Mom has this kind of program.

chapter 30

....

graham learns his lesson

What Graham did was pretty good. At Lampedusa's we were given a table for four so he would have room to spread out his papers. 'I want to start with the good part,' he said. 'Where I took good advertising and continue the campaign. I'm going to start with Absolut.

'I did "Absolut Knockout".' He had done a little drawing with a boxing ring in the shape of the Absolut bottle and two miniature boxers going at it amidst a roaring crowd. Not bad.

He also did 'Absolut Nightmare', with someone sleeping in an Absolut-shaped bed, tossing and turning in crumpled sheets and 'Absolut Fright', with a man's hair standing on end in the shape of an Absolut bottle. I rather liked that. It looked like the ads for the movie *Eraserhead*.

The first ad in his Saab campaign had the headline 'Reality Goes Hollywood' with a drawing of the car zipping down a canyon road with everyone in it wearing black sunglasses. And I liked 'Enjoy The First Snow . . . Safely.' The passengers had on ski caps and had their heads back and their mouths open as the snow fell on their open convertible. 'This headline's a little flat. What else could we say?' I asked.

'Enjoy The First Snow . . . It's Cool?' Graham suggested.

'Not bad,' I said. 'I wonder if people will understand we're talking about car safety. I guess it's all right. I like it.'

'You're not just being nice to me to encourage me, are you?' he said.

'Please,' I said.

His last one for Saab convertibles had people on a pier fishing from the car with the headline 'Stop Fishing Around'. 'I love the visual. But I don't think the headlines are consistent. All the rest have this sort of "it's fun but it's a great car" concept. I think you need to work a little more on this one,' I told him. He wasn't crestfallen. He was doing great.

His Tag Hauer watch ads were visual concepts, but he seemed to be a good visual thinker. He had people bobsledding between walls of fire. Pretty good. He had skiers going down the inclined roof of a glass skyscraper. His best were croquet players on a lawn planted on the wing of an airplane, high over the ocean.

'I think you get it. Prestige sports activities. Unreal and slightly scary situations,' I said.

'Visceral,' he said. 'It should make you feel a little something in your guts.'

And I noticed he'd made the headline a little dialogue. It was written so there seemed to be two voices. One said, 'Success'. The other replied 'It's a Mind Game'. And the first voice responded 'Precisely'. That was good, too. He was adding a little something.

'*Voilà*. Excellent. Now let's see how you rescued the advertising you don't like.' I had finished my pesto by this time, having gotten only a little bit of it on his work papers. The salad came just as we got started on the next section and he moved his work out of range of any splattering dressing.

'First, the dreaded Bijan. I guess we know that Bijan will have to be in the ads, don't we? And that he will have to be laughing that awful laugh of his. All those teeth. So I thought maybe the campaign should use recognizable comedians, like Sandra Bernhard and Bette Midler and Joan Rivers. And we could have some men, too. Jim Carrey. And they can be telling him a joke.'

'I think that's brilliant, Graham. Absolutely brilliant. Do I sound gushy?' I really meant it. I would have never thought of that solution. Bijan obviously likes stars and if he were a client it would be the only way around it.

'I thought we could use lines like "So he drove me to New Jersey". You know, the punch lines to really raunchy jokes.'

I said, 'Or at worst, you could leave them out altogether, because you have recognizable comedians in the ads.' I loved it.

'Want to hear my other lines?'

'Let's see if I've ever heard any of the jokes.'

'I have "Then she hit me right here with a nine iron".'

'I don't know that one.'

'And "He doesn't even belong to this club".'

'I know that one. The alternate punch line is "Hey, Red, come on out. We know it's you".'

Graham said, 'That's great. I never heard that. And I have "Is that right? What team is she on?" and "Mine's as big as my hat".'

'I think the last one is rather guessable, don't you? You make me feel as though I've led a rather sheltered life, though,' I said.

'Women don't really like dirty jokes anyway,' he told me. 'I think they get them. They just don't like them.'

I said, 'It's true. I'm always feeling sorry for the people in the jokes. I *love* this campaign! What else have you got?'

'Here's Johnny Walker Black Label.

'I thought of just having the one word headline "Smart" and endorsements by leading intellectuals. Like Stephen Hawking, people like that. Deadly dull. Not good-looking. Invade a whole new world of endorsers. I mean, brains are kind of fashionable, aren't they?'

'Our problem is thinking of the Nobel Prize winners to do

this campaign. Of course, they don't have to be known at all to be effective. I just feel like such a dunce not being able to think of any.'

'And lastly. I was torn between Tommy Hilfiger and The Gap. They're both so sort of exhausted and seen-it-all-before. I decided to give Tommy Hilfiger the makeover,' he said.

'*Digame,*' I said. 'You may have come upon something the whole sportswear industry is waiting to hear.'

'I thought we should create a group called Hilfiger's Angels. And have them all on motorcycles, or hanging around in grungie bars. Exactly the same clothes, but in a kind of tough environment. All the kids in the projects wear Hilfiger or steal it. It would make a great contrast to nicey-nice Ralph Lauren. But I think the models should be these clean-cut types, just roughed up in a rough world. Like Jonathan Schaech in that Gregg Araki movie. What's it called?'

'*The Doom Generation,*' I told him.

'What do you think?'

'I think you're right. Next step is getting you a portfolio. You have to work on getting your visuals together. You have to write some body copy to go with some of these things,' I said.

'And then what?' he said.

'The big what. We haven't even really talked about this. If you could get a job as a writer would you take it? It's not going to pay a lot of money. Look, let's not think about it right now. You have to do some television commercials to put in your book, too. Let's just work on that stuff and we'll think about the rest later. Am I going to hoist myself on my own petard?'

'Meaning?' Graham said.

'I'm going to train you to be a copywriter and you're going to go to New York and leave me here, a porn queen,' I said.

'The waiter would love to have us order dessert and get the hell out of here,' he said. I looked around. There was only one other table with people eating. We passed on dessert and ordered cappuccino and the check at the same time, so they'd know we were okay people.

'I used to be a dishwasher in a restaurant,' he told me. 'I know the feeling of standing around waiting for the last table to go. You're standing there shifting from one foot to the other waiting for them to get out. I never want to be the last table.'

'We'll gulp this down and beat it,' I said. And we did. Our papers and pencils tucked under our arms.

'This is fun,' Graham said in the car. 'I like working with you. I like being with you. I like sleeping with you. You're the perfect woman.' He slipped his hand in between my legs. I loved that but I took it out and put it back on the wheel. 'I'd love to die in your arms but not in a car crash on La Cienaga,' I said.

'We're not going fast enough to get killed,' he said.

'Only horribly scarred. And you know how they hate that in Hollywood. They prefer you killed.'

When we got home there were two calls on the answering machine. One from Freddy asking me to line up his plane ticket for him and one from Mimi asking if we could do the stills for the box on Tuesday evening. Perfect. How did one explain to a teenager that Mom has to be out for the evening because she's doing nude stills for the box cover of her porn movie?

chapter 31

....

freddy arrives

'Are you two guys going to get married or what?' Freddy asked. He had taken over one of the couches and had his Walkman on. Evidently he can hear on two channels as he consistently listens and talks at the same time and expects answers.

He came Sunday afternoon early. He looked bigger as he came out of the door at American's Gate 33. A little taller than me, not as tall as Graham. They had never met. 'Freddy, this is Graham Grant. Graham, this is my son, Frederick De Rochemont.'

Freddy stepped right up and shook Graham's hand, a well brought-up little gent.

'How do you do. I'm very glad to meet you,' he said. He had his skateboard under his arm.

'Planning to use that?' Graham asked. 'I'll take you out to the skateboarders' arena if you'd like. It's pretty hairy.'

As we headed for the luggage Freddy said, 'I thought I'd test my nerve and at least go see what they do. I'm just doing prep-school kind of stuff but I thought it would be worth it to see what extremes it's possible to go to.'

'Let's break something while you're here,' I said.

'Oh, Mom,' Freddy said and put his arm around my waist and planted a big kiss on my cheek. We hadn't kissed when he arrived. I wasn't quite sure what to do. We were never separated for any length of time in New York so we never had any real reason to kiss hello and good-bye. And I guessed teenagers were squeamish about kissing their mothers in public, anyway.

His luggage was one great near-exploding canvas bag.

'Is that full of dirty laundry?' I asked Freddy. He could hardly lift it on to his shoulder.

'Not all,' he said. 'And it's heavy because I brought books. Not just for school. For reading, in case it's very boring here.'

'You little wretch,' I said, leading the way toward the parking lot. Freddy looked more like Bertrand than me but blond. It's hard to say what he'll look like finally. He hasn't gotten his growth yet. Maybe he'll be tall, like Uncle Fred. He probably will have that kind of body.

Graham left us alone to unpack. We planned to go to dinner at Spago so Freddy would have a chance of seeing a movie star or a rock star or someone he could brag about when he got back to school.

We dragged his soiled underwear out of his canvas carryall. Freddy said, 'Alicia claimed to have had a very good time here with you.'

'Are you calling your grandmother Alicia these days?' I said as I carried an armload of unspeakable undershorts and T-shirts to the washing machine.

He followed me to the kitchen door. 'Not to her face. But I've been calling her from school to talk once in a while. She's cool. She gets the picture on what's going on in your life.'

'I wish she'd tell me,' I said and put the machine on hot and normal.

'I knew about Claire a long time ago,' Freddy said. 'I just never said anything because I knew you'd get all shook up. And probably walk out on the old geezer.'

'How did you figure that out?' I said.

'Her niece goes to my school. She thought it would be very

cool to tell me that her aunt was my father's girlfriend. Pretty dorky, huh?'

'Not being very nice seems to run in the family,' I said.

'You're right. Claire acts nice but she's not. And Dad's too stupid to figure that out. If he marries her he's going to find out in a hurry.'

'Do you think he's planning to marry her?' I asked.

'She's sure planning to marry him. She doesn't leave him alone for a second. They spend all day together at the office and then she comes home with him at night.'

'Must be quite a temptress.'

'Naah. She's not as good-looking as you are. It's the same old thing. She gives head.' Freddy looked scornful.

'I don't know how you would know that and I don't want to know how you know that. That's your father's business. And you know, Freddy, *I* left your father. And not just because of Claire. That was just part of the problem. Let's have a cup of coffee.'

First, my mother and I really become friends, and now Freddy. Fuck up everybody's lives and they become your friends.

'We didn't really talk about it, Freddy. I hated leaving you. And I probably wouldn't have if the Claire thing hadn't come up. That's true. But I was just so crazy – really crazy I guess – about Graham, I felt I had to grab on to a new life. I didn't want my life to become like your grandmother's and I didn't just want to be a working woman like Edwina.'

'It took a lot of nerve to do what you did, Mom. Dad wasn't treating you right and a new guy showed up. I mean, emotions are what it's all about, right? It's not about making money or being famous is it?'

'I don't think I've ever fixed you a cup of real coffee before. Cream and sugar?' I said.

'Black,' he said. 'I drink it black when I'm staying up studying. I'm not going to take any pills or anything. Alicia said your new boyfriend was a really great guy and she liked him a lot and not to worry about what he was doing for a living as it was just a sort of crazy period in his life and you were going to straighten it all out. He seems like a real nice guy.'

I didn't tell Freddy about the movie we were planning to make. He was in such a loving mood I know he'd approve if I told him Graham and I were going to join a Zen nude bikers' society.

And then Graham came in and we went to Spago and we did see Carl Reiner and Traci Lords and Mr and Mrs Lloyd Bridges and Sly Stallone. Freddy noticed that everyone in the movie business was shorter than you'd expect them to be.

'Who would you have liked to see?' I asked him.

'Kate Moss,' he said firmly.

'She's not a film actress,' I said.

'But she goes with Johnny Depp,' he reminded me. 'I thought she might be here in Hollywood.'

'Do not give up hope,' Graham told him. 'Kate Moss may be here and we may see her yet. I've seen her playing pool in one of the clubs. Tuesday night I'm going to arrange for someone I know to take you out club-hopping. Maybe you'll see her out with Johnny.'

Graham is, of course, a genius. He'd figured out that we'd have to have the decks cleared on Tuesday night for our still photo session. A mother didn't have to do everything after all.

Freddy ran around with Graham all week. I had to go to work. We were closing in on the fragrance project. It looked like Mr Duress would make a name choice this week. We had it narrowed down to twenty and were presenting them with rough layouts and visuals to guide our thinking. Guide *his* thinking.

A bizarre thing happened in a Cleanola fragrance meeting that shook me up. We were discussing whether Filigree or

Nuage might be better to suggest an elusive or evanescent quality when Claude Duress looked at me and said, 'How does the name *Chase My Love* sound to you?' This was the working title of the movie I was purportedly going to make. I didn't blink an eye.

'It doesn't make any sense, really, does it? Or am I missing something?'

Both Fiona and Ashley looked confused.

Fiona said, 'I don't get it. It doesn't sound like a fragrance name. Maybe that's what's good about it?'

Mr Duress said, 'Ashley?' but he didn't take his eyes off me. He has eyes like a gila monster. There are depths beyond depths there and you really don't want to know what those depths contain.

Ashley said, 'It really isn't a Cleanola kind of name is it? It sounds frivolous.'

I shifted my eyes to Ashley. She didn't know what was going on but, game girl that she was, rallied to my cause without knowing why.

'Let's work on it,' I said. 'Mr Duress always has a lot of insight. We'll come back tomorrow with a layout and see how it stacks up against the others. How about that?'

The gila monster had withdrawn into its hooded look. He muttered and left the room.

'Where does this stuff come from?' Fiona said. 'We're just closing in on something and suddenly he has a vision.'

'He's just trying to make us think very hard about what we've done, I think. I'm sure we'll go with one of the others. But we'll do a layout anyway.' We packed up and split.

I can't believe Duress came out with the line by chance. He knew something. I would have to mull this over.

chapter 32

....

photo session

'We're going to Noblesse Candor's in Coldwater Canyon,' Graham said when he picked me up Tuesday evening. He had arranged for a young guy from his acting class to take Freddy clubbing. And had told him no drugs and no hookers. So in principle all would be well.

'Noblesse Candor? That can't be right,' I said. 'She does *Vogue* and *Harper's*. She can't be doing box covers for porn films. It must be at her house.'

But it was Noblesse Candor all right. She opened the door. I hadn't seen her in several years since she was doing all those bandaged nudes lying around in men's washrooms. She still looked like Vita Sackville-West on a bummer. Like someone who works in those little store-front places in Greenwich Village with weird lights who want to look into your future.

'Nina De Rochemont? How did you *find* me? Come in, come in. But you can't stay long. I'm doing a shoot tonight.'

'I *am* the shoot tonight, Noblesse,' I said as she caught sight of Graham coming up the walk from parking the car. 'This is it, Noblesse, Chase Manhattan and Nina De Rochemont in the nude.'

I was brazen. I'd passed the point of no return.

chapter 33

....

written in the stars

Do you believe in the passage of the planets and their effect
on our lives? Neither do I. But then again. I was in Woodstock
once and on a telephone pole someone had tacked up a notice
on lavender paper. 'Full Moon Today.' Just to warn you I
guessed.

First, the naked shooting. Noblesse Candor did a nice job
on the pictures. She had a big romantic draped bed in her
bedroom and set the shooting up there. There were no private
parts showing and Graham and I were entwined about one
another in a series of poses on the bed. I did my own hair
and makeup, which I can do very well when I put my mind
to it. I've certainly seen enough of it done. And I wasn't
about to put myself together with big hair and lots of eyes.

Noblesse had the good sense to do some shots with me
kneeling instead of lying down so my breasts fell into place.
Nobody's breasts look good when they're lying on their back.
Unless they're completely plastic. And my breasts are quite
okay given half a chance.

Once you're naked it's not like being naked anyway. There
may be a little rivalry as far as breasts are concerned, but
breasts are sort of in the public domain. We're always semi-
exposing them or revealing them in tight sweaters, or in some

way making it quite clear what their shape and size is, even when we're faking it.

Whatever, it didn't bother me to romp around nude. Noblesse had a young guy assistant, but he seemed very unconcerned also, checking the light, holding filters and moving around us with special lights as Noblesse instructed him. I suppose they do these things rather regularly.

I felt a little sorry for Noblesse. She probably thought I was going to squeal to everyone in New York that the fabulous and demanding Noblesse Candor was reduced to doing porn movie box covers. Imagine the conversation. 'My *dear*, I was doing this nude shoot for a porn movie box cover . . . or should it be . . . I was doing this nude shoot for one of *my* porn movie box covers and who do you think the photographer was?' Her secrets were safe with me and my secrets were safe with her.

During the week we went to the movies a lot with Freddy. And I managed a couple of afternoons off to go to the Museum of Modern Art and the Getty. I think he enjoyed his days with Graham much more, fooling around in Venice watching the skaters and bodybuilders. And trying a little modest surfing. Freddy told me that Graham surfed quite well. They didn't roller blade when they were in Venice because Freddy preferred his skateboard. They went to see the skateboarders do their thing on that specially built skating area and Freddy, who will not readily admit to being impressed, was impressed. It showed him worlds to conquer.

He didn't see Kate Moss but since he was too young to get into any of the heavy-hitter clubs he wasn't too miffed.

On my way home on Thursday night to take Graham and Freddy to my favorite Hamburger Hamlet, I took a swing by Mimi's office to look at the chromes from the box cover shoot. I told her I insisted on doing this as a creative director as well as a nude model. She didn't have a light box so I was holding them up to the light on her desk. When I put them down I saw an envelope with the Cleanola logo.

'What's this?' I asked Mimi. Bad manners, but I thought we ought to get things out in the open.

'It's nothing,' she said. 'I have a friend who works over there and writes me a note from time to time.' 'Who?' I asked. 'You know that's my big client, Mimi. I might be loony enough to make a porn film but I'm not so loony that I want it advertised in my place of business.' 'It's no one you know.' Mimi was fidgeting. 'I have contacts over there. They invest in these movies quite regularly. As private investors. Not the company.'

'Claude Duress?' I asked her.

'I'd rather not say. They don't have anything to do with the movie-making part. They just turn money over to me and I pay them a profit. It's all very above board.'

'This doesn't look good, Mimi. Maybe I'm a complete idiot but Duress was on my case when I first showed up out here. He chilled when he found out I was involved with someone. Now suddenly I find he is putting up the money for this movie!'

'A. He is not putting up *the* money,' Mimi said loudly. 'He's putting up *some* of it and not really all that much. And B, he's certainly not going to be calling any plays. And C, I don't think he even knows you're going to be in it.'

'I'm quite sure he does,' I said. 'He was making references to our movie title in a meeting. There's no way he doesn't know now he's putting up money. Mimi, I have to talk this over with Graham. I don't mind losing my job and I don't mind having my reputation besmirched. It's that already. But I *do* mind being involved with someone like Claude Duress, who is an old lech and perhaps dangerous. Am I wrong?'

'Not entirely. But I think you're exaggerating what's going on here. Claude is amused that someone who works for him is making a porn film. Almost proud. He *is* an old lech and

he likes the idea of everyone becoming lecherous right along
with him. I don't think it means he's going to make any moves
on you. Let's face it, Nina, there are a lot of young, beautiful
women around this town who would be thrilled to have
Claude Duress on their trail. He isn't lacking for date
material.'

I went home. And smiled and talked and had my hamburger
at Hamburger Hamlet. Graham hadn't been staying over so
as to give Freddy and me as much contact time as possible.
I would have loved to discuss these new developments with
Freddy – somehow I had a feeling he could give me good
advice – but I decided having your mother discuss her future
as a porn star was perhaps too much of a Hollywood experience. Edwina was clearly out, too.

At least that was what I thought until I got in to the office
on Friday morning and had a message from Fred Farmer.
I couldn't place Fred Farmer for a moment. And then I
remembered the evening out with Edwina and Claude Duress
and the little man who came to our table and was such a pest.
I called him back.

'I'd like to have lunch with you, Nina,' he said. 'My spies
tell me you're about to make a movie.' 'Me?' I said. 'I'm
about to make a television commercial for Cleanola, but it
really doesn't qualify as a movie.'

'No, I understand you're about to appear in a movie. Is
that right?' he said.

As always in an emergency I model myself on Edwina.

'Mr Farmer, this is all nonsense. I am a writer not an
actress. But I think we should have lunch. I want to know
where you heard something like that and I want to tell you
what I *am* doing.' Take the offensive; always the best policy.
'Let's have lunch today. I'll make myself free. Domitala. On
Melrose. Near the corner of Detroit? One o'clock? If I have
trouble getting a reservation I'll call you back.' I took his

number. I sounded strong even to myself. Something was definitely in the air. There always was in Los Angeles.

There was no trouble getting a reservation. Fred Farmer was at the bar when I arrived. Shorter than I remembered. Fatter than I remembered.

'How's your fiancé?' he said as he slid off the stool and shook my hand. His hand was wetter than I remembered, too.

We sat down. We ordered our pasta and green salad and white wine and I stared thoughtfully at him. Knowing that something was up made me calm. At least I knew I wasn't going mad.

'So. About this movie, Mr Farmer?' I said. I have never made anyone squirm in my life but I was rather enjoying making the little worm uncomfortable. And then, of course, I realized that he isn't *just* a little worm, but a little worm from Massillon, Ohio, or someplace like that who came to Hollywood to make his way. And is doing so. And I felt a little sorry for him. He mustered himself.

'The fact that Chase Manhattan is making another porn movie isn't news, Mrs De Rochemont. But if my information is correct, the fact that the elegant Nina De Rochemont, prominent Hollywood advertising lady, is making a movie with him, that's news.'

'If you really have any serious information, why would you tell me?' I asked. 'Wouldn't it be newsier after this movie is done? I don't make any bones about the fact that Graham Grant is my boyfriend, Mr Farmer. We're not living together, but in fact, we might as well be. And he does make adult films under the name of Chase Manhattan. Perhaps there are people here in Hollywood who don't know, but you don't try to conceal something like that. Not here. But that's a long way from my making a movie with him, don't you think?'

'Of course. And I didn't believe it at first. But you develop a chain of information in my kind of job, and one of my contacts works freelance for Mimi Fandango. He does the contracts. And he told me he'd drawn one up for you.'

'That's news to me,' I said. Which it was. No lie there.

'If this news breaks, it's a good story for me,' Fred Farmer said. 'But I have a feeling you don't know who the principal backer is for your movie. A lot of people know this here in Hollywood but nobody is going to break that story because they don't want to get into trouble and lose their jobs.'

'Cleanola?' I asked.

He looked surprised. So far in the 'who looks surprised' competition I was faring better than he was.

'You *do* know. Are you getting a big cut out of this? Is this part of the agency's deal with Claude Duress? Is Chase Manhattan just a beard for Duress? Excuse me. You kind of caught me offguard. If you *do* know then there are a lot of other questions to be asked. You New York people. You look like one thing and turn out to be something else altogether. At least out here people tend to look like what they are.' The poor guy. He could see his story disappearing into thin air. He wouldn't dare squeal on Claude Duress's girlfriend.

'Mr Farmer,' I said, 'I think you were trying to tell me something to help me. And that's much appreciated. I think maybe you were going to try to pull half the plug on this story, without pulling the other half. Or maybe you were warning me to bail out. I'm not sure. Maybe you hadn't figured it out completely yourself. But I'm taking it in the way, hopefully, it was intended. I'll tell you I'm not Claude Duress's girlfriend. I am in love with Graham. That's all I can tell you now. But if I have more news, you are going to be the first one to know.'

I paid for our lunch. It was a little too tense to linger over coffee. I think Fred Farmer is a not too bad guy who's scrambling for a living but the facts are that what he knows a lot of people can know very rapidly.

This was the kind of mess from which only big girls can extricate themselves. I wasn't that big a girl yet. I called Edwina and told her everything.

'This is clumsy,' she said.

'Quite clumsy,' I said, 'and I'm among the clumsiest.'

'Not at all, my darling. Not at all. Although I will not say that it could have happened to anybody.' And she laughed.

I laughed, too.

'Let me think about this,' she said. 'But I do think you are going to have to give up your plans to make this little film effort, Nina. It's one thing if a society lady wants to do a little nudity for the fun of it, but I think this is beginning to go beyond the fun of it. Here's what I don't get,' she went on. 'I can understand Duress backing a skinflick, he's a dirty old man. I can understand Duress being on your case. You're a good-looking woman. But why is he putting up the money for your movie and letting you know – however subtly, at least for him subtly – that he knows you're doing it? There's something cooking. I'll mention no names, my darling.'

I hung up. Something *was* cooking. Mr Steer's secretary called and asked me to stop by his office before I went home.

'I just wanted you to know that Mr Duress just called from Cleanola.'

'Yes,' I said.

Nice bland Mr Steer. His face so empty. His manner so reassuring. What could it possibly be like to go to bed with a man like that? It would be the only time you might have some idea who he really was. I, for one, was never going to find out.

'He called to tell me how well he thought we were doing with the account and how highly he thought of you,' Mr Steer smiled. Mr Steer was happy.

'That's awfully nice to hear,' I said. 'The writers have been working hard on the new fragrance project and they'll be happy to hear it's appreciated.'

'They're good kids.' Fiona would be delighted to hear she'd
been referred to as a kid. 'But you're the reason it's all going
so well. We're certainly going to do something salary-wise
after you've been here for six months. Which is pretty soon.
What is it, next month?'

'April. That's very nice of you, Mr Steer,' I told him.

'I think we know each other well enough that you can call
me John,' he said. Now I certainly never would. 'And Nina,
what you do in your private life is entirely your concern. I
want you to know that. This is an all-business agency. If
you're delivering the goods for us, we really believe your life
is your own to lead.' All this delivered in the same pleasant,
lifeless manner he has whether discussing the oleomargarine
account or expected tidal waves. He knew something, but
what?

'That's very nice of you to say. I'm really not planning to
embarrass you or come in here with a ring through my nose.
I'm the kind of woman who would never do anything that
would displease her mother.' A flicker of confusion was in the
back of his eyes. But he's good, very good. He could easily
have been sitting there wearing black lace panties under his
gabardine suit and none of us would ever be the wiser.

So I tried to put the seed of doubt in his mind that whatever
Duress had told him might be untrue. Or that he had misun-
derstood what Duress meant.

'I'm very happy here . . . ' I hesitated for a moment with
the desire to say 'Mr Steer' but fought it down and let the
sentence end. 'Everyone's been so nice to me and the work
is really interesting and exciting.' I can deliver meaningless
phrases along with the best of them. If Mr Steer thought I
was going to be up front with him he was to be sorely disappointed. He can say little dumb things with hidden intentions
and I'll say little dumb things right back. Like *Noh* drama.

Freddy was waiting when I got back home to my gnomes
cottage. He was in a mood to complain. 'We never eat in,

Mom. I thought maybe you'd be doing some cooking and we could have that meat loaf you make that's like grandma's.' When he wasn't thinking about it, Freddy forgot to call my mother Alicia.

'I know, my love, but somehow here I just don't seem to get around to do the marketing the way I did in New York.'

'You have more on your mind, I guess,' he said. And he wasn't smirking. He followed me into the bedroom and lay down on the bed. 'I'd like to come and live with you, Mom. It would be more fun.' He was staring at the ceiling when I turned to look at him.

'I thought you liked it at boarding school, Freddy. You were planning to go even if I hadn't left your father. To get your grades up so you had a better chance at Princeton.'

'It's not really fun. It's okay, but I'm lonely there. I miss you. And I'm going to be going to college before long and then I'll really be away from you. Forever.'

I lay down beside him and hugged him to me the way I used to when he was a little boy. He didn't resist me but he didn't hug me back.

'I feel so stupid about what I've done, Freddy. I've screwed your life all up and put myself in such a dumb situation. Here I am in love with a man who is a lot younger than myself in a city I don't particularly like.'

'If I came to live with you you'd like it more, maybe,' Freddy said. We were very comfortable lying there, my son and I.

'What about Graham?' I asked.

'He's cool. He loves you and wants to marry you.' He turned over and looked at me, slipping out of my grasp. 'Actually he's *very* cool. I told him I already had a father when he started counseling me on something. And you know what he said? "So do I."'

I sat up. 'He *is* cool. We have to think about this, Freddy. Of course I'm not going to say "no". It's just that there are a lot of things going on right now. You have to at least finish this semester at Groward. That I insist upon and it isn't going to kill you.'

We left it at that and Graham and I had no time to talk together until we were coming back from the airport early the next morning.

Now that Freddy was gone I could stop worrying about him for a little while and start worrying about myself a little bit.

'Something is going on, with this movie,' I said and told Graham what I knew.

'Maybe Duress is so crazy about you he just wants a movie of you in the buff so he can sit home and get off to it.'

'What a very attractive idea.'

'Well, that's what these movies are for.'

'It seems so sad somehow. People all over the world masturbating to movies about other people making love.'

'They're not all masturbating alone.'

'Even so. It's unhealthy.'

He looked at me sideways.

'You're one of a kind. Really one of a kind. How'd you get to be your age and still be so nice? How'd you get to be your age and be interested in a guy like me?'

'You're nice. Very nice.'

'I'm a porn pig.'

'That's what's so nice about you.'

chapter 34

....

the real story on graham

We were walking on the beach at Malibu when Graham finally spilled the beans. About himself, his life, his everything. A rare occasion. Maybe the only time he ever had. Or ever will.

We were walking along the water's edge with our arms around each other. So sappy. That high school side to our romance coming out.

'This is how I always thought it would be someday, Nina,' he said. 'When we were being dragged around from army base to army base. When I was a kid we lived in Germany, North Dakota, California, Guam and Germany again in about seven years. Nobody ever liked us. My mother drank a lot. Finally my father left us altogether for some *fräulein*. It was really shitty.'

'Who is "us"?' I said.

'My two brothers. One older, one younger. The older one's with my mother in Kentucky. Married. My other brother's living in Portland with a hairdresser now. I got out of there as soon as I could.'

His arm tightened around me. He was looking at the horizon. The sun was thinking about setting. I tightened my arm around him, too.

'I went to Santa Barbara Junior College for a semester. I wanted to get as far away from them as possible, short of living in the ocean. I washed dishes. Parked cars. All that kind of stuff. It was too hard for me. And everybody was always on my case.'

'Because you were, you are, so beautiful,' I said.

'I suppose. I was always getting letters from home about how they needed money. So I did some wrestling videos. You know that kind where you're all greased up, but no sex. That's what the good-looking straight guys are always willing to do.

'And then I did Chippendales for a year. But I really hated being expected to screw drunk women in order to make any money. At least I learned how to dance. And then I did some jack-off videos. The money was much better. So I could go to acting school and get an agent and start going to auditions. A lot of guys do that. And then I did some magazines. I used Stet Walton as a name in those days. A lot of those photographers are women. So it's not a real gay, gay world. And I went to night school and studied English Lit. I thought I might be a teacher someday.'

'You'd be a good teacher,' I said. 'I can imagine it.'

'And I slept with a lot of people. A lot of them nice people. But none of them were like you, Nina. They just weren't smart enough or nice enough. Some of them, men and women, loved me a lot. And I tried to reciprocate. I never treated anybody really shabbily. But I didn't really need to be kept. I had some money, so it was share and share alike. And we always drifted apart because I couldn't be there for them emotionally. And we weren't really using each other, like a lot of relationships out here. I always knew there was someone like you out there, waiting for me.'

'*This is my message to the world, who never wrote to me,*' I quoted.

'Yeah, exactly. Despite screwing a lot I was like Emily Dickinson, shut up upstairs. I never felt like anybody knew who I was. Some of them tried. Most not. So wrapped up in their concerns for themselves. And now, here I am. Doing these sex videos. I know I'll never have an acting career. That's a kind of joke. It's much too late for that. When you've done over fifty titles, you can't just switch into adventure movies.'

'But you haven't been doing these films that long,' I said.

'Longer than you think, maybe. Mimi got me into the major leagues. Let's walk some more.'

We had stopped and were just staring out where the sky was getting that coppery color only the Pacific has at sunset.

'Mimi saw some of that Mr Bigge stuff I did and had heard I was easy to work with. No drugs. No attitude. A stiff prick with no problems.' He looked at me, not really embarrassed, more to see how I was taking all this. 'Her company is the top of the line. They take care of their talent. Don't try to do a whole movie in one day like some of them do. Mimi created my Chase Manhattan image. Actually Mimi gave me my Graham Grant name too. He always calls me Graham.'

'I don't know that your name matters so much,' I said to him. 'I'm never going to think of you as anyone but Graham Grant. I guess you're so close to me now I don't even think of you as a name. More as a presence. So you're never confusing to me, even with all those names.'

'I'm not going to tell you I never peddled my ass here in Hollywood either, Nina. Or my dick actually.'

'You already told me you didn't,' I said.

'I was lying. But I never peddled it much. And only for very big money. And only if I did the fucking. And only if I found the person attractive in some way.'

'Men and women?' I said.

'Mostly men. Some women. The men are actually nicer. I guess the reason I'm telling you all this is because I had already met Claude Duress before we had dinner at Le Dome. In the line of work.'

'You slept with him?' After this, nothing would surprise me in Hollywood. I promised myself that.

'Not actually. I might have, but when I got to his home he

only wanted to be degraded. You know, ordered around. Told to do humiliating things.'

'The other side of Claude Duress,' I said. 'I wonder if Edwina knows about this?'

'He wasn't really into S and M. No black leather slings or things like that. It was more "force me to kneel down and clean that toilet", but I couldn't do it.'

'Because in fact he was humiliating you, forcing you to humiliate him for money,' I said.

'That's pretty fucking brilliant, Nina,' he said. 'I didn't figure that out right away, I just knew I wasn't up for it, even for $500. So I left. He was really in a rage, calling me all kinds of names.'

'He was pretty cool at dinner,' I said.

'He's the best. Masterful. But now I worry about you because I'm sure he thinks I've already told you and you'll tell Edwina and so on. I've really been sweating it out trying to figure out how to discuss this with you.'

'He's right,' I said. 'You have told me and I don't know if I would tell Edwina, but I certainly want to discuss it with her. Something went on between Claude and Edwina at one time I'm sure. Maybe she knows all about this.'

'I got that feeling, too. There was too much good behavior that night.'

'So are you still sleeping with people for money?' I said. I hate it when I get that perky little tone in my voice.

'I still get a lot of calls, not "no". Not since you came out here. I haven't had time.'

'I work all day,' I said.

'So does everyone else. And what I really meant was I didn't have emotional time. I'm getting my virginity back with you, Nina. I don't really want to just go stick my cock in somebody. Because that means I'm just sticking my cock in you. And I think I'm actually doing much more than that with you. I'm sticking my life in you, Nina. I just can't imagine my life without you. It would be awful.' He stopped and pulled me to him, my face in his chest. It sounded like tears in his voice.

I looked up at him.

I said, 'The only way you'll ever get rid of me is by kicking me out. You're it for me. I'm going to be your girlfriend and your Mom and your baby and everything else from here on out.'

I grabbed him by the hand and we ran off through the dusk towards the parking lot, lights glimmering on the hills above us. The smell of kelp and salt in the air that was suddenly cold.

'Let's go home and snuggle,' I said.

chapter 35

....

nina gets the picture

Mimi picked me up after work. She didn't come up to the
office. I didn't say she couldn't but good taste prevailed I
guess. She had called me in the middle of the afternoon and
asked if we could have a drink after work. Quite calm. Quite
masculine. I told her I'd walked to work so she agreed to pick
me up.

'Where to?' she said in the car. She was wearing her captain's cap with the gold braid on the visor and a new wig.
Longer, more like the way I wear my hair. It suited her better.
Less Marilyn Monroe. And a Moschino jacket with gold
buttons. Short skirt of course. Her pantyhose were sheerer
than usual and she was wearing those Bally flats the Upper
East Side ladies wear in New York.

'Nautical but nice,' I said, looking her over.

'I saw a picture of Leona Helmsley dressed like this and
thought it looked good,' she said. 'Except her jewelry was
Bulgari.'

'I think you're much younger than she is, Mimi,' I said.
'You don't need all the real jewelry.'

'And I've never been in the pokey,' she laughed loudly,
slapping the wheel with both hands. Cars swerved to the side
to avoid us.

'Do you shave your legs, Mimi?'

'Doesn't everybody? Not all the time actually. But for you I did. Where are we going?' she said.

'You're driving. But we seem to be drifting inexorably towards the inevitable Hamburger Hamlet.'

'Inexorably. Only you would use that word in Hollywood, Nina.'

'You seem to know what it means,' I said.

'I read,' she said. 'I just don't speak.'

We pulled up and parked on an uphill side street and walked to the front door of the Hamburger Hamlet on Sunset. Drag queens are not a daily staple at Hamburger Hamlet, but in Hollywood nobody stares. Not even the children. It would suggest you haven't seen everything. Mimi and I are about the same height. Possibly the woman who seated us thought we were mother and daughter. I flatter myself. Maybe sisters. Mimi's not really old enough to be my parent.

I ordered a margarita. I needed a little bracing for this conversation I was sure. Even if I didn't know what it was about. Mimi ordered a martini. No olive.

Before the drinks arrived she said, 'We're not doing the movie. I gave the money back. It broke my heart to do it but I had to.'

'Explain,' I said as our drinks came.

'I'm sure you suspected that most of the money was coming from Claude Duress. You were right. I lied to you.'

'Everybody lies in Hollywood,' I said.

'Only to keep things from you that it would do you no good to know.'

'Actually I do know, Mimi. Fred Farmer told me yesterday. He knew I was planning to do the movie, too. He warned me to stay clear.'

'That little slut,' she said. 'He can never keep his mouth shut. I'll kill him.'

'Somehow I thought he was being nice. As nice as he knows how to be. He thinks Claude Duress wants the movie made so he has something on Graham and me. To harm us in some way.'

'Not harm. Control. Claude is a very strange guy. He has a yen for humiliation and power at the same time. Very strange. So he has to have power over the people who humiliate him.'

'Like yourself,' I said. I had just gotten the picture.

'Oooh, naughty, *naughty*, Nina. Do you think I humiliate Claude? Order him around? Make him clean the toilet bowl wearing a little apron?'

'I think that's exactly what you do, Mimi. And he couldn't have a better dominatrix for the job.'

'Claude and I don't have sex,' Mimi said.

'I was sure you didn't. This is all rather beyond sex, isn't it? But I knew about this, Mimi. Graham told me he had a run in with Claude, who wanted to be abused. I haven't known this for any length of time.' I sounded so collected. At least I didn't sound perky. The Madison Avenue Nina cleaning under her son's bed seemed long ago and faraway and now I could feel that cold wind blowing when the seasons change and you shift into another phase of your life. Phase into a new persona. Nina in Hollywood, though so new, was already closing down as a chapter in my life.

'How did all this affect the movie?' I asked.

'Claude wanted this movie so he could have something on you. He wasn't ever going to let it be released. He wanted something big. And now, I see, through you to keep Graham quiet. Graham isn't very vulnerable on his own. Just another porn star. And who's going to pay much attention if he talks about Claude's little whims. But you're another story. You know a lot of people. You probably think making a porn movie isn't that important. That you're not important. But Claude can be a real bastard. Turn on him and you could be on the front page of *People* magazine. Like the Mayflower Madam. You'd never hear the end of it. Not to mention all those rags at the checkout line. They'd be bringing it up every time news got slow.

'He could really fuck up your life, Nina. And he would. Because I know you. You wouldn't let him control you, even for Graham. So I saw disaster ahead and I talked him out of it. I pretended I had no idea why he wanted this movie made and I said we'd never make any money with it. Too arty. And he took the money back. He's not such a terrible guy, deep down, but even so I think you should split, Nina. Go back to New York. He's intimidated by New York.'

'Decisions clearly have to be made,' I said, picking up my bag. Mimi picked up hers, too, signaling for the waiter.

'One thing more, Nina,' Mimi said. 'Now that I'm never going to be seeing you again, I suppose a fuck is completely out of the question?'

'Oh, Mimi, you wouldn't want to ruin a wonderful friendship, would you?' I said and stood up.

Now I knew I had really arrived in Hollywood. Just as it was time to go.

chapter 36

....

rue pigalle

We went to Paris. To Uncle Fred's apartment in the Rue Pigalle. The Red Light district. His apartment is a Russian fantasy in pastels. Uncle Fred always says he has tried to re-create the apartment of one of *Les Grandes Horizontales*.

Each room is in a different color and everything in each room is in that color. The salon is turquoise. Turquoise walls frosted heavily with white moldings. Turquoise from the swoop of the watered satin damask draperies, practically vomiting fringe, to the turquoise velvet upholstery on the settee and chairs. A turquoise oriental carpet. A turquoise sky behind the sulking Spanish lady over the settee. Up above, a painted turquoise sky with clouds billowing up to the chandelier, which was tied to the sky with a turquoise velvet ribbon. It's turquoise, no mistake. And so on through the pale green dining room, the pale blue bedroom, to the yellow, yellow guest room and the peach foyer. Only the bathroom is in black and white with 1920s fixtures. That's as far into this century as Uncle Fred is willing to go.

Mother and I used to come here before I was married and Bertrand and I were here with Freddy a number of times visiting Bertrand's parents. Who never came to this apartment because it's a fourth-floor walkup and because Bertrand was sure they would be shocked. We were here once when Uncle

Fred was in residence with his huge gray Persian cat. Bertrand said, 'Even the cat is decadent.'

Not at all Bertrand's geometric Mies van der Rohe kind of taste but with great heating and hot water, which is not that common in Paris. One was safe in this apartment, swaddled and cocooned against the outside world.

Graham loved it. He said, 'I knew apartments like this existed but I've never actually been in one. It's so overpowering it makes you love being overpowered.'

'I think Uncle Fred decorated it this way to make him forget that Paris is on the same latitude with Newfoundland. And has much the same weather. The sun seems to be shining in here even when it's foggy and murky outside.'

'So foggy you can hardly see the whores.'

So why were we here? Edwina made me do it. She called me over the weekend after the week of 'alarums and excursions'. 'I think you better get the hell out of there,' she said. 'I'm not able to piece this whole thing together exactly but you're in a very bum situation. I couldn't weasel the whole story out of Claude Duress, who is a brute. He's going to make sure that you never work in advertising again, even if you don't make the movie. He's going to spring the word through Fred Farmer that you planned to. Which is just about the same thing. And he bought the whole shooting that you did from Noblesse Candor. He told me that much. That person, Mimi Fandango, he has in his hip pocket and I wouldn't be surprised if he doesn't have a finger in a lot of what's going on in the porn industry. He's bad news, my darling, and you've had the bad luck to capture his fancy.'

'But this is ridiculous, Edwina. I don't work for him. I have nothing to do with him. It doesn't make sense.' I could hardly speak.

'It makes a lot of sense. He's a *very* rich man. You *do* work for him in that you wouldn't be at Steers, Stark, Staring Mad if you weren't working on his business. And he's pissed-off.

In a way he's probably trying to get at me, too. We were never really lovers. And he has this little S and M side to him I don't cotton to. He never really had any control over me. And he resents it. The notch in his bow that never got cut. And you made a second. In a way this is my fault for ever sending you out to the coast in the first place.'

I was trying to think fast. I can be well-balanced but I realized I was not going to be able to leave Los Angeles without Graham. Would he leave with me?

Edwina went on.

'I've got something for you to do right away if you want to do it. We have to have location scouting done immediately in France for the new blonde hair shades we're doing for the Nixtrix hair division. They're called Châteaux Blondes, if you please. I didn't dream that one up, they did. And we need a series of châteaux to shoot in. You speak French and you've been in France a lot. Your former husband is French. At last, a real purpose for him, background for you.'

'My present husband,' I said.

'My God, haven't you gotten a divorce yet? You can't even get married again. You're something, Nina. You really are. Sitting there telling that Duress person you're getting married in the autumn. You're just like Marlene Dietrich. She never got divorced either.'

'Bertrand is getting the divorce. I left it in his hands,' I said.

'It's too late now, sugar. You have to get your little *derrière* out of Los Angeles *tout de suite*. I think you should leave Monday at the latest. Best to just drop it. You can call the agency and tell them you're not coming in anymore. It's all a farce anyway. Duress is going to move the business somewhere else as soon as he drops the bomb on you. You are holding no winning cards, my angel. Except for Graham. You'd better talk this over with him, make your plans, get your reservations and let me know when you'll be in France. I can pay you

$500 a day and you can have a couple of weeks. That'll give you some pocket money until you get re-organized.

'I have one last thing to say to you, Nina,' Edwina said. 'The Indians have a concept that your conscience is like a little tin triangle that turns around in your head. It has three sharp points that hurt a lot at first, but the points wear down and become dull. It doesn't hurt so much after awhile. Finally it doesn't hurt at all. Personally, I think guilt pushes you into a larger view of what life is all about, as long as you face it. And it does stop hurting. So just keep on trucking, my darling. Remember we've both gone through tough times, but we always looked good and we were always fun to be with. That's important.' She hung up.

Graham was a prince.

'Let's go, it will be fun,' was his reaction when I told him. He wasn't outraged and didn't threaten to kill Claude Duress, even though he'd once said he wished there was someone to kill for me. We both knew there was no hope of winning this hand. And there was no question of my leaving without him. None. It was a feeling I'd never had before in my life. Not with my mother. Not with Bertrand. But with Graham it was immediately 'whither thou goest there go I'. You want to stay forever with someone who is so much on your side.

'We'll put what you don't want to take at my place,' he told me. 'I'm going to keep my apartment until we see what gives. You can call your landlord and say you have an emergency and you're going to have to sacrifice your deposit. We'll pack our little bags and we'll take the Monday night flight to Paris.'

So here we were, up to our necks in turquoise. I called Freddy and explained that my life was totally up in the air but as soon as it settled down we'd make a plan. He said, 'I'd *prefer* to live in Paris with you Mom, even over LA. That is truly superbly cool.' The poor child must have thought I was on drugs or something.

When I had called Uncle Fred to see if we could stay in

his flat he said, 'It sounds as though you are having the most adventurous time, Nina. I was always rather disappointed that there was no one else in the family who was tempted to walk on the wild side. But you seem to not only have been tempted but to have fallen. I think it's wonderful.' He added that Graham and I should use his country house in the Loire Valley whenever we wanted to. Gurney and he might be there for awhile next summer but there would always be room for all of us. I didn't tell him that I'd have to keep my eyes open to make sure the occasional blowjob wasn't being slipped over on me. There was no need for him to know anything about Gurney's little indiscretions.

My mother didn't even ask why I was leaving but only said, 'Oh, lovely. I'll come over in May when the weather gets good.' She did add, 'You are alright, aren't you, Nina? I mean, you want to do this don't you?'

I told her I was looking forward to it very much. Who wouldn't enjoy taking a running leap off the edge of the earth? The fact Graham would be with me reassured her.

That little self-starter Graham immediately enrolled himself at the Alliance Française to study French when we arrived. And although my French is pretty good I was planning to *perfectionner* it a little at the Alliance myself.

I knew Paris a little better than Graham, who had been over in the days when he was pursuing a modeling career somewhat sporadically. For a breath of the eighteenth century I'd dragged him to the Nissim-Camondo Museum, where each room is purely of its time down to the smallest detail. And we hung around the Place des Vosges in the fog, having chocolate cake and tea on a little upstairs balcony with beams so low Graham couldn't really stand up straight. Looking down on fat little ladies and mysterious teenagers and all-business waiters pushing through them as though there was really somewhere to go. We went to the movies on the Champs-Elysées when we needed to hear American voices.

Once we walked into a theater a little late. It was pitch black and he reached out for my hand just as I reached automatically for his so as not to lose each other. It was so tender and reassuring. We're becoming one person.

We walked the streets surrounded by people with the quick and witty look of those with small concerns. Eating. Vacation. Clothes. France.

And we ate at little places where one wondered how they could possibly make any money serving all these courses to the handful of people that were there, until you got the bill.

And finally I found things I wanted to buy, lurking in antique store windows. Little bronze paperweights of ladies with curls over their ears. Bonbons with twisted ends made of silver. Things you never knew you wanted until you saw them in the window. Wanted? Needed!

We'd go home, take all our clothes off and and climb on to Uncle Fred's bed with the drooping garlands of wooden roses and do the kinds of things that seemed even more intimate swaddled in this apartment, the draperies let down against the night fog. Winding up with my head on the floor or piled up against those huge French pillows, Graham's fingers clutching deep in my buttocks. Him frantic. Me watching his face. Where his greatest pleasure looked like great pain.

chapter 37

....

the château hunt

On our hunt for châteaux for Edwina, we stayed in Uncle Freddy's house in Sully-sur-Loire. Not so far from where Edwina had been brought up. An old sixteenth-century stone house that had originally been three houses but was now cobbled together into one sprawling arrangement with an interior courtyard. Uncle Freddy always said he had no idea how big it was when he bought it. Once he took possession he realized that there were strange staircases and rooms at an angle and rooms lost in the attics and back wings with the roof falling in. It was quite a project but he didn't Americanize it. He only bought a refrigerator a few years back because his guests wanted ice cubes. And it was a little one. Brown. He said he had a lot of trouble putting a big white shiny fridge in that big old room with the heavy beams and square red tiles on the floor. The house feels kind of crumbly and cozy. He installed the only central heating in the entire town because one night he was so cold he had to get up and put the bedroom carpet over the bed. Now he only comes in the summertime. But it's not all that warm even then.

We scouted out Gué-Pean, an ancient place lost in the woods, quite romantic, with basset hounds in the courtyard. I wasn't sure the interiors were up to snuff. I was fascinated to see a bottle of American catsup sitting on the dining table in the half-acre dining room. The old vicomte was thrilled at the prospect of Americans doing a commercial there.

We went to Cheverny, which is quite splendid but a little glossy for Edwina. It was so submerged in tourists that it almost looks like a Disney reconstruction.

My favorite of all was Montrésor, a wonderful medieval castle perched on an outcrop of rock with a wall around it. A Polish family bought it early in the nineteenth century at the time of one of those sub-dividings of Poland that left no real country at all. They did manage to depart with their fortune, which was substantial, and bought this château and a vast townhouse in Paris.

The château was decorated in the 1850s and has never been touched since. Gloomy and dusty, cobwebby and filled with spurious Renaissance masterpieces, as well as a number of gigantic paintings of every major Polish disaster, with dying citizens and defeated troops sprawled everywhere. What atmosphere! Topped off with a dining room filled with stuffed trophies of the chase. Eagles and boar heads and deer heads from the homeland, all protruding from the walls. And at the head of the table, a gigantic wolf hanging by its ankles with its tongue protruding. I loved it. And that odor of ancient books, decaying paint, frayed carpets that makes an old house old. Nothing at all like the spiffy Cheverny.

The Polish prince and princess lived just across the lawns in what had been the servants' quarters, another vast stone barrack. Probably all wall-to-wall carpeting and television in there.

We wanted to give Edwina ten choices, to give her her money's worth, so we traveled a long way to La Garguillière one day, out of the Loire actually near Châteauroux. Some neighbors at Sully-sur-Loire had recommended it. They knew the owners. He was a brother to the wife of some high-ranking government office holder and had a title. Le Comte de Quelque-Chose. And they said we would like his American wife.

It was a lovely place with a big sweep of lawn in front of it. Late eighteenth century, a squarish château with a balustrade across its top and a staircase pyramiding up to the front door. We got out and squished across the gravel and up the stairs.

A maid let us in and took us into a dark blue drawing room. There were fires in the fireplaces at each end of the paneled room and huge bouquets of fresh flowers on the mantelpieces of each fireplace, reflected in the mirrors. The floor-length windows looked out on another great stretch of lawn that swept down to the forest's edge. A flock of sheep were nibbling their way across the lawn, a shepherd with his crook supervising them.

'Exactly as it was done in the eighteenth and the nineteenth centuries before there were lawnmowers,' I said to Graham. He held me by the shoulders and looked out.

'The little turds must have been fun when they played croquet,' he said.

We heard footsteps behind us and turned. The Comtesse was Cinda Marquardt.

'Nina,' she said. 'What a surprise. Are you doing television commercials now?'

Cinda was in my crowd in high school and we had gone to the same college. Wellesley. We weren't friends there particularly but always said hello since we were from the same hometown. She was blonde, rangy, not really pretty, but long-nosed and toothy, that Wasp look that many people prefer to pretty. Taller than I am.

'Should I call you Comtesse?' I said, shaking her hand.

'Not at all, darling. I tell Jean-Claude I don't give a damn about that kind of thing.' But of course she did. Being a countess in a château in France was about as much of a trump card as you could play. 'Let's have a drink, shall we?' I introduced her to Graham. She is very well bred; no asking if we were a couple or working together or what. She would weasel all of that out in her own good time.

I remembered that she had worked at *Vogue* at one time and gone to Paris to work on the magazine there. That must have led to her encounter with old Jean-Claude. It had started to rain slightly and I could see the shepherd had put on a large-brimmed hat and a cape. Extraordinary, this large, gleaming room filled with Louis Quinze furniture, gold-framed pictures, the flames flickering in the fireplaces, fresh-cut flowers here at the end of winter in the middle of central France, the middle of nowhere.

A handsome dark young man came in. Booted and wearing a riding jacket. Could this be Jean-Claude? No. He was introduced as Marc Something. Cinda said, 'Marc is the head of our stables.' Cinda said Marc spoke no English and she switched from one language to the other. I spoke to him briefly in French, but couldn't really think of anything to say. He stood with his drink in his hand by the fireplace. Cinda was cool but she certainly knew that *I* realized that handsome young men who work for you don't hang around in your salon by chance. You know when something is going on between people and there was definitely something going on between these two.

And as we chatted about school friends and what we'd been doing . . . 'Did I hear your husband is French? Your married name is? . . . ' of course I knew that Cinda was sussing out that Graham and I were involved with each other. You don't have to have these things spelled out.

On the other hand we didn't know each other so well that I needed to spill my guts about leaving Bertrand and being in love with a younger man. I did say that I had left my husband and that we were location hunting for an American television commercial production and how wonderful it would be to work in France.

'Oh, but you should call Betsy Bucknell right away. She's

been the creative director at McCann for Arenelle, you know, the big hair people, for years. And she's leaving. She and I worked at *Vogue* together and then she switched over to advertising. She's married to some man at *Woman's Wear Daily* and they're going back to the States. Do call her. You never know.'

Certainly she doped out my situation and, trouper that she is, did her bit to give aid and assistance. We didn't really look at the rest of the house. She seemed unsure that Jean-Claude would want television people tramping about. And I also sensed that she didn't want me to see much more of her lifestyle, complete with handsome leader of the hunt.

She said good-bye to us on the stairs, in her plaid pleated skirt, dark blue cashmere sweater and matching tights, feet in flat black patent leather pumps, a barrette holding back her straight blonde hair. The perfect picture of a country lady. I felt as though I was abandoning her in a way, although she certainly seemed pleased to be where she was. She, too, had got what she wanted and was now being a good sport about it.

I put my head on Graham's shoulder as we drove through the light rain back to Sully.

'I wouldn't want Cinda's life, even with the shepherd on the lawn,' I said.

'Not even with that handsome little jodhpur-wearing gigolo on hand to hammer your clam?' he said.

'What a nice expression,' I said.

'It's a Mimi Fandango special,' he said. 'I kind of miss the fat old fart.'

'Can you imagine her here?' I said. 'She'd never know what to wear in the country. Certainly not pants. But the folks in Sully would probably love her. She'd be like someone from the future. We certainly seem to have flung ourselves into our own future, haven't we?'

'I had nothing to leave behind,' he said.

chapter 38

....

turquoise world

It was dank and gloomy outside, but I didn't care. I was lolling in a turquoise velvet armchair with my feet up on a turquoise *repose-pied*, coddled in a turquoise world of heavy draperies, oriental rugs and walls covered in moldings. Uncle Fred knows how to do cozy.

I was learning how to live in a completely insecure world and feel secure. Graham was off at the Alliance Française. We'd sent off our châteaux selection to Edwina, and now next steps needed to be taken.

When we came back from our châteaux hunt I called Betsy Bucknell, the woman whom La Comtesse Cinda suggested I call. At McCann-Erickson. I was seeing her tomorrow. They did need a new Creative Director on Arenelle and she said I sounded good. Of course, Edwina's name always does the trick. I said I had been her senior writer in New York on Nixtrix and she said, 'There's no better recommendation.' Evidently there was no problem getting working papers since it's a New York-based agency.

What I hadn't told anyone was that I was pregnant. I wasn't telling anyone except Graham until I saw how things shook out. I was definitely having this child. My love child. My trophy from the love affair of the century. Freddy the Second always needed a sibling.

What a slut! An unmarried mother at my age. And in my circumstances. Just myself and a much younger out-of-work lover to depend on. I liked it.

I had saved a fair amount of my salary in Los Angeles. I suspect Graham had oodles of dough from his ill-gotten motion picture career, but we certainly weren't going to spend it maintaining ourselves here. He seemed to love being in France and particularly in the Loire Valley. As we walked around Sully he had said, 'Not only have I never seen a town like this, I didn't even know there were towns like this.'

It was a good feeling to be in an all-stone city that had seen the Vikings come and go and Arab invaders almost reach it and the Germans rage in or nearby any number of times, and nevertheless, was still here. The same moon shining down on the same glittering slate roofs, the same old wooden shutters slamming shut every night, the same croissant served up fragile and warm every morning. Here you felt there was something steady and secure under your feet.

Graham believes that we each have our destiny and we only get off the track when we do things we don't *feel* like doing but only *think* we should do. He believes we've been heading for each other since we were born and now our paths have crossed we'll continue on together to the end.

I wonder. I know for now our paths have synchronized emotionally. We get up in the morning wanting to be together and go to bed at night feeling the same way. And if he was taken away from me it would leave a great gaping torn-away place in my being. Which I would have to limp along with. I wouldn't want to fill it with someone else, that I know. I never felt that way with Bertrand. There was always someplace inside of Bertrand I never knew and I don't think Claire knows and no one will ever now.

But Graham is accessible and I do know what is going on in there and he wants me to. What can I say? He completes me and I have to play the hand I've got. And little Alicia or

Graham junior who is lurking inside my belly will benefit from it. From having a Mommy who really loves her Daddy. Whatever may happen finally with handsome Daddy and older Mommy.

And when Graham came home we went up to the corner and had mussels and I told him about baby. He was startled. But excited I think. And now we'll just see how it goes.

chapter 39

au revoir to all that

So Betsy Bucknell loved me. I went for the interview in my black Jil Sander and a raincoat and dark lipstick and we clicked right away. Same age range, same background, what was not to like? I showed her my book and my television reel and she said, 'You're perfect. *And* you speak French.'

Then went on to say that they needed an Art Director, too, as hers was freelance and was going under contract to Chanel. Did I know anyone?

I've gotten so gutsy with my new winging-it-around-the-world lifestyle I said, 'How about my husband? He's not as senior as I am but he's very talented.'

And they agreed to see Graham's portfolio, which is really a copywriter's, but we'll wing it.

Of course he knows absolutely nothing about art direction, but he showed real flair in that little writing project he did for me, and what's to learn? All art directors are learning to do their thing on a computer anyway, so he might as well start from scratch along with everyone else.

He wasn't daunted when I told him about it.

'With you to coach me we'll give it a go,' he said.

He wasn't even terribly surprised that I was pregnant. 'I certainly was trying to be careful,' he said. 'But you can't fuck as much as we do without one of those little tadpoles sneaking through.'

He's been very sweet and gentle with me since. I told him he didn't really need to be solicitous for quite a few months, but it makes me love him even more that he isn't at all burdened and worried about fatherhood.

By then we'll have our own flat and be really installed in Paris. I don't want to devastate Uncle Fred's flat by bringing up a baby here. And the four floors to walk up could quickly pall with a baby and a stroller and all the other debris I remember from Freddy's early days.

I called Bertrand, very reluctantly, and told him I was living in Paris and will very likely stay here. He hasn't really taken any steps towards a divorce, but I told him I wanted to remarry and that seemed to galvanize him. He's a perfect gentleman, and didn't ask me whom I planned to marry, but I thought I caught a note there that perhaps he thought I might one day have returned. He would like the convenience of it and it would give him a perfect reason to shuck Claire, but I'm afraid that's out of the question. Always was. A woman obsessed is a woman obsessed.

He said he'll get a divorce in the next few months and would start the process in the next few weeks. And then Graham Grant, my love, and I will get married. Here in Paris.

I called my mother and told her the news. 'Would it be too much of a good thing for me to come over soon for a visit,' she said. 'And then come back when you have the baby to help you out? Of course, I want to see you but I want to see Graham, too. I have to tell you that I like him a great deal more than Bertrand. Imagine Bertrand singing with me at the piano.'

'I think he brings out the worst in you, Mother,' I said. 'The next thing I know you're going to launch a cabaret act.'

'I would have loved to do that,' my mother said. 'I always thought I was born to be a Big Band singer, like Helen

O'Connell and June Christie. Unfortunately when I got big
enough the big bands were small again.' She added, 'All
Freddy talks about is coming to live with you so that's something you're going to have to face, dear.'

'Well, what do you think?'

'You're going to have another child around the house, you
might as well have two. It will be better for both of them
when the new baby gets older. It will have a real brother. You
have to work that out, honey, but I think if you can swing it
you ought to have little Freddy on hand. He seems to have
liked Graham. It's unconventional but I don't think it's a
problem. I think Freddy's so excited about one-upping his
friends and moving to Europe that he'll make an effort to get
along. And he's a teenager. As soon as he has a little French
he'll be out of the house pursuing some fetching little made-
moiselle.'

There's the deal. Life looks like it will be getting organized
here in the Rue Pigalle. Here's the surprising news of the day.
It seems Edwina met Angela in New York and they became
friends. They liked each other very much and then they fell
in love. When Edwina called and said, 'You have to brace
yourself for this, Nina, but I think we're going to become
lovers. I've never been involved with a woman before. I mean
I've fooled around a little, but not in any serious way. But
Angela is a really large-scale person and I think this is perhaps
something I have always wanted to do. I mean, it's quite
obvious I could never be anyone's wife anymore. Ordering
food and planning parties and that kind of thing. And men
in my age range don't seem very loving.'

'Or very attractive,' I said.

'There's that, too,' Edwina said. 'Angela is very beautiful I
think.'

'You and the rest of the world. She's been enormously
successful for those hosiery people. She's the queen of
Fabulegs.'

'At any rate, there you have it. You started the ball rolling by deciding you would try something new, and now I'm doing the same thing.'

'I can only encourage you, Edwina,' I said. 'We have to fight our way through to find out who we are as people. There really isn't any other point to being here, is there? You were always my inspiration, Edwina.'

'And now you're mine, Nina. Naughty Nina. And Naughty Edwina. We're quite a pair.'

'I love you, Edwina.'

'And I love you, Nina.'

And there we leave it. New people to love. New places to go. New things to do. It never ends. Which is as it should be.